RIDE THE WHITE STALLION

D1334034

SWANSEA LIBRARIES
WITHDRAWN

6000286375

William Glynne-Jones (1907–1977) was a novelist, children's writer, broadcaster and journalist. He was born and grew up in Llanelli and following school he worked at the Glanmor Foundry in the town. He left the foundry on medical grounds in 1943 and moved to London to pursue a career as a writer and journalist. During his time working in industry he developed his skills as a writer and observed and took part in much of the world he was later to use in his fiction. He wrote a number of novels of which *Farewell Innocence*, published in 1950, and followed by *Ride the White Stallion* in 1951, are semi-autobiographical accounts of the journey of Ieuan Morgan from foundry worker to man of letters.

RIDE THE WHITE STALLION

WILLIAM GLYNNE-JONES

LIBRARY ᴏꜰ WALES

Parthian, Cardigan SA43 1ED
www.parthianbooks.com
The Library of Wales is a Welsh Government initiative which highlights and
celebrates Wales' literary heritage in the English language.
Published with the financial support of the Welsh Books Council.
www.thelibraryofwales.com
Series Editor: Dai Smith
First published in 1951
© The estate of William Glynne-Jones
Library of Wales edition published 2016
Foreword © Jon Gower
ISBN: 9781910901311
Cover Art: *Farmer in a Field* by John Bowen. With kind permission of the estate
of John Bowen and Carmarthenshire Museums Service Collection. The painting
is in the collection at the Parc Howard Museum and Art Gallery.
Typeset by Elaine Sharples
Printed and bound by Pulsio SARL

FOREWORD

Growing up in Llanelli it was all too easy to envy those other parts of industrial Wales that had been hymned into being in novels and short fictions. It made them more real, somehow. Certainly the coal industry had been well and truly mined in the sensational-realist novels of Lewis Jones such as *Cwmardy* and *We Live* and the fabulous short stories of Ron Berry, who suggested in *History is What You Live* that "coal mining had to be experienced day by day, year in and year out, the whole ingested for as long as oxygen fans the skull-mix".

So, where were our experiences, our fictions, our histories, then? This was, after all, Tinopolis, a town with a mega-productive past of making tinplate and steel, not to mention coal, iron, vanadium, explosives, white lead, arsenic and zinc. As a schoolboy I remember the high chimneys of foundries and works rising like birch thickets on the lowlands next to the Loughor and this was well after the industrial heyday of the town. And yet the hooters of not one, but two steelworks next to the Grammar School still divided our days into shifts as well as lessons. It was a town with a fascinating history, a place of hard work and proud of it. Where was this reflected in prose or poetry?

It came as some relief, a decade or so ago, to finally encounter the work of William Glynne-Jones, the author of several novels and going on for a hundred short stories, as well as a dozen books for children. He was successful both here and further afield and indeed was the winner of the Rockefeller Foundation Atlantic Award for Literature in 1946. William Glynne-Jones is perhaps a less showy writer than, say, the loquacious Gwyn Thomas, or the lyrical Glyn Jones but he is nevertheless an author who honestly and unflinchingly depicts the grit and un-bending-ness of workers and the acrid fumes of their workplaces.

Glynne-Jones' novels thus helped put Llanelli on the map, albeit as Abermor, with sunshine-drenched tales of childhood antics in works such as *Summer Long Ago* and *This Childhood Land*, where the language of the kids is shot through with bits of Welsh, reflecting the fact that this was once the largest Welsh speaking town in Wales. This is interesting, not least when one charts the decline in the language in the town: but when it comes to tapping into life in the foundries for inspiration we find something more unique, prefiguring books such as Christopher Meredith's novel of Tredegar steel and social dislocation, *Shifts*, published in 1985. *Ride the White Stallion* shares the same gritty authenticity of someone writing about industry who knows all too well the sweat and strain of very hard work:

> Clouds of gritty silica dust billowed into the air. Perspiration dripped from the men's arms and faces in the almost unbearable heat. Their movements were restricted: there was hardly room to turn in the confined area in which they worked.

Ride the White Stallion, first published in 1950, is the sequel to *Farewell Innocence*, advancing the story of the young idealist and aspiring writer, Ieuan Morgan who works at the Glanmôr Foundry (herein named Bevan's Foundry) just like young William, who started working there at the unripe age of fifteen.

By now Ieuan is twenty-one years of age and fully a steel moulder, taking his place among the specialisms and pecking orders of foundry jobs – the fettlers, labourers, pattern makers, apprentices and roll-turners.

Time and the foundry have made their mark on him and his hands, "once familiar only with the feel of books, were dark, knotted and fiercely strong." Yet he does not like the work a single jot more than when he started and hates the foundry "as intensely, now, as he had on that first day when he had risen before the sun, and seen its ugliness in a greying light." Now, at the beginning of the 1930s Ieuan's troubles have amplified. Sadly, his young love, Sally, is by now consumptive, confined to a nearby sanatorium for three testing years to treat the tuberculosis. Work in the foundry is drying up and periods of unemployment act as corrosively on the workers' spirits as any laboratory acid. Men stand around on street corners, waiting for news of work, beggars of bread.

To turn around the foundry's fortunes, or at least to make the place more competitive Ieuan is offered the Judas job of conducting time and motion studies, which earn him the right to both a white collar and the opprobrium of his butties. With Sally well again, and a wedding and marriage to fund, Ieuan reluctantly accepts the job. This affects his health in unexpected ways, his feet swelling from standing around too much and his stomach aching from the stress of acting as spy on his own comrades. For comrades they are, and Ieuan's politics are heavily left leaning, such that he has to try to justify his timekeeping as an act of solidarity with the workers rather than with the owners, a moral juggling trick and a half. It is a trick he fails to pull off, alienating and even fighting his closest friends.

Meanwhile Ieuan's fractious relationship with his mother continues to develop around kernels of harshness rather than love and the old lady dies of cancer just before they have time to properly reconcile. There are tensions, too, with his mother-in-law, Mrs Marvin, not least when she tries to bring in a backstreet abortionist – who belongs to the same religious sect, the Christian Brotherhood – to act as midwife to Sally as she gives birth to her first child.

In due course a baby is born and shortly thereafter life changes again for Ieuan when he starts to achieve a modicum of success with his writing (as did William Glynne-Jones, who was variously published by the *Welsh Review*, *Strand* and *Esquire* in America) not least when Stella Courtland, the vampish editor of *The New Forum* starts to treat him as her protégé, initially seducing him by letters and then quite literally when she visits him in south Wales. The novel closes with an account of Ieuan's witheringly embarrassing visit to Hampstead to seek her out, and of her dismissive reception of him, when he realises, with all the impact of an emotional sledgehammer, that he has been nothing more than a plaything to her.

One of the pleasures of this novel comes in the form of counterpoint, when Ieuan and Sally leave the grey grimness of the town for a three day honeymoon in Brecon and Glynne-Jones is given free rein to compare country idyll with the sullied landscape of Abermor:

> Farmers in breeches and leggings, bow-legged, red-faced. Long-maned horses nodding along the quiet streets. An archway of trees glistening after a shower and casting across the lane a greenish-black cloak.

Such brief moments of escape, elsewhere captured in descriptions of a Saturday spent fishing for sea-bass on the silken stretches of Cefn Sidan sands, serve to remind us of the poisonous fug of the foundry and help explain Ieuan's aching need to escape, if only in those flights of imagination that are his stories, to soar above the stench.

Ride the White Stallion is both honest storytelling and social history, capturing the hard graft and honest sweat that helped build my hometown. I have sunk many a pint of Double Dragon ale in the Drovers, where Ieuan celebrates his twenty-first. I have also recently visited the foundry, or what's left of it, which is now a centre for Christian missionaries from Korea who want to spark off a new revival in Wales. And this in a town that abounds with empty chapels. Nowadays there is little physical evidence left of the super abundance of factories that once typified the landscape here, demolition-balled in the name of progress and the beautifying processes of the Millennium Coastal Park.

So there is the real and present danger of the town suffering from what the late artist and critic Osi Rhys Osmond described as "cultural Alzheimer's", a creeping fog of forgetfulness about how this town, and others like it, came into being and of the labours that entailed and the myriad workplaces there once were, such as Dunkin's Arsenic Works, Cambrian Tinplate and New Vanadium Alloys: Stradey Galvanizing, St David's Tin and Llanelli Steel.

William Glynne-Jones's novels therefore serve as important and elegantly readable *aides memoire*, just as the books themselves remind us of a lamentably forgotten writer, now deservingly brought back into the light.

Ride the White Stallion and its prequel serve to illuminate our histories and thus our understanding of ourselves. They do so simply by redacting a bloody good tale and involving us fully in the travails of their working class characters. These are the sort of people who – by dint of wearying labours and collective political convictions – built our towns and bequeathed us a better future.

Jon Gower

RIDE THE WHITE STALLION

PARTHIAN
LIBRARY OF WALES

CHAPTER ONE

Three young men stooped through the low doorway from the coreshop into the foundry yard.

The first, Ieuan Morgan, was of medium height, dark haired and good looking, with a quick eye and tanned complexion. Under his arm he carried a blue dungaree jacket rolled into a tight bundle.

Behind him came Thomas Hughes, deep of chest, broad shouldered, dressed in a faded grey tweed jacket and moleskin trousers. The third, a trifle older than his companions, wore a dirty boiler suit that was far too big for his small frame, and which hung about him in greasy folds. As he appeared through the doorway he looked nervously around.

"Couple o' minutes to go again before the hooter blows, boys. What d'you say we hang around for a bit? The bug-house—we could have a sit down there." His voice came forth thickly as if it were oppressed and stifled by a feather bed.

Thomas shrugged.

"Okay, Titus. Hell! you're a fine one to come to the 'do'. Ieuan's big day, and all you can think of is a couple o' minutes and the bug-house! The sooner we get to the Drovers' the better. On Saturday mornings the place is as crammed as a tin of sardines."

Titus mumbled under his breath. "Thinking of Lu, I was," he said presently as they passed the tall mound of scrap iron facing the steel furnace. "He's been up the pole this morning. Caught me having a spell in Jonah's shanty and played merry hell with me. Don't want to rub him up the wrong way again."

"Why bother about foremen, Titus, when I'm feeling like a millionaire?" Ieuan now spoke. "As Thomas says, this is my big day. From now on I'm a fully fledged sand rat. Next week I get

1

the journeyman's rate, and this afternoon I'm seeing Sally. You and your Lu! Come on, the drinks are on me. By the time we reach the fitting shop the hooter'll be on the blow."

"How is Sally?" Thomas asked, his good-humoured face solemn for the moment.

"Fine. She's getting on fine. The doctors say she'll be out soon. Next month, or maybe June."

"Good! That's grand news, indeed, and I'm glad to hear it."

Titus, still apprehensive, sidled in between them.

"Who else's coming? Reg Bowen, Charlie?"

Ieuan nodded. "Yes, we're meeting them outside the main gate. Bingo and Abraham promised they'd be along, too. And Dummy."

Titus grinned. Tiny wrinkles appeared on the side of his impudent, tossed-up nose. "Don't tell me old Abie takes a pint! I thought he'd signed the pledge."

"This is a special occasion," Thomas reminded him.

"But he's a deacon. Never heard of a deacon who walked into a pub the front way. Round the back, and a swig on the sly— that's the usual."

"Old Abraham's broad minded," Thomas winked. "Besides, he has a right to be asked to the 'do'. A fat lot we'd know about things if old Abie hadn't shown us." He paused. "Why the hell I ever chose to be a moulder, beats me. It'd have been better if my old man had apprenticed me to Parry the Undertaker. Now, there's the job where a feller needn't worry about unemployment. Always plenty of corpses knocking around waiting to be buried."

Turning to Ieuan, he smiled. "Well, boyo—what's it feel like to be a journeyman at last? And better still, what's it feel like to be twenty-one on this fine and glorious April morning? How's that, Titus? Damn it, I'm talking like a book."

Time and the foundry had made their mark on Ieuan. His face, sensitive and thoughtful, was deeply tanned and glowing with health, and his hands, once familiar only with the feel of books, were dark, knotted, and fiercely strong. Though somewhat slight in build, he looked tough and muscular. He carried himself with an air, and walked with a quick, nervous step.

Thomas's question had disturbed him, and for a while he did not answer. He felt deflated, somehow, and no longer eager for the Drovers' Arms, and the pint to celebrate his twenty-first birthday. His mind flashed back to a dark and rainy November morning in 1924, six dreary years ago, when he had suddenly been pitchforked by his mother from the County School into Bevan's foundry. The coreshop and his apprenticeship were now far behind him, but the agony of that beginning, and the suffering which followed it, would remain with him always.

He hated the foundry as intensely, now, as he had on that first day when he had risen before the sun, and seen its ugliness in a greying light. He remembered how near tears he had been then as he passed through its gates and stumbled across the yard to the coreshop. He remembered Frank, too. Frank, who had put an arm around his shoulder that morning and had become his friend and adviser. Frank was married, and Frank had been killed in the foundry. He had seen him being burnt alive.

That was five years ago, and in spite of it the foundry had continued to hold him, and, with the few shillings it gave him to take home to his mother, had frustrated all his efforts to shake himself free. It should do so no longer, however. He was now twenty-one, and, if he were going to be a writer it was time he did something better than just letters to the press.

But he would have to see that Sally was all right, first.

Dear Sally! She had pleaded with him so desperately to leave Bevan's before she was taken away to the sanatorium. How he hated to think of her there, alone. The doctor had assured him she would get well again. She was getting better, too. He had seen that she was, and he had just told Thomas that she was.

Thomas—

Ieuan pulled himself together as Thomas spoke again.

"I said, 'What does it feel like to be twenty-one, Ieuan?'"

"Sorry, Thomas. I was just thinking..."

"Not worrying about the new lad who started this morning?"

"Well, now that you've mentioned it, I do feel sorry for the kid."

"Oh, come on, snap out of it. The young improvers are not half as bad as the lot we had to face when we were in the coreshop," Thomas said light-heartedly. "Reg, Bingo and Charlie have grown a bit wiser now that they've got kids of their own. As for Bull Jackson, I reckon since he's been made shop steward he's got his hands pretty full. I suppose the youngster'll get his leg pulled plenty. And why shouldn't he? It'll do him good. But I don't think he'll get the rough-housing we went through as kids."

"Maybe you're right, Thomas. Reg and the crowd have certainly changed, but Bull's just as likely to have it in for the kid as he had it in for me."

"You sure don't have any liking for him."

"No, frankly I haven't—not after what happened to Dummy the other week."

Thomas stopped. His face went hard. "Yes, that was a nasty business." He shrugged again and continued down the yard. "But Bull copped a packet—got paid back in his own coin, didn't he?"

They had now reached the pattern shop. The door was slightly open and a group of pattern-makers crowded inside the doorway, waiting for the hooter to release them for their week-end respite. They nodded to the three moulders as they passed.

Titus made to cross over to the bug-house, a corrugated iron lean-to near the steel furnace where another group of men, moulders, fettlers and labourers were gathered ready for the road.

Just then the hooter blew. Its loud, penetrating wail was deafening. The clamour increased as other hooters from neighbouring factories, steel and tinplate mills joined in to form a discordant symphony that echoed far out over the town and its environs.

Soon, the yard was black with workers who sprang into view from every obscure corner and hurried in thick procession down the sunlit yard towards the time-office. The only people who seemed not to hurry were the white-collared office workers.

Conscious of their superiority they strolled leisurely through the main gateway, the morning newspapers tucked under their arms.

Later, in the wake of the stream of overalled and grimy workmen came the departmental foremen, dignified and aloof as the office staff.

Ieuan and his two workmates stood at the time-office door where they were soon joined by Reg Bowen, Charlie, Bingo, and old Abraham, the coreshop charge-hand. Presently Dummy, a wiry, thin-faced youth, greeted them with a smile. He patted Ieuan on the back and his expressive fingers spoke to wish him a happy birthday.

"Well, lads—let's go."

They swung to the right over the level-crossing, passed Joe Marasiano's ice-cream shop and ambled up the hill to the Drovers' Arms. When they came to the front door of the pub, Abraham hesitated. He fixed his attention on a poster glued on to the saloon bar window.

CAPEL SILOAM
Thursday, April 10th 1930, at 7 p.m.

GRAND CONCERT

by

THE ABERMOR LADIES' CHOIR
(Conductor: Arwel Jones, A.R.C.M.)
(Accompanist: Madam Gomer-Lewis-Rees, L.R.A.M.)
EMINENT LOCAL ARTISTES WILL ALSO APPEAR.
Admission 2s. 6d. (Reserved)
Gallery 1s. 6d. (Unreserved)

Titus smirked. He nudged Ieuan. "Better show him where the back door is. He's a bit shy."

Abraham overheard the remark. He straightened himself, and, glancing quickly around, hurried in through the open door.

5

The tiny bar parlour of the Drovers' was, as Thomas had predicted, "full as a sardine tin". On the wooden benches ranged round the room with its one small, curtained window opening out on to the grey, drab street of cement walls and tipsy chimney-pots, sat the regular customers.

Lean, red-faced steel millmen in their canvas aprons and iron-shod clogs, foundry workers, dock-trimmers, young lads who had not yet started to shave, three commercial travellers who sat apart from the shag-smoking millmen—of such was the Saturday noon company.

Pint mugs of beer, stout and shandies sparkled on the zinc-surfaced tables. There was a low hum of conversation broken now and then by the musical tinkling of glasses as the pot-man shuffled over the sawdust-strewn floor and gathered up the empties expertly, impatient with the men's demands to "fill 'em up again, Dai *bach.*"

Thomas walked to the bar and rapped a coin on the polished mahogany. Mrs. Jenkins, the landlady, her grey hair screwed into a bun on the back of her head, bustled into the room. She peered at him short-sightedly over her spectacles.

"Hullo, Thomas Hughes, not much patience you've got this morning, I must say. A Saturday thirst you must be suffering from, after the foundry—is it?"

She saw Ieuan and the others who were edging into a seat on the near side of the room.

"Hullo, Ieuan, how are you today, my boy? And Titus—looking well you are. Started courting yet?"

"Mrs. Jenkins, come now, my girl," Thomas protested. "This is no time for idle gossip. Six pints of mild and bitter if you please, and..." He threw a glance over his shoulder at Abraham who fidgeted uncomfortably in his seat, "a bottle of pop."

The drinks were brought to the table, and Ieuan paid the landlady. She regarded him dubiously, weighing the money in her hand.

"That's all right, Mrs. Jenkins—this is my round," Ieuan smiled.

6

"But Thomas, he…" she began.

"This is a day for celebration," Thomas interrupted. He placed an arm about her shoulder and held his cheek close to hers. "today, Mrs. Jenkins *fach,* Ieuan pays his footing."

She threw up her arms. Her eyes twinkled.

"Dear me! So Ieuan Morgan is out of his trade at last? Well, well, fancy that now. And only the other day his mother was coming to meet him at the gate! There's quick the time goes, doesn't it?"

"Indeed, Mrs. Jenkins." Titus clutched his pint mug with both hands and blew off the froth. "If you hinder us any more there won't be time for one for the road, so off with you, woman, and back to your station. Customers waiting for booze, you know."

The landlady took no notice. "Then five years he's been at his trade," she went on. "Gracious! A man he has become all of a sudden."

"Twenty-one today," said Thomas.

"Twenty-one, there's lovely!" Mrs. Jenkins giggled self-consciously and without warning began to sing in a quavering soprano:

"I've got the key of the door,
Never been twenty-one before."

She sighed. "Wish I was twenty-one again." Her voice dropped to a confidential whisper. She jerked a thumb to indicate her husband who was serving in the public bar in the next room. "Though he wouldn't h'appreciate it. A beauty I was in them days, believe me, boys, with half the fellows in town ready to give up their right arms to marry me. Never had a bit of life in him, did Ezra. And now he's gone beyond everything—if you know what I mean?"

Titus leaned over and dug her playfully in the ribs. "There's a one you are, Mrs. Jenkins. Fancy mentioning things like that in company. I remember once when Farmer Moody's bull…"

7

Thomas kicked him hard on the shin. He held up his glass.

"Here's to Ieuan. Good luck, and all the best!"

The six glasses were raised.

"*Iechyd da!*"

"Best o' luck."

"Bottoms up, and all the best."

"Cheers, Ieuan!"

"Long life and happiness to you, my boy."

Mrs. Jenkins sighed once more as the toast was drunk.

"One on the house you'll have now, eh, boys?" she invited, summoning Dai the pot-man to her side.

"No—no more, thank you," Abraham hastened to say.

"But twenty-one years old today, my man! Another drink that calls for."

"You can fill me another," said Titus.

"Same here, Mrs. Jenkins." Reg, Bingo and Charlie slid their glasses towards her. Dummy swallowed the remainder of his beer and waited expectantly.

Ieuan laughed. "Right-ho, fill them up again, Mrs. Jenkins. Then we'll all go home quietly."

The glasses were refilled. A second toast was called, when Bull Jackson stepped into the room. He glanced casually at the party, then shouldered his way to the far side of the room. His right hand was heavily bandaged, and he was dressed in his street clothes.

Thomas was the first to notice him.

"How you feeling, Bull?" he called. "Think of starting Monday?"

The other nodded slowly. "Hope so," he said cursorily. "Been feeling pretty bloody all last week." His eyes fell on Dummy who, meeting his gaze, looked away and fumbled nervously at his cigarette-case.

Jackson called for a drink and sat down on the bench near the window. He turned to the man seated next to him, evidently an acquaintance, and ignored his workmates.

Dummy's cigarette-case clattered to the floor. He smiled

sheepishly when Ieuan retrieved it and handed it back to him. He appeared to be ill at ease, and occasionally his eyes wandered across the floor to where Bull was seated.

There was an awkward silence. Dummy snapped open the case and offered a cigarette to his mates. Each took one, with the exception of Abraham who preferred his pipe. Ieuan and Thomas exchanged a look deep with significance. They knew, even as the others did, why Dummy felt embarrassed in Bull's presence.

The incident had happened a fortnight ago, barely three months after the young mute was given a job in Bevan's foundry.

Any dirty jobs to be done in the foundry, and Dummy was the one who was sent to do them. Filling the tar bosh, mixing wet loam for the mould joints, carrying the heavy, steel digging bars to the smithy to be resharpened, changing the heavy chains on the crane—these were some of the tasks which the other men avoided when Dummy was near at hand.

They exploited his good nature, but he accepted their impositions without protest, as though he were anxious to make friends and establish himself with the moulders.

He was a little, "four feet and a farthing" chap, and pasty-faced, a midget in dungarees, with eyes full of pity like a spaniel's.

On that day, a fortnight ago, Johnny Blewitt, a moulder in the English union, came into the steel shop with a huge paper parcel under his arm. The hooter had blown for the first half-hour break, and the moulders who ate their breakfast in the foundry and compo-shed crowded round him, curious to find out what the parcel held.

Johnny had a reputation as an angler and most of his leisure time was spent in casting into the surf on the beach which lay about a quarter of a mile or so from the foundry. He would often bring in his catch and offer to sell it to anyone for the price of a couple of pints of beer.

White-haired Owen Matthews, the machine moulder, was the first to question Johnny. He nosed around the parcel, prodding it with his calloused hands.

"What have you got in there, Johnny *bach*?"

Johnny dropped the parcel to the floor and began to unwrap it. "Just wait till you see it, boys."

The stench that rose from the half-putrefied salmon bass which the parcel revealed made Owen jump back a pace, his nostrils tightly pinched between thumb and forefinger.

"*Jiw, jiw*—what a stink there is," he gasped. "That fish, Johnny—where did you catch it, man? It must be a month old, indeed. Or p'raps it giv'd itself up?"

A burst of laughter followed Owen's query. Johnny Blewitt stooped over the fish and grimaced as he turned it over gingerly on to its belly.

"Found it washed up near the sewers by the Ballast Tip," he explained, wiping his hands briskly on the seat of his trousers.

"But what the hell's the idea of bringing it in here?" someone asked. "It stinks like a backyard."

Johnny chuckled. "I thought it'd be a lark to palm it off on to someone. Arrange a kind o' raffle, with the winner ready marked. We'd have a bloody good laugh to see the feller's face when he gets the prize." He rubbed his bristled chin. "You chaps know of anyone who'd like a salmon bass? Mighty fine fish, that," he tittered like a schoolboy, "when fresh."

Bull Jackson, attracted by the laughter, pushed his way to the front. He turned the bass over with his foot.

"Listen, Johnny," he grinned, "there's no need to go to the trouble of fixing a raffle. I got a better idea." He swung round to the others. "If you fellers want a laugh, just watch me."

Owen Matthews walked away. "I don't like your ideas. Smell they do, like the fish," he mumbled. "Always putting someone in trouble, and I'll be no party to that."

"Christ! Hark at him. Gone sanctimonious all of a sudden." Bull wrapped the fish in the brown paper and thrust it under his arm.

"Who's coming over to see the fun?"

Johnny Blewitt and the others followed him down the foundry, clambered after him over a dry bank of moulding sand and stood in a half-circle a few yards away as he headed for a corner under the furnace landing where Dummy was eating his breakfast.

"Here y'are, Dummy. Got a present for you." Bull tossed the parcel into his lap.

Dummy looked at him. His eyes lighted with pleasure. Then all at once he became suspicious. He shook his head vigorously.

"Come on, take it," Bull cajoled. "I'm telling you, Dummy, it's a—it's a kind of gift for you from us chaps. We've been pretty rough on you ever since you came here, getting you to do all the muck work and we feel—well, we're sorry and all that. This parcel's for you, Dummy, a sort o' compensation for all you've done for us. Isn't that right, boys?"

"'Course, too bloody true."

"Just to show there's no hard feelings."

"It's yours, Dummy. And there's no catch in it, either."

Dummy looked up again at Bull, then at the parcel. His eyes began to smile. He opened his mouth. No sound came from it as his lips framed the word, "Thanks."

"Forget it." Bull waved his hands airily. "We owe you plenty."

Dummy took the parcel and held it in his arms as though it were something precious. He turned and walked over to his tool cupboard built between the girders in the archway leading under the furnace. The men waited to see the fun.

Bull hurried after him. "Hey, hold hard a bit, Dummy! Don't be in such a hurry, *mun*. Open up... Let's see what you got." He called the moulders around. "Come on over, fellers."

Dummy glanced at the crowd. He was still smiling in a shy sort of way, embarrassed by the sudden friendliness shown towards him.

"Come on. Dummy. Open up. Show some gratitude," Bull coaxed.

Dummy hung his head. He acted like a child and it was evident that he wished to open the parcel privately. At last he placed it on a mould and unwrapped the paper. Johnny Blewitt and his fellow conspirators sniggered and held their noses. Bull gave the wink.

In a moment the putrefying bass was exposed, its dull, dead eyes staring up at Dummy.

"There! Isn't that a nice surprise?" someone laughed.

Bull guffawed loudly. He slapped Dummy on the back. "What d'you think of it? Nice of the boys to remember you, eh? 'Tisn't every day that a feller gets a present. That's a good piece of fish flesh, that."

Dummy just stood there. At first it seemed he was going to cry. He was badly hurt. Then suddenly he got mad. His mouth opened. His lips moved.

"Look out. Bull!" Johnny Blewitt shouted with a laugh.

Dummy stooped. He caught the bass by the tail with both hands and swung it fiercely upwards. Bull ducked. The greasy tail slipped from Dummy's hands and the gaping onlookers saw the bass hurtle through the air and land in the water bosh on the other side of the foundry.

"What the...!"

Johnny and the moulders started laughing; not at Dummy, but at Bull who made a ridiculous figure as he crouched with head down, his arms shielding his face.

The insinuating laughter made him wild. He swore at the men under his breath, then, springing forward on his toes, he reached out and gripped Dummy by the collar. He thrust his right fist under his victim's nose.

"See that!" he blazed. "The good ol' right, and you're going to get it plonk under your chin, Dummy... the old one-two, one-two. Now, get that fish out of the bosh, d'you hear?"

Dummy shook his head. He looked around appealingly. His whole body trembled. He tried to step back, but Bull jerked him round and dragged him to the bosh.

"Get it out!" he shouted.

Dummy choked. Again he shook his head. Bull's mouth tightened. He grasped Dummy by the nape of the neck. His fingers

12

sank into the thin flesh. Dummy's body twisted with pain. A horrible cry, half human, half animal, escaped from his throat.

Johnny Blewitt's laughter died. He turned and walked up the steel shop. The rest of the men followed him slowly and waited near the moulding machine at the top end of the foundry.

Dummy struggled to free himself, the awful noises still coming from his throat as Bull forced him forward over the edge of the bosh. The pressure of his fingers increased. Dummy's hands disappeared into the dank water. Lower, lower they sank until his arms were submerged to the shoulder. He groped for the fish; but the bosh was too deep.

"I'll make you get it out, you little bastard!" Bull raged. Gripping Dummy by the seat of his trousers with his left hand he lifted him off the floor and pressed his head down viciously.

It seemed Dummy was under for good. Then up popped his head. He gasped for breath. Streaks of black slime trailed down his cheeks. His hair was matted with oil and grease. He lashed out with his arms and kicked wildly at his assailant, but Bull was too strong for him.

"Get that damn fish out!" Bull behaved like a madman. Once more he forced Dummy's head under the water. The next time Dummy came up spluttering and choking, he had the fish in his hands. Sobbing with fear and rage he threw it down on a mould.

Bull released his grip. He leaned back against the bosh, panting with exertion, his face livid. "Let that teach you not to get tough with me."

Dummy lay on the floor, the grey dust clinging to his clothes, his face smudged with slime, and it was as he was lying there that Ieuan and Thomas, on their way to the coreshop, saw him, and Bull near by. Before Thomas could prevent him, Ieuan was confronting Bull.

"You did that, of course," he said, pointing to Dummy on the ground. "It would be just like you, you skunk."

Bull jerked himself upright. "Damn you! Who d'you think you're calling a skunk? I'll bust you into pulp for that."

13

Thomas was now standing at Ieuan's side, and Thomas, as Bull knew, was a match even for him. But it was a cold, stern voice, and not Thomas, which held Bull where he stood.

"What's the game?"

All three turned slowly to face the speaker. A few yards away stood Lu Davies, the foreman. The nine o'clock hooter had blown and the moulders scuttled back to their jobs as he spoke again.

"What's the game?"

Bull sneered. "Nothing's the game. Why?"

"Then what's happened? Did you do this to Dummy?"

"Ask him."

The foreman stooped over Dummy. "What's wrong? Did Jackson do this to you?"

"Hey! Who the hell d'you think I am?" Bull shouted, but Lu took no notice. He put the question again. Dummy shook his head. Bull grinned.

"There! What did I tell you?"

The foreman scowled. He looked Bull straight in the eyes. Then at Dummy, and the wet, slimy fish.

"I think I know who's who in this place. You and some of the other fellows here keep picking on Dummy, and I'm going to put a stop to it, once and for all. You ought to be damn well ashamed of yourselves, the lot of you. If the chap was big enough to stand up for himself I suppose you'd steer clear of him."

Lu turned to Ieuan and Thomas. "You two, see to Dummy, will you? You, Bull—take that stinking fish out of here."

Bull sunk his hands into his pockets and stood, feet astride. "It's not mine," he grunted.

"You heard me. Throw it out. If you don't, I'll make you."

Bull's lips compressed into a thin line. He clenched his right hand and brought it slowly to his side.

"You can put away that good ol' right. I'm not scared of you. Bull Jackson, or of your one-two, one-two." The foreman tossed his head. "I've pasted better fellows than you before breakfast. Now, clear that—that thing out o' here when I tell you."

14

Bull made no move to obey. He dropped his right hand. "I'm not bloody well scared of you either, Lu," he challenged. "I gave Dummy a ducking, but he had it coming to him." He sniffed. "The feller can't take a joke."

Lu brushed the excuse aside with a contemptuous toss of the head. "I know the kind of jokes you and the others play on Dummy, and I tell you again it's got to stop."

"Oh, for Christ's sake, go take a flying jump at yourself. I've told you something, too. I'm not scared of you."

"Maybe." The foreman smiled sardonically. "I know you and your kind, Jackson. Not scared of me, perhaps, but damn scared of losing your job. And that's what's going to happen if you don't take my orders. I'm the boss in this hole. Outside, I'm nothing. If you don't do what I tell you then I'll pack you out through the gates, and see that you won't get a job elsewhere in this town— shop steward or no shop steward." He pointed to the bass. "Now, throw that stinking carcass out. It's your last chance."

Bull cursed. Wheeling round, he lunged at the bass with his foot. The fish toppled to the floor and rolled into the dust.

"Out! You heard me. Out with it! Pick it up!"

"What the hell!" Setting his teeth, Bull bent down and grabbed the bass. As his fingers closed over the greasy scales he gave a sharp yell of pain. Then, gathering all his strength, he flung the fish through the archway.

"That's better." Lu gave a hand to Dummy and helped him to his feet. He spoke over his shoulder to Bull.

"Back on your job, if you know what's good for you."

But the latter wasn't listening. He felt the ball of his thumb, pressing out the globule of blood that had formed there when the sharp, spiked fin had punctured the skin. He sucked it, then, flapping his hand, walked slowly back to his job.

The next day Dummy had peace, and the moulders never imposed on him again. Bull came to work, his hand swollen and painful.

"What's up?" asked Johnny Blewitt when he saw the injured hand.

15

Bull Jackson grunted. "Nothing. I got scratched with that lousy fish of yours… just a scratch, that's all."

"On the good ol' right, indeed. No good for the old one-two, one-two now, eh, Bull?" Dan Price, a labourer, grinned. "Whatever will you do?"

Bull swung round on him. His right arm shot out from the shoulder. The blow never contacted, and he dropped his hand sharply, wincing with pain.

"Just a scratch, is it?" Dan asked with a sneer.

Bull got more than he bargained for. The following day the hand grew worse. Then it began to turn black. When Pritchard, the foundry's time-keeper and first-aid man, saw it, he told Bull he'd caught a packet.

"You've got blood-poisoning there, my lad. Better go up to the doctor's and have something done to it."

Pritchard's diagnosis proved correct. Bull Jackson remained off work the next day and no one saw him at the foundry for the following two weeks.

Old Owen Matthews was very happy at the result. "If Dummy didn't get his own back on our shouting shop steward, that fish of Johnny Blewitt's did, ay indeed. And thank goodness, too, I say. Time it is that Jimmy Jackson was made a bit quiet. Too handy he's been with his fists for a long time."

No one disagreed with Owen's remarks.

CHAPTER TWO

It was almost one o'clock when Ieuan and his companions rose to go.

"Half a mo', boyo. I've got to go out to measure a donkey's ears." Thomas opened the door which led to the public bar. A loud, strident voice raised in argument in the next room made him pause. He smiled wryly. "Badger Made to Measure's at it again," he remarked. "What the hell's the matter with the chap. Always on the grouse over something or other."

"Let's see the fun," said Bingo. He pushed past Thomas, while Ieuan and the others stepped into the bar. Sitting at a corner table was a tall, vicious-looking man of about forty-five or so, clad in a smartly tailored suit and bowler hat. From beneath heavy eyebrows his small eyes flickered restlessly over every article in the room, from ceiling to floor, corner to corner, and he regarded everything and everyone with vindictiveness.

This was J.M. Badger, town councillor and owner of a chain of clothing stores, who was known to the townspeople as Badger Made to Measure, a business term he had advertised so extensively that the phrase had replaced his initials.

A tinworker, a half-empty pint at his elbow on the bar counter, swallowed nervously during the momentary silence caused by the appearance of the newcomers.

Badger tapped his pipe violently against his knee. His eyes fastened on the tinworker.

"You fellows, you're never satisfied," he snapped like a terrier. "You earn the best money in town. You're never out of work, I mean to say, no one has ever seen you queueing at the Labour Exchange. And now you have the temerity to put forward a claim for a bonus..."

The tinworker hitched up his soiled apron. He reached for the pint. "Now look here, Mr. Badger," he began in a quiet tone. "I don't want to argue with, you, but ..."

"I beg your pardon!" Badger's thick eyebrows seemed to leap up his forehead. "Me, argue! Why, I mean to say..."

"Take the millmen in Calcutta," the tinworker went on, but Badger's look of scorn and indignation made him stop.

"Calcutta, my foot! Who wants to talk of millmen out there? It's this place, Abermor, we are concerned with, and the other tinplate towns of South Wales. I suppose you want to say that the tinplate worker in Calcutta is paid more handsomely than you, that he has these—these certain privileges and bonuses? Perhaps you would care to go to Calcutta, Evan Harries?"

"And why not? If I had the chance, I'd go. Tommy Flagons didn't do so bad when he went out there in 'twenty-two. Owns his own house he does, and his kids got a good education on the strength of what he earned."

"There!" Badger opened wide his arms and addressed the crowded room, the occupants of which were deeply interested in the argument. "You see, friends, Evan Harries isn't satisfied with his lot here. He wants to go to India." He jammed the pipe into his mouth. "England is a fine country to live in," he blurted with a vehemence that forced Evan to seek refuge in his pint. "I mean to say, it's the finest country in the world. Where, I mean to say, can you get more freedom, more justice?"

The tinworker groped for an answer, but before he could utter a word, Badger held up a hand.

"You don't answer, do you?" he challenged aggressively. "Well, silence is golden. I mean to say, silence is all right in its place, but, after all, it's common courtesy to speak when one's spoken to, I mean to say."

"Mr. Badger!" A voice cut into the room, and the irritable councillor turned in his seat. He frowned at Ieuan who now stood at the bar with Thomas and Bingo.

"Yes, and what have you to say for yourself, young man?"

"Nothing," Ieuan replied, "but it seems your attitude is not quite fair, is it?"

"And what's wrong with my attitude? I mean to say, this is a private discussion between Mr. Harries and myself and I see no reason for your interference. You'd better clear off, young man."

Ieuan smiled. "If I'm interfering, I'm sorry, but I happen to know Evan and I'm sure if you give him a chance to explain his point, he'll—"

"I've already heard his point," Badger retorted.

"And, incidentally, young Morgan, the less you say in a public bar the wiser you'll become... Oh, yes, I know you all right, I mean to say, you've been pointed out to me."

"Indeed?"

"You are the young crusader with a torch. The fiery young idealist who will put the world in shape again, I mean to say, in a few words."

Titus tiptoed to the bar and ordered a pint of beer for Charlie and himself, then leaned against the door, a half-grin on his face. Abraham was apprehensive and, excusing himself, made a quick exit into a side street.

"Yes, I've heard of you. I'm familiar with your various letters to the local *Guardian*, Mr. Morgan," Badger continued, his spleen now doubly aggravated by Ieuan's intrusion. "I mean to say, your epistles of criticism."

He tapped the bowl of his pipe against a table leg and smothered the embers into the sawdust-covered floor. "You're one of those bolshies, aren't you?"

"I'm a socialist, if that's what you mean," Ieuan replied. "I believe economics was made for man, and not man for economics."

"I said you're a bolshie."

"What you call me and what I am are entirely two different things, Mr. Badger. I'm not a member of the Communist Party."

Badger sniffed. Once again he sought to address the room. "You heard him, friends. He's a socialist. But I ask you, I mean

19

to say, what right has a so-called socialist to criticise his own government? Ramsay Macdonald, Jimmy Thomas, Snowden and Clynes—now I wonder if young Morgan here could, I mean to say—well, has he the intellect, the experience, to challenge the integrity of these men whom we have elected to govern us? Why, I mean to say, we shall soon be having our young friend speaking on the Town Hall Square one of these fine Sundays. And then perhaps we shall enjoy the fun of seeing his name on the list of candidates for the next parliamentary election, I mean to say."

Before Ieuan could reply to the taunt, Thomas strode from the bar and advanced towards the argumentative business man. His face clouded with suppressed anger.

"Now, look here, Badger... Yes, you heard me— I said, 'Badger'. I don't want to listen to no more of your slanging. You know Ieuan, you say. Well, I know you, too, and so does everybody else in this room. Everybody in every pub in town knows you. Not because you sell Made to Measures but because you're a damned old fusspot who goes round from pub to pub looking for arguments."

"Why, how dare you! I'm a town councillor, I'll have you know." Badger rose to his feet, red with indignation. "I mean to say—"

Thomas pushed him firmly back into his seat, heedless of the murmured protests around him.

"'I mean to say, I mean to say'," he mimicked. "Now, what do you mean? Stop yammering, and spit it out. You're a councillor, yes, and you call yourself a socialist... a socialist who makes profit on the backs of the likes of us."

Badger shook himself like a dusty hen. He reached again for his pipe and tobacco pouch. His fingers trembled and his efforts to fill the pipe bowl were completely ineffective. He looked up to see Thomas face him pugnaciously. He made another attempt to appeal to the men in the bar.

"Did you hear that, friends? Slander, that's what it is. A deliberate slander... I—I mean to say, the man's getting personal, and I—"

"Personal, by damn!" Thomas brushed Ieuan's hand away as he tried to restrain him. "You got more than personal with Ieuan just now. A free country this is, you say? Well, a chap can write to the papers if he likes..."

"Certainly, certainly, I am not disputing the fact," Badger's voice dropped to a whisper. His aggressiveness melted.

"He signs his name to the letters, that's more'n what some other fellers do. He's got the courage of his convictions, he's got guts."

"Indeed, indeed, I don't deny it. I mean to say..."

"Then shut your trap and stop trying to be funny about him."

Thomas crossed to the door that opened into the street. "One thing more, Badger—you'll not get my bloody vote again. Not after this."

"Now then, now then, boys, no bad language in here, if you please," Mrs. Jenkins protested, poking her head into the room. She scowled at her husband, who had listened with relish to the long argument.

"Ought to be ashamed of yourself, Ezra Jenkins. No decent public house'd stand for all this nonsense. This isn't the House of Parliaments, you know."

She caught sight of Ieuan who was on the point of leaving. "A nice birthday party this has turned out to be, my boy. I hope you get more sense into your head by the time you are twice twenty-one."

Thomas saluted her gravely. "All right, Mrs. Jenkins, the war is over now, and we are leaving you nice and quietly and as sober as little judges. So long, my girl. I'll be coming back to see you again, soon."

21

CHAPTER THREE

Ieuan and Thomas left the Drovers' together. As they walked down the hill, Thomas spat into the gutter.

"That Badger chap gives me the pip. By damn! It's time he was kicked out of the town council to make room for someone with a bit of sense." He scowled, and dug his hands into his pockets.

Ieuan smiled. Thomas looked at him, puzzled.

"What the…" he began. Suddenly, they both burst out laughing.

"Aw, to hell with Badger."

"Yes, to hell with him."

They walked on for a while in silence.

"Say, Bull was a quieter fellow today, wasn't he, Ieuan?" Thomas said presently. "There's something mighty queer about that chap. D'you know," he stopped to light a cigarette stub, "he's not all that bad. They tell me he's a grand chap at home with his old mother. Funny, isn't it?"

"Is that right?"

"Yes, it's true enough. He thinks the world of her. Can't say he had any respect for his old man when he was alive, though. The old man used to lam hell out of him. Kept him away from school, too, until the education authorities brought him over the coals. Ay, old man Jackson was a terror by all accounts."

"That puts a different face on it, Thomas."

"I know. Well, that's the story. Don't ask me why he's such a bloody fool in the foundry."

"Kind to his mother… Yet look at the way he treated Dummy. I don't understand it."

Thomas shrugged.

The Town Hall clock chimed, the echoes reverberating along the narrow streets. Thomas flicked his cigarette stub into the road.

"Which way you going, Ieuan?"

"Up Deacon's Hill."

"Good! I'll come with you as far as the Square."

A crocodile of red-bereted, orphaned children from the Cottage Homes marched into Station Square, led by a morose young woman in a plain brown dress and straw hat. Thomas watched them, his eyes darkening into deep and musing tenderness.

"Suffer little children," Ieuan heard him say, and saw his mouth tighten.

A tramcar swerved noisily into the Square. The young woman gave a sharp command, and the children wheeled towards the terminus. They were bound for Howard's Park and a day in the April sunshine, to have a cup of tea and a bun generously provided by the ladies of the Howard's Welfare Committee.

The friends parted, and Ieuan continued his walk homewards. From Deacon's Hill he could see the face of the Town Hall clock. It read a quarter to two. He hurried along past the grey school building. Below him lay the town, ugly, forbidding even in the yellow sunshine, and his eyes were instinctively drawn away to the distant fields and woods that sloped from the outskirts to the blue-rimmed horizon, to a beauty untouched by industrialism.

There, on high ground beyond the town, screened from it by trees, and clear of its smoke and grime, its foul river, its bursting cemeteries, its clangorous mills and roaring foundries, and its roads pinched by strings of drab houses, stood the gracious homes of the factory owners and business men. Their sleek lawns, paved drives, and proud frontages turned away from the town, and their windows and balconies faced the wide sweep of a blue bay that reached out to the world's end; a blue, shimmering bay protected on the remoter side by an arc of green-topped cliffs and undulating hills of a richer green dotted with white farmhouses and the holiday bungalows of the industrialists.

Except for the slight differences in contour, the steel towns of south Wales are identical. The rolling mills, steel and iron foundries, chemical factories and tin-plate works sprawl untidily along the coast. There is no grandeur here, no Manhattan skyline of towering skyscrapers; no sharp burst of colour, but a monotonous greyness that wearies the eye and deadens the spirit of all save the exile who willingly returns to this, his home, again.

From the Bristol Channel and the bays of Glamorgan and Carmarthenshire, one is faced with a vista of tall, soot-begrimed chimney stacks from which clouds of black smoke belch unceasingly. The salt tang of the air gives way to the pungent smell and taste of acrid fumes. The little rivers, once pastoral, laughing and clear, are now black with coal dust, yellow with acid, polluted and unclean, the home of rats and refuse. They flow sluggishly through the towns, under rusty, unsightly iron bridges; past burial grounds that bear not a blade of grass, the laughter they once knew now silenced for ever by the thunder of the rolling mills.

And it is only when they reach the final stage of their weary journey into the estuaries and bays that they gather speed, as if happy at last to find release from their confinement in the bleak hills and barren wastelands of the industrial area.

Ieuan shielded his eyes from the sun. Far out to his right he saw the long, golden stretch of the lonely *Cefn* sands washed by the blue waters of Carmarthen Bay. *Cefn Sidan,* "silken back", the treacherous beach, windblown and savage in the dreary winters; where the sailing vessels of long ago met their fate, blown in from the open bay on to the shallows, never to be launched again. On the yellow sands lay the rotting hulks of many vessels, and below lay buried the bleached bones of the million nameless mariners of childhood imaginings.

But when summer came, the *Cefn* extended a promise of solitude, and inveigled one away from the sprawling, dingy towns. Its cool breezes caressed the sun-frowning brow. The surf ran high over the powdered beach, and its waters were clear as a spring. Here the salmon bass frolicked, and the sea-angler found contentment.

Ieuan knew the beach well. He had his own secret nook there which he had discovered last year when he had been unemployed for months. He remembered how on occasions he would hurry to it to escape from the defeatism of idleness, and how, as he lay on his back in the sun, the unvarying rush of the surf soothed his rebellious thoughts. He had found peace in the solitude of the *Cefn* and new hope and a respect for life.

"Suffer little children…" What a grand chap Thomas was!

The hollow chimes of the Town Hall clock boomed again, over and beyond the Saturday town. Two o'clock!

In three hours' time he hoped to be at the sanatorium. There was a dinner to be eaten, a change of clothing to be made, a journey to town and a rush for the bus. He'd have to hurry!

The prospect of his visit to Sally roused him from his mood of quiet despondency, and he turned his eyes away from the shimmering beach.

A freckled boy with a basket over his arm trotted by, bouncing a rubber ball.

"'Ello, Ieuan, Sammy Rowlands is over in your house," he called, as he passed.

"Thanks, Davie." Ieuan loosened his collar. He turned into the back-lane of the street where he lived and began to run.

A motor-cycle drawn up outside the back door confirmed the boy's story.

"Well, son, you're later than usual today." Dick Morgan stood in the kitchen doorway, watch in hand. He smiled. "Didn't see you go out this morning, Ieuan, so I s'pose I'm not too late to say many happy returns to you?"

"Thanks, Dad."

His mother paused in her preparation of the dinner and glanced at them. She wiped her hands on her apron. "Thank goodness you've come at last. Where've you been, Ieuan? Dinner's in the middle room today," she went on. "Dick! Tell Gweneira to come and give me a hand. Phyllis can talk to him in there till we're ready."

"*Him!* That's Sam right enough," Ieuan grinned, but his mother was in no mood to appreciate his banter.

25

"All this fuss every time he comes here," she grumbled. "Gweneira and him courting! I don't mind making dinner in the middle room on Sundays, but it means a lot of extra work when I have visitors on a Saturday."

"Never mind. Mam. It's my birthday today... Let me help you."

"No, be off with you and have a wash. Gweneira's job it is to help me. Besides, you're off to see that girl, aren't you?"

"I'm going to see Sally, if that's what you mean, Mam."

"Well, 'Sally' then, if it pleases you. Some day your father and me's going to be left alone in this house. You and Gweneira with your notions about courting, indeed! Phyllis is gone her fourteen, she'll be the next one to be having young fellows chasing after her. A woman brings children into the world, then just when they've grown up a bit and able to lend a hand they off to go and get married. Young Sam, a farm labourer he is... A grand match for my daughter, isn't it?" She brushed a wisp of grey hair from her damp forehead. "Where's that girl? Why don't she come when she's told... Gweneira!"

A slim, black-haired girl with laughing brown eyes came in answer to her call. A tight-fitting red woolen jumper accentuated her firm breasts, and she walked with the same quick energy that her brother possessed.

"Ieuan!" She threw her arms around his neck and kissed him impulsively on the cheek. "Many happy returns of the day to you, big brother. How does it feel like to be twenty-one?"

"I've answered that one before," he smiled. "There! That's enough... no more kisses for me. You'll get yourself all dirty."

"Gweneira!" her mother called impatiently. "Cut some bread and butter, will you, or it'll be tea-time before we look round?"

When Ieuan returned from his bedroom, washed and changed, the family were already seated at the dinner table. His younger sister, Phyllis, welcomed him with a kiss. Sam Rowlands, jovial and ruddy-cheeked, shook his hand heartily.

"Happy birthday, Ieuan."

26

"Thanks, Sam."

"You going up the San this afternoon?"

Ieuan nodded.

"Good. I'll run you up on the pillion. That all right, boy?"

"But I thought you were taking Gweneira out for a ride?" Phyllis enquired, glancing dubiously at her sister.

"I can go another time," said Gweneira. "Ieuan's late today. It's half-past two already. He'll never catch the bus."

"Oh, yes I will," Ieuan interposed. "If you and Sam have made arrangements, then you carry them out. I'm not going to spoil your day. I'll catch the bus all right, it doesn't leave till three."

"If you're going by bus, Ieuan—can I come?" Phyllis asked.

Her mother frowned in angry disapproval. "You'll stay at home, my girl, and give me a bit of help with the dishes... Dick! speak to her." She then addressed Gweneira. "You be careful on that pillion thing. A lot of accidents there are on the roads these days. I don't believe in young girls sitting on those things, with their legs all showing."

Sam fumbled embarrassingly with his fork.

"These so-called modern misses, always tearing around in a hurry as if they haven't got a minute to lose," she continued. She viewed Gweneira's red jumper with disapprobation. "And the way they dress! When I was a young woman—"

"Oh, Mam," Gweneira protested, "there's nonsense you speak sometimes. Sam is very careful, and as for me—well, I always try to keep my skirt down over my... Oh, dear, never mind."

Mrs. Morgan appealed to Dick. "There! just listen to that. There's gratitude for you! Just like our Ieuan is, all cheek when I try to give a bit of good advice. Respect for my elders I was taught when I was young, but today nothing but cheek and impudence one gets."

Dick fingered a piece of bread and butter.

"Now, now, Millie—the children do respect you. Eat your dinner, there's a good girl. You've had a hard morning and the heat in that kitchen's enough to roast an elephant. Sam'll take care of Gweneira, all right... and she won't be showing her legs at all, though it's a pity I say. Lovely little legs she's got."

"You never saw my legs when you was courting me, Dick Morgan."

"No, girl. Funny if I found out after we were married that you had a wooden one, eh?" Dick laughed, and the others joined in. But Mrs. Morgan frowned.

Later that evening when she and her husband were alone in the house she reminded him of all he had said.

"For ever trying to make light of everything you are, Dick. It's no joke for me, I can tell you, to be losing Gweneira so soon."

"But the girl is bound to marry some time, Millie. We can't expect to have her with us always."

"She's only nineteen—far too young to be marrying this year," came the quick retort.

"Old enough to know her own mind, Millie. I've no objections. Sam's a decent little chap, steady and hard working. They should be happy in Brecon..."

Mrs. Morgan was determined that he should not have the last word.

"I let Ieuan know this afternoon that just when I need the children's help most they start talking of getting married. Children ought to help their parents is what I say—especially after all the sacrifices I've made for them."

Dick placed his feet on the brass fender and began to untie his bootlaces.

"They didn't ask to be born, Millie," he said, tired of the argument.

She flared. "That's it! Go on at me like you always do. Taking the children's side against me... Alone we'll be, I'm telling you, with not a soul earning a penny in the house..."

"Oh, don't fret, girl." Dick kicked off his boots and sank back in the armchair. "We won't be alone, not for years to come. And when that time does come, we'll just have to make the best of it. If Gweneira and Ieuan get married, there's still Phyllis... She does help, you know?"

"With the few shillings wages she gets from Mrs. Barrington 'Oakhurst' you mean? It was useful last year when you and Ieuan was out for that long spell... but what she earns, well, you can put it in your eye."

Dick sighed. "All right, then," he said sharply. "Even if Phyllis leaves us you'll still have me, won't you? Don't cross your bridges before you come to them, Millie." He leaned forward in his chair and sought her hand. "Oh, don't let's argue all the time—what's the use of it? I've never prejudiced the children against you, but you've done nothing but nag at them ever since they were little. They've grown up now, remember, and it's only natural that they won't stand for it any more... Come on, girl, let's go to bed. It's very happy you and I should be, really. We've got three lovely children... and every one of them as handsome as their mother."

Her face softened for an instant. "That was a very nice thing to say, Dick... I mean, about them being good-looking."

He tightened his hand on hers. "A real beauty you were, Millie, my girl, and proud of you they are... Oh yes, you take it from me."

CHAPTER FOUR

As Ieuan approached the Town Hall Square, a tall, thin woman, hatless, and dressed in a cheap black summer coat and cotton frock, stepped out to meet him from the shadow of the cenotaph.

"Hello, Mrs. Marvin!" He smiled, and took from her the heavy basket of food she was carrying. "A lovely day, isn't it?"

Mrs. Marvin was about fifty, with a face deeply furrowed with wrinkles. Her eyes had a peculiar brilliance, and the rigid parting of her greying hair, carefully smoothed in Victorian fashion, marked the reserve and reticence of a bygone age.

Ieuan was in a happy mood as he escorted her to the parking-ground behind the dilapidated Butler's Cinedrome on the other side of the Square.

Two or three weeks more, and Sally would be home again. Gone the anxiety, the torment, the months of fear when her letters brought news of a relapse, when he had begun to despair of her recovery.

He recalled the many visits he had paid her, and the pain and grief he felt on his return home. And of the evenings he had spent with Mr. and Mrs. Marvin, nerve-shattered and torn with anguish. Her parents had accepted her illness as inevitable, and as time passed Mrs. Marvin had sought the comfort of religion more and more. Her prayers, her exhortations, and her absorption in the Bible had become an obsession. She had reached the stage where she was intolerant of criticism, fanatically religious.

And then, suddenly, Jim Marvin was taken seriously ill. A heart attack, and within a week he was dead. The news was withheld from Sally for some time. It was feared that the shock might excite another relapse. But she took the tragedy bravely.

The third year of her stay at *Calon y Nôs* brought happier

tidings. She was responding favourably to the various treatments. Her rest periods were shortened, her walks increased, and at the end of the year she was placed on "grades".

During Mrs. Marvin's last visit, a week ago, she had spoken to the Medical Superintendent. He was highly pleased with Sally's remarkable progress and assured her mother that she was due to be placed on top grade which meant that soon she would be discharged.

"Good afternoon, Mrs. Marvin, and to you, too, my boy. Lovely day for the trip, isn't it?"

Buxom, matronly Mrs. Jane 'Cardiff', a Crooked Row neighbour, poked her head out of the bus. Her ponderous double chin obscured the large cameo brooch she wore on her black satin blouse as she leaned over and extended a plump hand to help Mrs. Marvin up the step.

"Come and sit by me, my dear," she invited. "I've kept a place 'specially for you. Nice news it is about Sally, isn't it?"

The driver strained at the starting-handle, and promptly at three o'clock the *Calon y Nôs* special bus, a ramshackle contrivance which, at one time, had been used to carry miners to and from the pits in the valley, rattled out from the Square.

The passengers, men and women, were dressed in their Sunday best, well-laden baskets and parcels of food in their laps. Everyone had a personal link with the sanatorium. There were relatives and friends to visit, and every Saturday afternoon the pilgrimage to the sanatorium was made.

The bus struggled up a steep gradient on the first lap of its journey out of town. The engine choked and spluttered. A sharp hiss of steam escaped from the radiator, and the passengers were rocked violently in their seats.

"Golly, like as if we are on one of them paddle excursion steamers to 'Combe," Mrs. Jane 'Cardiff' laughed as she held on to her seat with both hands, the cloth-covered basket bobbing up and down in her ample lap.

A sudden crack from the exhaust, and a series of bangs which threatened to shatter the vehicle in two, forced a few stray pedestrians on the hill to scramble anxiously into the safety of the hedge. The stench of petrol and exhaust fumes filled the bus, and Mrs. Jane 'Cardiff' swayed to her feet and struggled with a window that defied opening.

Finally, the bus panted valiantly over the crest of the hill. Released from the ardour of its climb it jogged merrily down the other side of the slope, the tin framework shaking convulsively, the mudguards rattling.

Ieuan relaxed in his seat. An hour passed. Before him the long white road twisted and turned as the bus jolted on its way through the many tiny villages that lay deep down in the valleys or breasted the hill-sides.

Rivers twinkled in the sun, and the sound of their rushing waters could be heard above the din of the bus as it struggled up the steep gradients. Towering forests of beech and pine swept along the mountainsides, silhouetted against the broad skyline. Bright ribbons of water trickled down between deep crevices worn out of the solid grey rock. Stone boundary walls, old as the Conquest, zigzagged over miles of bleak moorland where black-faced sheep and wild mountain ponies roamed. On the summits of massive crags stood the ivy-entwined, ruined walls of ancient castles.

"Indeed, I'm glad your Sally will be out soon, Mrs. Marvin." Mrs. Jane 'Cardiff' was speaking.

"A lot of trouble you've had with the poor thing. Pity for her, I say. Such a pretty little girl, too… A shame you didn't find out years ago, I say. They do tell me that if they catch it early enough, there is every chance—"

"It is the will of God. There is nothing we can do about such things."

Ieuan gritted his teeth. "The will of God"—how often he had heard her say those words! A sudden anger rose within him. He remembered the days when he had pleaded with Sally's mother to apply for a new house. He had begged her to speak to the local M.O., but she had refused to listen.

"None of us ever had T.B. The house is clean and it is well looked after ... I say that what is to be, will be."

In the end he himself had approached the M.O.

"Too late, Mr. Morgan, I'm afraid. The Council have a long waiting list of over three thousand applicants. Deplorable, I admit, but the housing situation here is desperate and it would be hopeless to expect any definite promise from me. Mrs. Marvin will have to wait her turn with the others. I'm very sorry." A shrug. "I wish I could help, but my hands are tied."

His enquiries on Mrs. Marvin's behalf had been abortive, and he received no thanks from her. His mother, on hearing of his endeavours, upbraided him:

"If you could go to the Council about a new house for the Marvins, you could have seen about one for us. After all, we are five in this little box of a place. No room is there to breathe properly. As for Mrs. Marvin—there's only her and the girl."

"But Mam, you know what the houses in Crooked Row are like? They're in a far worse condition than ours. That's what took Sally to the sanatorium. That's how the Williams' boy got T.B."

"Yes, T.B. It's we'll be having it next. I'm telling you. It wouldn't have been much for you to have had a word with Rogers, the chap who's on the housing committee. Or p'raps Badger Made to Measure could have put in a word for us. Bought plenty from him, we have."

Realising the futility of reasoning with her, he had said no more.

The bus swung round a bend. A cloud came to hide the sun. The shadows raced across the white road, and suddenly a shower of rain hissed on the roof and spat angrily at the closed windows. The scene changed. The real countryside was left behind and replaced now by a valley, dark and sombre.

Rivers ran black, covered with a thick layer of coal dust, and the trees on the banks were withered and bare.

The tumbling streets where the miners and their families lived were shabby and depressing. Children played at their games, oblivious of the ugliness of their surroundings. They had no eyes for the pit-heads and the black pyramids of slag that lay along the valley, disfiguring the land and robbing it of its fertility.

A foursome of miners squatted on their heels against a low stone wall, their cloth caps askew, their white mufflers flapping in the wind. They looked up through the shower as the bus rumbled into the village. Their lean, blue-scarred faces smiled. They waved their hands, and some of the passengers acknowledged the greeting.

Further along the street a group of ragged children played at cricket. Shrieking at the top of their voices, they scampered out of the way of the speeding bus. A drain cover had been raised and placed on end against the kerbstone to serve as their wicket. On the wet roadway a rough-shaped wooden bat and a ball of screwed-up paper lay abandoned.

Nostalgic recollections of his own childhood in the smoky town besieged Ieuan's mind as he saw the crude bat and the paper ball.

Cricket in the back-lane on summer days, amongst the sweepings from the houses, potato peelings, cabbage stumps, broken bottles, jam jars, empty tins, grease-stained newspapers, tea-leaves, mussel shells, cinder-dust and horse-dung.

Spit on a stone, throw it into the air ... "Toss up for sides, Jamesie" ... "What's it—wet or dry?" ... "No slamming, mind. And remember—six for lost ball."

A game of cricket in the old brewery yard, in the shadow of the derelict building... sinister, weird; a building of cobwebbed rafters and ghostly echoes; haunted rooms, and a spiral staircase that wound its way to heaven. Where a child would laugh and scamper with his friends, but tread with bated breath and dilated eye when alone.

Cricket, with orange-box for wicket on Sunday School outings to a holiday beach in Tenby, the dreaming summer town where blue boats sailed on a blue bay, and old seafarers with salt in

34

their beards sat on the harbour wall and spoke of the days that were dead and drowned.

A bat to hold, a ball to throw! And other games to play in the yellow noons of childhood. Quoits in the silent, tree-shaded field near Moody's farm, where little girls picnicked in a fairy ring, with bread and cheese and bottles of Spanish water!

How pleasant it was to see the ring of silver fly from upraised arm and curve into the sun's eye; to feel the yielding softness of the blue clay bed beneath the arched foot! Then, to hear the sharp kiss of metal as the quoit struck downwards against the iron centre-peg, and to feel the air of proudness swell within you until you had to open your throat and let it out into the world in a shout of exultation!

The bus jolted. A woman laughed. Ieuan drew his face away from the window. He dismissed the longing thoughts of childhood from his mind. This was no time for day-dreaming. The past was gone. Sally was coming home... Sally was coming home soon. Nothing else mattered.

There had been no shaping of his ambition to become a writer, no incentive to study, since she had gone from him. His mind had been a chasm of doubt and despair, but now, there was hope for the future. When she came home again he would work at his writing as he had never done before. No more procrastinating, no more the futile thoughts of disillusionment!

The bus swerved into a street of derelict houses, grey-faced, silent, where only shadows lived, and a cloud swept across the sun's face.

No more procrastinations? He looked out of the window at the spreading valley below where a river had lost its song. Deep within him he felt a weariness that made him old. No more procrastinations? How often in the past had he resolved that nothing would interfere with his ambition?

"Life is a tissue of expectations that are never realised, of anticipations that are never fulfilled, of toil for unsatisfying ends..."

To hell with it all! Forget it, forget it! Sally was coming home.

CHAPTER FIVE

The bus chugged up the last hill. In the distance stood *Calon y Nôs,* grey-walled, austere, hidden among the trees and sheltered on three sides by a massive cliff which rose high above the clock tower and the faded weathercock.

The sanatorium, once the country home of Welsh aristocracy, had been vacant for many years. An air of desolation still hovered there, no matter how bright the day or how blue the sky.

Even the walled-in garden with its miniature fountain and a rustic bridge over the lily pond failed to add a touch of beauty to the scene. The building was grim, prison-like, shadowed by the grey cliff, hemmed in and dwarfed by it. The red soil in the terraced field beyond the garden, where the produce for the sanatorium was grown, lacked the fertility of the richer earth in the wide, farm-scattered valley beyond. Spring plants drooped listlessly in the furrows. It was as if nature had abandoned *Calon y Nôs* and bestowed her bounties upon a terrain which welcomed more the sun, the wind and the rain.

From the bus Ieuan could see the iron-trellised balconies, the orderly row of beds and the patients who waited eagerly for the friends and relatives who were coming to visit them. Nurses, prim and efficient, flitted past the wide open windows.

The passengers alighted, and the elderly porter at the gate put away his pipe and stepped into the road-way to chat with the driver.

Ieuan passed into the gravelled courtyard. Mrs. Marvin touched him lightly on the arm.

"Shall we go this way, Ieuan? She's in Block A."

He took the basket from her, and together they walked along the drive and up the three wide stone steps leading into the hallway.

"Would you mind very much if I saw Sally alone?"

Mrs. Marvin shook her head. "Of course not, my boy." She sat down on a chair in the ante- room, the basket clasped in her lap. "Do you want to go first, or would you rather wait till I've seen her?"

"I'll wait here."

"I understand, my boy."

Presently a nurse, starched and rustling, appeared in the doorway.

"Visitors for?" she enquired.

"Sally—Sally Marvin."

"You are Mrs. Marvin, her mother?"

"Yes, Nurse."

"And you—her brother?"

"No, just a—a friend."

The nurse regarded them dourly. "Do you wish to see her together? She's resting at the moment."

Mrs. Marvin rose. She smoothed her dress and coughed nervously. "I'll come first, Nurse... Ieuan, he would like to see her by himself."

"Very well. This way. Follow me, please."

The patter of their feet died along the tiled corridor. Across the hallway came the murmur of voices, and Mrs. Jane 'Cardiff's' high, incessant chatter as she led the other visitors into the waiting-room.

Ieuan stared at the clock on the wall. It ticked solemnly. He began to count each second, then tired of it. A sheaf of magazines lay on the table. *Sketch, Illustrated London News, Tatler, Britannia and Eve, Punch*, covers purple-stamped *'Calon y Nôs'*, pages well-thumbed. He scanned through them.

His hands trembled. He grew conscious of the echo his feet made as he stepped back to his chair, a copy of *Punch* tucked under his arm. He sat down. The clock ticked louder. Through the window he saw the bus-driver and the porter still in animated conversation.

37

Sally. He would be with her any minute now! And she was coming home in June.

Abie, Abie, Abie my boy
What are you waiting for now?
You promised to marry me someday in June,
It's never too late, it's never too soon...

The song lilted through his mind. He tapped his feet boyishly on the gleaming tiles and tossed the magazine back to the table. Make a noise... who cares? Scrape your feet against the floor. He had come to see Sally. She was cured. Let him shout, dance, sing, laugh... Soon it would be good-bye to *Calon y Nôs*. Shout and sing to the glorious heavens. Laugh and dance. A hornpipe, Irish jig, tango and fandango...

Oh, Sally is my darling, my darling,
And she's coming home in June...

The clock moved on. The bus-driver and his companion disappeared into the white-curtained lodge at the gateway. Mrs. Jane 'Cardiff's' voice was silenced in the sound of footsteps which echoed once again in the hollow corridor.

The same dour nurse appeared in the doorway. She stood aside to let Mrs. Marvin in.

"Oh, Ieuan *bach*, there's happy I am. My little darling, she's been delivered to us. The good Lord in His mercy has given her back to me again."

Mrs. Marvin's eyes were red with tears. "So grateful I am, so thankful to the Lord ..."

The nurse beckoned Ieuan.

"Follow me, please."

He pressed Mrs. Marvin's hand. His knees shook, and he could hardly control his excitement as he followed the nurse to the cubicle where Sally waited.

"In there. I'll call you in fifteen minutes."

He tiptoed into the tiny, white-walled room, not knowing whether to laugh or cry. His lips were pressed tightly together. His heart beat loudly. He swallowed hard.

"Oh, Ieuan... Ieuan, love!"

She lay propped up on the spotless pillows, her rich dark hair cascading about her shoulders. A ribbon to match the pale blue of her woollen bed-jacket was tied in a small bow on the top of her head. Her cheeks, once so pale and thin, were flushed with a ruddy glow of renewed health. The eyes that had known many tears sparkled with happiness.

"Oh, I'm so glad... so happy to see you again, Ieuan. Come, let me touch you, let me feel you again. Oh, it's so lovely, so lovely to see you."

He took her outstretched hand and gripped it warmly, reluctant to leave it go.

"Sally, *cariad*..." His voice broke. He turned his head sharply. "Oh, Sally..."

He dropped to his knees and buried his face in the coverlet. His shoulders heaved.

"Ieuan, darling boy... you're crying." Her voice was soft and low. He felt her trembling as she leaned over to stroke his hair. She rested her cheek against his head. A tear dropped and mingled with his own.

Unashamed, they wept together.

"Please, Ieuan... don't cry. This—this is such a happy day. It's—it's so silly of us... Laughing we should be, what with all the grand news I have to tell you. Oh, please, Ieuan..."

He pressed her hand to his lips and kissed it lovingly. Again he felt the gentle touch on his head. Her lips brushed his wet cheeks.

He rose slowly, her small, fragile hand still clasped in his. With a rough male gesture he rubbed away the tears.

"I'm daft, Sally, honest I am. Acting like a big baby."

"No, Ieuan, it's I'm the baby... Just look at me. And I tried so hard to make myself pretty for you. Even a blue ribbon I put in my hair. That's the colour you like, Ieuan, isn't it? Remember that night in the fair when we met?" Her eyes were moist with tenderness, and when he turned his face to her a radiant smile greeted him.

"Gee, Sally... you are beautiful. More beautiful than ever."

She gave an infectious little laugh. "Compliments you are giving freely this afternoon, Ieuan Morgan. Come now, sit you down over here by my side, you handsome Welshman." She directed him round the bed to a chair by the open window. "A lot I have to tell you. So much that I don't know where to start."

She clicked her tongue and tossed back her head.

"There's silly we've been behaving, wasting time with crying when we should have been talking and laughing."

"Now," she sat upright in the bed and folded her arms, "Mr. Ieuan Morgan, I'll have you know that in five weeks from today I am to be discharged. Isn't that the grandest news! Dr. Phillips has said the word. Mam knows, and now you have been told. And what is more important, Dr. Phillips says I'll not need to come here ever again. I'm cured. Cured, Ieuan..."

Her mock solemnity vanished. Ieuan saw the tears form again. Her lips quivered, and before he could say a word she had thrown herself into his arms.

"That's wonderful, Sally love. Wonderful." His words came hoarsely. There was a tightness in his throat. This time the tears were stemmed. He kissed her smooth forehead, then playfully ruffling her hair, held her gently at arms' length.

"Red herring's eyes again, is it?" he smiled. "They don't go well with blue ribbons. Come now, my girl, let me hear all the little bits of gossip I know you're dying to tell me... But first of all, tell me—whose girl are you?"

He saw the smile blossom. The lowered eyes gazed shyly up at him.

"Ieuan's girl," she whispered.

"That's right." He kissed the tip of her nose. "And now, Miss Marvin, you will please to tell me what you have to say in the short time at our disposal."

40

Sally held his hand. She sank back on the pillows.

"Oh, so much, Ieuan, so much there is to say." She fanned her face. "Whew! First of all, I've been on top grade for a long time. Doing a bit of housework, I'll have you know. And shopping, too. I'm feeling grand, Ieuan, and oh, so happy to hear that at last I'm going home again. I've counted every minute since Dr. Phillips told me, and oh, you can't imagine how much I've been longing to see you again, my lovely boy."

She spoke rapidly, her eyes intent on his, her hands restless, expressive in her excitement.

"We'll go for lovely walks together—just you and me, Ieuan. I'll have more time now..." She paused, and a note of sadness was born into her voice. "Mr. Simpson the Dyers, he wrote to me... a very nice letter. I—I won't be able to work there any more. They had a new girl just after I left. Dr. Phillips—he said I should take things easy for a long time and take my rests every afternoon. It'll be a year, or perhaps more, before I can go and look for a job."

He raised her chin and smiled. "What is that to worry about, Sally *cariad?* You are coming home, that's the happy thing. You are well and strong again." He snapped his fingers to the air. "That! To Simpson. You were too good for his place, anyway. It's a queen you are, and a queen is not supposed to work. As for the lovely walks, of course we'll go. To Dinas Wood, River Valley, Howard's Park and all the places we used to know... What's more, I've got a surprise trip planned for you! No—no guesses allowed. I'll tell you... It's to the *Cefn* we'll be off one fine day. A picnic on the sands, that's what. You can boil the kettle while I do my fishing, see?"

"Good! That's settled. Now, another item—"

A sudden flutter of wings startled him, and he drew back instinctively to glance over his shoulder. He heard Sally laugh and when he turned again he saw a tiny sparrow perched at the foot of the bed.

He rubbed his eyes and blinked.

"Am I seeing things?" He addressed the sparrow, which, quite unperturbed by his presence, hopped into Sally's lap. "And please tell me, who invited you?"

Sally's eyes twinkled. "A surprise for you to know that I have other visitors, too, eh, Ieuan Morgan? And regular ones, I may tell you." She held out a hand to the little bird.

"This is Tommy," she explained. "He's just one of my country friends, and quite tame. Like those London sparrows we read about in the papers. We have lots of them here in the san, and we feed them with bits of bread."

She looked round furtively. "Of course," she whispered, "Matron and the nurses don't like it, because... well, the little birds make a mess on the sheets. You know what I mean?"

"I think I do," he laughed. "Didn't I keep pigeons once when I was a little boy... And rabbits, too," he added.

The sparrow, finding no tit-bits, soon tired of his visit and flew through the open window in search of more fruitful pastures.

For a while there was a silence, and Ieuan sensed that Sally was worried over something. He leaned over the edge of the bed.

"Ieuan!"

"Yes, love?" He relaxed back into the chair.

"There is something else I want to say to you... You won't be cross?"

"'Course not, sweetheart."

"It's—it's about your writing."

"My writing?"

"I mean your letters to the papers."

He laughed. "You've been studying my style, eh? I bet you've got a *Nesfield's Grammar* tucked away under the pillow somewhere."

She did not smile, but bit her lip and glanced at him nervously. "It's serious, Ieuan..." She hesitated. "You—you won't mind if I say what I think?"

"Surely not, *fach*. Go ahead."

"Well." She averted her gaze. Her long, tapered fingers toyed with the edge of the coverlet. "I've been reading the *Guardian*, Ieuan. I have it every week, and nearly always I find your letter in it."

"Yes..."

"Last month you wrote about the new housing scheme on the Brynhill estate... You said the contractors were delaying the work."

"They were, Sally."

"But, Ieuan, you should be careful. People have to prove statements like that. What if you got into trouble? They could have you up for libel."

"It's the truth I said, dear. Now, don't you go worrying your pretty head, there's a good girl."

"I am worried, Ieuan. I can't help it." She hung her head. "Then, in that same letter you mentioned our street... the houses—they should have been condemned years ago, that's what you wrote."

"Yes, I did, and meant it. Listen, dear, there are plenty of people in Abermor who think that the houses in Crooked Row should have been pulled down. Just look at the house you live in, Sally. Why, it isn't fit for human beings, not by a long way. It made me angry and savage to think that you should have to come back and live under those conditions—the very conditions that sent you to—to this place. It wouldn't be fair to you, nor to the hundreds of other people who have to live in such houses."

"The house has been repaired now," she whispered. "It's much more comfortable, Mam says."

"All right, then, but there are other houses that have to be seen to... "

"And there's other things you write about, Ieuan. Mam is getting a bit worried. She's heard the neighbours talking. 'Who does that young man of Sally Marvin's think he is? With his ravings in the paper every week, a proper nuisance he is.' That's what they are saying, Ieuan."

She paused. "And there's your job in the foundry... The management, they'll victimise you."

Ieuan got up from the chair. He took her hands from the coverlet and squeezed them gently.

"Let people say what they like, Sally love," he said firmly. "As for my job." He shrugged. "I'll be out of the foundry one day. I never intended sticking there. And my writing... well, I feel that's the way I can best express what I feel about everything. I'm young, I know, but I've learnt a lot, Sally, and there's a great deal more that I know nothing of. If I could speak, I'd take a soap-box to the Town Hall Square every Sunday—"

"Oh, don't say that, Ieuan," she pleaded, her voice subdued. "You are true and sincere, I know, but... Oh, why don't you write stories like you said you would some day. If you feel that writing means so much to you."

He smiled sadly. "I've tried to, Sally, but it's no good. Some day, perhaps, it will come. I'll try hard, I promise you. But now, there is so much to do, and my letters help a little, I'm sure."

"Yes, Ieuan." She looked up at him. "Your—father and mother, I forgot to ask you. How are they? And Gweneira and Phyllis, are they all right?"

Taken aback by the unexpectedness of her query, he fumbled for a reply.

"Fine, dear... fine. It seems likely that Gweneira will be married this year."

"Gee, there's nice for her."

"Yes, yes, it will be grand. Sam's a real good sort, and I'm sure they'll be very happy... But, Sally—my writing. As I was saying—"

The pained look in her eyes made him hesitate. He sat on the edge of the bed and rested his cheek against her shining hair.

"Please don't let's quarrel, Ieuan," she breathed. "This is too happy a day, and I've been waiting for such a long, long time to see you... I'm sorry for what I've said this afternoon. I didn't really mean it. Cross my heart, I didn't."

He kissed her forehead. "Quarrel, my sweetheart! Why, we're

just having a little talk. After all, you are entitled to your opinion. Come now, a nice big smile, please... Please!"

"No, Ieuan, it isn't an opinion. It's just my... oh dear, I don't know what to say."

"Then smile, *cariad*. Smile for me, eh?"

She placed a hand on his arm. Her breath warmed his cheek as she turned her face towards him. The sad look had not gone from her eyes, and he began to feel sorry for her once more.

"Ieuan!"

"Yes?"

"You—you still love me?"

Suddenly, he laughed. A loud, happy laugh that rang down the echoing corridor. He ruffled her hair, and, leaning over, took her small, enquiring face into his hands.

"I'm going to marry you," he said.

And at that moment, as she lay sobbing in his arms, the voice of the nurse called from the doorway.

CHAPTER SIX

The foundry was working at full pressure. In spite of the dismal conditions—the stifling heat, the silica dust that hung in clouds in the air, the crude ventilation, and the strenuous labour—the men seemed happy and companionable. A certain measure of security had come at last after the long years of unemployment; the dread of the dole was behind them.

Yet beneath the good humour, the camaraderie, lurked the same fear that some day the foundry would close down again.

Bull Jackson had been elected shop-steward for the year. His blustering and bullying, his powerful physique and bellowing voice kept the more timid members of the union in subjugation, and he found, with the exception of Ieuan, Thomas, and a few others who were unmoved by his loud assertiveness, that he could dominate and control the Shop Committee even to the extent of having his own decisions accepted.

But Ieuan was not unduly concerned. It was the last week in June, and his thoughts revolved mainly around Sally. On Sunday she was coming home, and the day could not arrive too soon for him. His mother said little to him, but it was evident that she resented his attachment to Sally. Gweneira's marriage at the end of the year would mean a wage packet less. And there was the prospect of Ieuan's leaving home to marry Sally.

"I don't mind the children marrying," she said to her husband on the eve of Sally's homecoming. "I suppose it wouldn't matter if I did raise any objections, but they ought to have some consideration for me, after me bringing them up and sacrificing myself. Plenty of time there is for marriage when a girl is in her twenties, but Gweneira—only a child she is. As for Ieuan—he could think of me for a change and give me his help for a couple of years. Besides, Dick, I don't have an easy mind about that girl, Sally Marvin. Consumption—catching it is, you know. All right to say she's cured and all that, but who can tell? And there's children to think of, too. In the blood it is, this consumption. Ieuan shouldn't think of marrying her, and that's the truth. But don't think I'm going to tell him so. An answer he'd have, pat. That boy's got an answer for everything. Proper independent he's become."

Dick Morgan accepted her long tirade with his usual silence, and she lashed at him again. "I must say one thing about you, Dick." The change in her tone made him look up. "You're consistent. You never say nothing, and it's a job for a woman to see what's going on in that mind of yours. But I'll wake you up to some facts, oh yes. Our Ieuan's wanting to marry that girl. All right! but you know what that means, don't you? It's to the Marvin house he'll go to live, and that Mrs. Marvin," she sniffed, "she'll be having the benefit of his wages. A widow's pension isn't much, and the girl won't be working any more, I'm thinking. Oh yes, that Mrs. Marvin—she'll have no objections to any wedding, and she'll welcome our Ieuan into her house. Better than any lodger he'll be."

They were sitting down to tea on the Sunday when Phyllis came rushing breathlessly into the house.

"She's home, Ieuan! Sally's home! I saw the motor coming just now. Crowds there are round the house, and Mrs. Marvin was crying and laughing, and—"

Ieuan left the table. His mother pursed her lips and glanced sideways at Dick. He smiled, and beckoned her to continue with her meal.

"The boy's in love," he remarked later. "What d'you expect him to do, Millie? Now, if you had been away for a long time, and I wasn't there to meet you when you came home, what would you think of me, eh?"

Ieuan hurried to Crooked Row. He saw the crowd of women neighbours Phyllis had described, chatting excitedly around the doorway.

"Lovely to see the poor thing home again, isn't it?"

"And there's well she's looking! Never think she'd been on her back for three years with the decline."

"Mrs. Marvin—sorry for her, I am, poor soul. Three years is a long time to be having your only child away from you, and not knowing whether the little thing is ever going to come back home again."

"Losing her husband was a big blow, too. Some folks gets all the bad luck. Troubles never come singly, so they say, and quite right the old saying is."

Ieuan pushed his way through the crowd of women. Mrs. Marvin welcomed him. "She's come home, my boy. Oh, there's happiness at last! The Lord has brought her safely into the light again. My prayers have been answered. The blessed Saviour has taken pity on me in my loneliness."

He did not hear her words, and as he stood in the parlour doorway a warm and tender smile greeted him. A pale hand reached out.

In a moment Sally was in his arms, and there were tears and laughter. He kissed her cheeks, her hair. There were no words to say.

Outside, the smiling neighbours crowded to the window.

"A lovely little couple they are, God bless them."

"Yes, indeed. Good luck to them, I say."

That evening it was tea in the front parlour. The best china, the lace-edged tablecloth. There was now much to say, and Sally and her mother were occupied in welcoming the families who had come to offer their congratulations.

"As soon as you've settled down, *cariad,* it's to the *Cefn* we'll go, on that picnic I promised you," Ieuan said when he and Sally were alone. "There're so many things we'll share together, Sally, so many things we've missed in the time you've been in... the time you've been away."

"Yes, Ieuan. Oh, I'm so glad to be home with all my people. And so—so very happy to know that I've got you to talk to me again."

48

"Talk! I'll talk you off your feet, my girl. Talk and walk, and get some sunshine into those eyes…"

Before he left, Mrs. Marvin took him into the kitchen.

"My boy, it's more than grateful I am to you for your kindness to my Sally. She thinks so much of you. You are a good son, Ieuan. So many young men today, they think of nothing but sinful pleasures, and it is hard to find one who is Christian and God-fearing." She sank into a chair, her thin hands resting on her lap. Her eyes were misty. "There is a providence in your meeting with my Sally. She loves you, my boy, and I know you will be good to her. The burden that I have carried has been made light again. The Lord comforted me in my sorrow when He took Jim away, and now He has given me hope again." She touched his hand. "You will come again, Ieuan, soon?"

"Yes, Mrs. Marvin, I will. Now… you've had a very trying day—all this excitement."

"God bless you, my boy."

In the following week he saw Sally every evening after work. One night after her visit to his home to meet his people, she seemed pensive and sad. They walked slowly through the dreary streets, arm in arm, her silence making him tense and nervous. He knew the cause. She had been hurt again. The visit to his home had not been a happy experience for her. Phyllis and Gweneira had welcomed her like a long-lost sister returned to home again, and his father, at first a little embarrassed and tongue-tied in her presence, had soon made her feel at ease.

And then his mother had entered the room. She had greeted Sally casually. A few brief remarks. "Pleased to meet you. A big relief it was for your mother to have you home, and I hope you'll soon be settling down again. But you'll have to look after yourself, you know?"

They came to a street corner. A gang of children were scampering noisily, chasing one another around the lamp-post, darting in and out of the yellow light, then disappearing into the darkness which was only the width of the street away, their voices echoing in the hollow night.

Around the corner the road widened. On one side lay St. Mary's cemetery, the common burial-ground. Facing it, on the opposite side and running parallel with the low boundary wall, was the Crooked Row chemical factory, high-walled, with sagging roof, the bricks red with dust, corroded by acid.

The tang of acid bit into the air. Ieuan coughed. A shawled woman stood in a darkened doorway and wished them good night as they involuntarily quickened their pace. The street lights grew dimmer. Soon, it began to rain.

Ieuan drew Sally into the shelter of the cemetery gate.

"What's worrying you, dear?" It was the first time he had spoken since they left the house. He put his hands on her shoulders and turned her gently towards him.

"Sally..."

She pressed herself close to him. The rain touched his face. He felt her shiver slightly.

"Come, let me take you home."

She did not move.

"Your mother, Ieuan... Why does she hate me?"

The question he had expected had come at last.

"Silly," he laughed with effort. "Mam doesn't hate you. No one hates you. You're too lovely a creature for anyone to feel that way about you."

"She does, Ieuan." Her voice was sad. "She hates me because I'm going to take you away from her."

"Then I'm just a little boy, and you're stealing me from my mammy, eh? Sally, sweetheart, you've got it all wrong. I'm going to marry you, and that's all there is to say. No one's going to stop me. Mam doesn't hate you. It's—it's just that she's not been well lately.

"Not well," he mused. "She has been ill for many years; an illness of spirit and not of the flesh. Bitterness has eaten into her like a canker." But had he the right to condemn her? What did he

50

know of his mother's struggles, her secret hopes? She had known poverty; it had lived with them constantly. Now, a measure of prosperity had come, and she wanted to cling to it, desperately. Gweneira's wages, his wages, his father's, and Phyllis's few shillings—this spelt prosperity to her, and she had never before been familiar with such opulence.

Gweneira was leaving. Sally had come home, and soon he would be leaving. And after—what? The continuation of the same endless struggle to make ends meet. Rent, food, clothing, insurances. Bills to meet, and not enough money to pay. No beauty, no joy. What had life to offer her? Was there no compensation? The children, Gweneira, Phyllis, himself—did they give her the love that was a mother's right? Did they share her fears, her frustrations? Who, then, was to blame?

That night he spoke to his mother. They were alone in the kitchen.

"Well, I do like that," she said scornfully. "Hardly said anything to her, indeed! What did you expect me to do? After all, I was feeling just as awkward as your father was. It's the first time I've met the girl, remember."

"That's no excuse, Mam. You were unkind. She's been ill, very ill, as you know. I've known Sally now for three years, and—"

"Yes, three years! Did you ever hear of someone waiting three years before he brings his ..." she hesitated, "his girl into his mother's house? I was introduced to your father's people the first week I met him. It's you are to blame, Ieuan, so don't go accusing me of being off-handed. Why, even Gweneira and Phyllis know her better than your father and me." Her lip curled. "But even they had to meet her on the street. Never once in this house."

Ieuan dropped into a chair. "I would have brought Sally here," he emphasised, "but you know, Mam, it wasn't long after we met that she was taken away. I never had a chance to introduce her to you. I want you and Sally to be—well, I want you to look on her as a daughter."

51

"And who says I won't?" came the sharp reply. "Trouble is, Ieuan, you're getting a bit too smart in the head. Suspicious of everyone, you are. I was quiet tonight, because... Oh, what's the use! I've got a lot on my mind. There's Gweneira to marry. In December it's going to be, and I've got plenty to think about."

"I'm sorry, Mam. I understand."

"I hope you do. There's no one else in this house seems to."

Ieuan rose from the chair. He walked to the door leading to the stairway. He had tried to reason with her, calmly, confidently. But what was the use?

"Good night, Mam."

She turned the edge of the cloth over the supper dishes left on the table, and stooped to rake the ashes from the fire.

"Good night," she called over her shoulder. Then, as he climbed the stairs he heard her mumbling to herself: "Next time she comes here I'll be blamed for talking too much. Some day I'll please everybody."

Sally's first meeting with Mrs. Morgan had unnerved her and she declined Ieuan's invitation to tea on Sunday a fortnight later. His father had enquired after her. He liked the girl, he confessed. "Plenty of common sense there, Ieuan. She looks dependable, too. I don't think you'll go far wrong if you stick to her. Of course, your mother... Now." He had looked swiftly down the passageway and closed the parlour door. "Ieuan, I want to talk to you about something. It's just between you and me, see? It concerns your mother. She's not half well, son." Ieuan was reluctant to listen. Dad was ready to defend her again, he thought. Why couldn't she accept Sally and make her welcome? It was preposterous, the treatment she was meting out to him; treating him as though he were a boy in his teens. There was no valid reason for her behavior. He felt angry and embittered. Sally had been hurt, cruelly.

Oh, the stupidity of it all! Why didn't Mam behave as a human being, and show at least some respect for the girl? If he had picked her up on the streets, a common, strident-voiced, uncouth

52

creature, painted and powdered, she would have had cause to show her disapproval. But Sally was decent and good.

"No, she's not half well, Ieuan." His father's voice was low. "For over a year I've watched her, and there's something radically wrong with her."

"Yes, it's my wanting to marry Sally—that's what's wrong with her." Ieuan returned his father's astonished gaze. "She's thinking of me in terms of wages, Dad. My happiness and Sally's means nothing to her. But, surely, I've a right to plan my own future?"

"You're too hasty in your judgment, my boy. Your mother will miss you more than you think, but she's prepared to help you all she can."

Ieuan felt ashamed. "I'm sorry, Dad. I didn't mean what I said."

"That's all right, son. I'm only trying to tell you that your mother's sick. We must have patience, all of us. You're a good boy, Ieuan, and I feel I can talk to you. I've got to talk to someone, and the girls—well, they're different, somehow. What it is with your mother, I don't know. She just won't say much, as you know, but now and then I've seen her put her hands to her stomach. Indigestion, she calls it—but it's something more than that, Ieuan, and I'm worried."

"Have you seen the doctor, Dad? Has Mam sent for him?"

"What's the use? Can you imagine what she'd say to him?"

"That's immaterial. If you suspect she's ill, then you'll have to send for him, or take her with you to his surgery one night. Look... if you like, I'll see him."

"No, no, Ieuan. Don't do anything rash. It'll only make her fretful. We—we'll wait a bit and see. I just wanted to tell you about it because of Sally. Your mam, she doesn't mean to be rude to the girl. It's her way, Ieuan. I know her. Deep down she's soft. Someday you'll see the truth of it. So we'll leave it at that now— what d'you say, son? And remember—not a word about our little talk."

"All right, Dad."

53

"Not even to Sally, you promise? I don't want to come between you."

"No, Dad, not even to Sally."

Ieuan considered his father's words. His mother's illness—what was the matter with her? The problem harassed him and troubled his conscience. Perhaps he was to blame? He should have been kinder, more tolerant, accepting her moods without resorting to his usual questioning and challenging?

From now on he would be patient. He would try to understand.

CHAPTER SEVEN

August Bank Holiday, and Abermor's industries, its shops, businesses, closed. The steel furnaces were damped down, the roar of the rolling-mills was silenced, and the town became a village overnight. It was the first day of the tinworkers' annual Stop Week, but to the other industrial workers it meant only twenty-four hours off.

The Town Council had prepared well for the holiday. There were many attractions planned that would keep the people at home. At Howard's Park, the annual bowling tournament; the town's football ground was taken over for the Agricultural Show, and the local annual regatta drew thousands to the beach. It would have been a reflection on the Council's administration if the Abermorites were enticed to the neighbouring towns with their rival attractions.

The local transport services were extended. There were buses to the Park, the football ground, the beach, and to the local beauty spots. From nine in the morning the main street was thronged with holiday-makers. The day was bright and sunny, and the long queues for the buses formed early. Everybody was happy. Children's faces were scrubbed and shining; their restlessness and exuberance were tolerated by their elders, and there were few reprimands.

Ieuan and Sally were away early from the crowded town. They were going to the *Cefn* for their picnic and their first holiday together. She looked beautiful in a white summer dress and wide-brimmed straw hat, but Ieuan had dressed himself in his oldest clothes.

He had planned to fish from the beach, and the previous night had been spent on the mudbanks along the estuary, where he had dug industriously for lug-worm bait.

The Sunday-dressed passengers in the bus from town stared at the pretty, dark-haired girl and her shabby companion, but Sally and Ieuan had no thought for them. They were to share a happy day together.

A long walk over the dunes brought them at last to the *Cefn* shore. Curving away from the path which had brought them there, the deserted beach, even in the strong sunshine, savoured of something mysterious and intangible.

No holiday crowds foregathered there as they did on other beaches that lined the Welsh coast. Bordered by the tall sand dunes, it lay exposed to the winds that blew in from the four corners of the sweeping bay. In winter-time it was difficult to walk across the beach, so strong and fierce were the gales that blew there.

But in the summer-time, the *Cefn*, with its silence broken only by the gentle sighing of the surf, held a nameless fascination for Ieuan. To him it seemed the world's end; a place remote from the everyday life he had known, the hurrying people, the clanging, nerve-shattering noise of the steel mills, the black smoke, the huddled houses, and the shouting children.

"Like to come to the *San Paula*, Sally?" He swung the heavy haversack from his shoulder on to the firm beach and unhitched the rod case.

She laughed. "Riddles now, is it? *San Paula!*—it sounds like some mysterious island hidden away somewhere. Indeed, I expect to see it rising from the water any minute at your magic word of command. But wherever it is, I'll follow you."

"Good for you, my girl! It's my favourite fishing spot, on my favourite beach," he replied, "and no mirage, let me tell you. So, if you'll take off your shoes, pick up your heels and trail along with me, I'll take you there."

"Then it *is* an island, and we have to paddle across to it?"

"No, my love, just a wreck. The schooner *San Paula*, that was. The proudest ship that ever sailed out of Carmarthen Bay in the leisurely golden days, the dream days of my grandfather's youth."

"So, a poet now speaks to me?"

"That's enough! Come on—to the *San Paula*!"

The hot sand burned their bare feet. They skipped hand in hand over the hard ridges formed by the ebbing tide, their voices and their laughter ringing across the lonely beach.

The *San Paula* lay in the distance on a brown-baked hillock of sand, her hull half buried, black, ugly, stained by the sun and the winds and rain that had beaten down upon her in the years she had lain on the *Cefn*. The paint had been washed away. Not a trace of the schooner's name could be seen on the once trim bow, and all that remained of the stout masts she once carried were three circular, splintered spars.

The shade cast by the wreck was the only sheltered spot on the blistering beach, and the young couple, flushed and breathless after their walk, sat down to rest a while.

"This is lovely, Ieuan." Sally leaned back against the hull. She tossed her wide-brimmed hat to the sand and shook her long black hair over her shoulders. Her eyes closed. A smile curved at the corners of her mouth.

Ieuan turned her face towards him and kissed her.

"It is," he said softly.

"Lovely," he heard her whisper again. "Oh, Ieuan, if life could always be like this. Just you and me, and this—this wonderful peace."

He sat up and looked out over the sun-shimmering waves and the long, undulating white line of surf that divided sea and sky.

"There will be rain, Sally," he said, as if to himself.

"Rain!" She opened her eyes and reached quickly for her hat.

"No, no," he laughed. "Silly! I don't mean it's going to rain now. I was just thinking ..."

"Of what, Ieuan?"

"Of life, Sally. It won't always be like this. There'll be grey skies, and sadness."

"My goodness, Ieuan Morgan, you are a Job's comforter, I must say." She jumped to her feet. "Fancy bringing a girl down

57

to the *Cefn* just to tell her that. And on such a glorious summer's day, too! Up, my boy! you're getting morbid. Time it is that you should be getting out your little worms." She shuddered. "Ugh! I'm getting morbid, too." She held out a hand. "Up you get, Ieuan Morgan, and don't you dare start preaching again—not while this lovely sun's shining, and not while I'm with you."

He clasped her hand and pulled her gently forward. "One kiss, and I'll forgive you." She drew her face away and laughed.

"Very well, then I'll steal one." He caught her round the waist and pressed her closely to him. Her soft hair brushed his cheeks.

"Sally *fach*, I do love you so much."

She returned his long kiss. "I'm your girl," he heard her breathe, "for always."

They sat down again in the shade, his head resting between her firm young breasts.

He felt her hands caress his forehead. Her fingers quivered. He turned swiftly and held her passionately. The sudden movement startled her. Her dress drew up over her knees and the sight of the bare, rounded flesh of her thighs excited him. He kissed her again and again, and she returned each kiss with equal fervour.

"Oh, Ieuan..." Then, without warning, she suddenly broke away from his embrace. She gave a little self-conscious laugh. Her eyes were cloudy. She bit her lip and looked at him, frightened. He watched her as she rose and stood before him, her black hair ruffled, her breasts heaving. He wanted to draw her down once more beside him, to feel her lips on his, to cup her timid breasts in his hands, to hold her, possess her.

Three years had been taken from their lives. He was now a man, with a man's longing for a woman. He loved her, and she loved him. Was it wrong, was it sinful to desire her?

Her voice broke into the silence of his thoughts.

"You—you *are* going to fish this afternoon, Ieuan?" Her composure was slowly returning. Her eyes were bright and smiling again. She picked up her hat and fitted it femininely over her head.

"I mean, the little fishes won't go away? Or are they just waiting for you?"

He felt angry. Then, abruptly, he said: "Of course I'm going to fish. What do you think I came here for..." He stopped short, embarrassed, as she quickly turned her eyes away from him. At once he felt sorry. He remembered her illness. That she had been away for three years and on the point of death. He forgot his passion and was overwhelmed by a sudden tenderness.

"Now," he took her hand, "you just sit down here in the shade, and I'll get my tackle ready." He gazed out over the bay. "Tide should be on the turn any minute..." He paused, still unsure of himself, conscious that his gaiety was forced even though he was desperately sincere. "You know what, love? You get the picnic ready, and I'll fish for—say, three-quarters of an hour. That'll make it one o'clock. Dinner at one, what d'you say?"

"Yes, Ieuan, that will be grand. You go after your little fish, and I'll have the cloth laid and the food prepared."

"Right, sweetheart!" He kissed her lightly on the cheek. Relieved and happy, he sat down on the beach, his legs straddled, and began to sort out his fishing gear.

He fitted the rod lengths into their brass sockets, clipped on the reel and ran the line through the porcelain rings. A yard of plaited brass wire from which three, short brass booms projected, was then tied to the line. Sally spread a small, embroidered cloth on the sand and took out from the haversack a packet of sandwiches, cakes, two large apples, bakelite cups and saucers, and a vacuum flask. She arranged them on the impromptu table, scurrying around on her knees, then sat back against the hull to watch Ieuan.

Selecting three gutted hooks from a wallet in his coat pocket, he looped them carefully over the booms. He winked at Sally, then, rubbing thumb and forefinger in the sand, took three lugworms from the bait tin and threaded them over the barbed hooks.

"I hope you'll wash your hands before you come to the table?"

He made a face at her, then tucked in his trouser hems and

pulled them tightly up to his thighs. Holding the rod at eye level, he sighted along it. Satisfied that the rings were in line with one another he tied an elongated, five-ounce lead weight to the end of the brass wire.

"Here I go. Wish me luck."

The tide was on the turn. Slowly, almost imperceptibly, the shallow river that lay between him and the wide bay began to swell, its becalmed surface shining with a yellow-greenish lustre. At this spot the incoming tides were helped by strong currents that swept across from the estuary into the bay. An hour's fishing was the most he could expect, for soon after the water would reach the foot of the dunes and cover the wreck.

The river filled and flooded over the intervening bank, merging into the waters of the bay. The breakers on the horizon raised their white faces and peeped shyly towards the shore. Higher and higher they rose. Then, with a thundering roar, they dipped their heads into the calmness before them, heaving it majestically upwards. A breeze blew in from the west. The bay reared and leapt, and line after line of racing white demons curled in wild pursuit towards the open beach.

He ran to the water's edge. The length of brass wire and the baited hooks hung down in front of him. The rod tip swayed, and the lead weight with its three-fingered grab of copper wire scraped in the sand, leaving a three-lined trail in its wake.

With one hand shielding his eyes from the sun, he waded into the tide, shuddering involuntarily as the cold surf fringe swirled around his ankles. He waded up to his knees.

The rod butt was gripped with both hands and swept backwards, shoulder high.

"One, two, three!"

A sharp jerk forward. The reel screeched, the lead weight, trace, and baited hooks whistled in a curve and plopped into the sea thirty yards from where he stood.

Satisfied with his casting, he held the rod butt hard against his stomach, then playing out the line, waded backwards on to the beach. In the meantime, Sally had stabbed the rod-rest into the sand. He placed the rod tip in its fork, looped the line over a reel knob, then screwed a small brass bell into a socket on the end of the rod.

"Now we can relax," said Sally. She poured out a cup of hot tea from the vacuum flask. He took it, his eyes still concentrated on the rod tip.

"My goodness, Ieuan, don't tell me you have to sit like that all the afternoon, staring at a little bell? Do you have to watch it? Doesn't it tinkle?"

"As sweetly as your voice," he returned, sipping the hot tea. "Sandwich, please."

Half an hour passed. The tide swept swiftly up the beach, forcing them to retreat farther from the wreck.

"Do we have to pick up our things and walk back all the time?" Sally fanned her face with her hat.

He laughed. "Unless you prefer to be a Canute."

"And isn't that little bell ever going to tinkle?"

"That's a matter I leave for the fish to decide."

"And when it does wiggle, that means you've caught a fish?"

"I hope so."

"You hope so! Why, is there anything else you can catch?"

He pushed the rest deeper into the sand and lowered the rod.

"A draught, a cold, a crab, jellyfish, seaweed, a chest of Spanish doubloons, or a drowned sailor... I once knew a chap who..."

"All right, dear, you can tell me again. I'm half-way through a sandwich just now."

The sun continued to blaze down on the burning beach. The sky shaded down at the sea level to the white of opals, and the summer afternoon glittered on the rising tide like laughter. Sally reclined on her back, her head pillowed on her arms, while Ieuan sat forward, his eyes still intent on the bell.

"How you men can spend hours and hours fishing puzzles me. What do you see in it?" she asked presently, in a voice that invited explanation.

Ieuan sighed. There seemed no hope of a bite. The tip of the rod had not moved since his first cast into the sea.

"I don't know, indeed," he said apathetically as he gathered together the bait-tin and rod-case. "A worm at one end of the line, and a fool at the other. Shall we go, love?"

He got up from the sand and began to reel in. "Ieuan, boy, I didn't mean to tease you. Please don't give up so soon."

"This reminds me of you girls with your knitting," he grinned. "Hours and hours, sitting down with a lump of wool and two preens."

She sat up and watched the glistening drops shower from the line as he reeled in rapidly.

"Well, we get something out of it in the end. A jumper, or a cardigan, or a pair of socks."

"And I get a fish—sometimes."

"Indeed, but there's no 'sometimes' about our knitting. Always we have something to show for it."

"You're deluding yourself, girl." Ieuan dismantled the rod and knelt down beside her. "You ought to come over to our house. Phyllis has started at least two pullovers for me, but..."

He saw her press her lips and look away.

"Have I said anything wrong, Sally?" He stroked her hair. "Have I?"

"Ieuan, we're so happy together. When—when do you think we could get married?"

For a while he remained silent, contemplative. "We'll be married, Sally," he assured, his fingers feeling the silk of her hair.

"When?"

"I'd marry you tomorrow, love, if everything were all right."

"But everything is all right, Ieuan. You haven't another girl, have you?"

"Silly!"

"Could we be married this year?"

He shook his head. "Listen, Sally—there're many things to think of. I mean..."

"The foundry, Ieuan? But you're working well, now. The slump is over and there's good money earned in Bevan's."

"Yes, that's true, but how long will it last—this little bit of prosperity that's come to Abermor?" He looked at her frankly. "I don't sound very enthusiastic, *cariad*, but I don't want to see you living in semi-poverty. I've had enough of it, I've seen what it does to people—this watching after every penny, wondering how next week's bills are to be paid. And the dole, Sally—we'd get twenty-six shillings to live on. A fine start to our married life!"

"But you're not on the dole, Ieuan." She lowered her eyes. "You—you do want to marry me?"

"I want nothing so much, dear, but I want us to have a good start, to make sure that the prospects at the foundry are brighter than they've been in the past. It's money, Sally... always money." He held her in his arms. "God knows I don't crave for it, but I want enough to let us live together in a little comfort."

"Money isn't everything, Ieuan. We love one another. We'll be happy. You—you could start saving now."

"Yes, love, I could, now while I've got the chance. There's talk that we're expecting a big contract at the foundry. I heard Lu Davies tell some of the moulders... twelve fifty-ton castings for some firm in Leicester. That should keep the place going on full-time for at least nine months. With a bit of overtime thrown in, I could earn... well, roughly, about five pounds a week. Save two out of that every week. In nine months that'd amount to, let's see," he traced the sum in the sand, "seventy-two pounds."

Sally gasped. "Seventy-two pounds! Why, that's wonderful! Seventy-two pounds! We—we could put it in the bank, Ieuan, it would last for years. Then you needn't worry about being out of work. Oh, that's marvellous news."

"It's very little really, Sally."

"Oh, Ieuan, you *are* a pessimist!"

"But it's true, Sally. How far would seventy-two pounds carry us? There's the wedding, there's furniture to be bought, new clothes... There'll be rent to pay, and..."

63

"Yes?"

"I'd like to have a little put aside. You see, Sally, some day it will be good-bye to the foundry. I'm going to be a writer." He stood up. "A writer!" he said bitterly, and she looked at him, perplexed. "That's a good joke, isn't it? I'm going to be a writer. How often have I said it? Ever since I left school. And what have I done about it? Nothing..."

"Oh, yes you have." She linked her arm in his. "On this lovely day you are as grumpy as anything, Ieuan Morgan," she said lightly, "and I am beginning to dislike you, yes, truly I am. Didn't you write all the time when I was at the san? And haven't you been sending letters to the *Guardian* every week?"

"I've done nothing, Sally," he repeated. "I did start, yes—full of enthusiasm, but Dad soon knocked that out of me. I had no experience of life, he said, so how could I ever hope to write anything? He was right. I had no experience—not then. Now, it's different. I've had the experience. I have something to write about. But I don't write. A writer who doesn't write, Sally—there are so many of them. Chaps like me, filled with ambition, but not prepared to sacrifice time or effort to achieve it."

"I was ill, Ieuan. How could you write with all that worry on your mind?... Oh yes, I know you were worried. Mam used to tell me. I had letters from Gweneira, and Thomas once wrote to me and said that you—you thought I was going to die. Please, Ieuan, please don't let things depress you so. You'll be a writer, I know you will. You are clever, the cleverest man I know in the world. Just you wait till we are married, I'll make you write, that's what. Then when your stories begin to sell you can save up your money and give up the old foundry. We'll have a little house of our own, Ieuan. We—we could take Mam with us, she wouldn't be much trouble."

He looked at her quickly.

"Your mother...?"

He held his tongue.

"Yes, Ieuan. When we get married we could live with Mam

64

until we find a house of our own. I—I wouldn't like to leave her, and your mother... well, I don't think there'd be room for us with her. There's your father, and Phyllis as well. It'd be impossible for us to get a council house, I know, for years. And as for living in apartments, I don't think you'd like that, Ieuan. I wouldn't."

They walked leisurely up the beach and crossed over the white sand dunes, the tall sea-grass cutting between their bare toes.

"Ieuan, sweetheart, we'll be very, very happy when we're married. Then some day you'll be a famous writer. I know you will, because," she smiled, "because I love you."

CHAPTER EIGHT

No engagement was announced in the local press. There was no ring, no congratulations. Mrs. Marvin was ready to welcome Ieuan as her future son-in-law, but his mother accepted the fact with a shrug.

"It's what I've been expecting you to tell me any day. I hope you'll be happy. What else can I say?"

The girls were delighted. Preparations were already being made for Gweneira's forthcoming marriage. The date had been fixed for the first week in December. Tentatively, Phyllis had suggested making it a double wedding, and had even told some of her friends that her brother and sister were to be married on the same day.

When the rumour circulated in the district and neighbours began to call at the house to offer their best wishes to Ieuan and Gweneira, Mrs. Morgan reprimanded her younger daughter and put an end to the rumours in her own dour fashion.

"Double wedding, indeed! Next you'll be expecting Gweneira to be dressed up all in white satin, with bridal veil and orange blossoms. No, indeed, our Ieuan won't be getting married for some time—and as for Gweneira, a quiet wedding it will be. We are not people to be making a fuss."

In spite of her attitude and apparent lack of sympathy, Ieuan sensed that his mother was happier now than he had ever seen her. For the first time in his life he saw her bring flowers into the house, and Sam Rowlands' visits became a pleasant interlude. She had been won over by Sam's simple ways and made him feel at home whenever he called.

The altercations, the arguments between her and his father, grew less. There was a happier spirit present in the home. The

66

foundry was working full-time. Luxuries never before afforded, were now tasted. There were occasional Tuesday afternoons when Mrs. Morgan and Gweneira went on an outing to Cardiff where they shopped, had tea at the Capitol restaurant, and spent the evening at the pictures.

A new hat, a new dress for Mrs. Morgan; the excitement of shopping in the city, the train journey, Gweneira's preparations for the wedding, these had given his mother a new interest in life.

Ieuan noticed the change in her, and it made him happy. But inwardly he had the old fear, the dread that some day unemployment would come again and destroy the happiness at which she grasped.

But the shadow of insecurity did fall. In December, in the week following Gweneira's wedding and her departure for her husband's home in Brecon, the foundry management issued notices to the moulders in the steel shop. It was said that the work to be done was insufficient to keep on all those employed in the department and, therefore, only the number of moulders which the management felt was needed would be re-engaged after the end of the week.

The moulders counteracted by refusing to accept the notices. A general meeting was called, and it was finally arranged that in order to prevent wholesale and indiscriminate sacking, the steel foundry would work on a part-time basis.

But why the sudden slump, the moulders demanded to know? The contract for the Midlands, the twelve fifty-ton castings—what had happened? It was understood that this contract would provide work at full-time for a period of at least nine months!

The management, faced by the Shop Committee's demand for an explanation, stated that there was no demand for what they termed "light work". There were no orders for the small type of castings upon which the foundry had depended in the past. The Midlands contract, it was true, had to be completed within the specified nine months, but it could be done in the stipulated time by only a sixth of the present number of moulders. One fifty-ton casting a week would require no more than a complement of fifteen men. There were ninety men in the foundry. Did the moulders expect the management to employ seventy-five redundant men each week? Were they not satisfied that the management had sympathised with their plight and had agreed to the Union's arrangement to work a part-time system? In that way, every man would have his fair share of employment.

Of course, the management itself could not be responsible for the organisation of the suggested part-time system. It would administer the scheme, naturally, and for that reason it would expect to be informed as soon as possible of whatever arrangements were reached by the moulders themselves, and their Union officials, possibly, for apportioning the work. It was evident that no one could expect more than six weeks employment in the next nine months, and it was for them as a body to decide how this should be done by each of them.

As to the question of a Christmas pay, the management was not inhuman. It would not care to see any single worker of Bevan's suffer during this season of peace and goodwill. For that week, it was prepared to let the ninety men work, so that no one would be without a Christmas pay. But this, it should be remembered, was prompted only by the management's consideration for its employees. After Christmas, if there were no more orders forthcoming, the foundry would continue on part-time.

Recriminations and threats would not help, and nothing more could be done about the matter. The fault lay, not with the management, but with the workers themselves. Too much time had been spent on various jobs. Production costs were rising. Bevan's was unable to compete with other foundries. It could not afford to reduce its tenders for contracts for the large industrial concerns in the Midlands and the North. The only solution lay in cutting down on production costs, and that could be achieved by the moulders if they were prepared to put their shoulders to the

wheel, and work with the interests of the firm borne in mind—
always! Production must be speeded up. Failure to do so would
eventually lead to the closing down of Bevan's.

The men accepted the decision to work part-time, but there
was much grumbling and discontent. Lu, with his own position
to consider, insisted on choosing whom he classified his most
capable craftsmen, and these fifteen men were given a greater
share of employment than the others. This led to further
discontent and bitter jealousy amongst the men themselves.

Lu was approached, but refused to listen to individual demands
for a fair share. Eventually a shop meeting was called one day
early in January.

Bull Jackson had been elected shop steward for another year,
and though reluctant to chair the meeting because he himself
was one of Lu's chosen fifteen, he was forced to do so by the
majority vote.

Ieuan and Thomas, who were in the younger group of moulders,
had at first agreed to stand aside and allow the married men to
have preference over them, and work one week in six. But now,
the married men were refusing to share. They had come to expect
the single men to sacrifice their week, asserting that it was easier
for those with no responsibilities to maintain themselves on the
dole, than it was for those with families. The thought of
unemployment had made them grasping. They considered only
themselves. What right had the single men to claim a share of the
work?

The moulders gathered round a coke brazier in the coreshop.
Those who were unemployed that week had come in their street
clothes and were careful not to brush against the soot-covered
walls and dusty core-boxes.

Bull Jackson clambered on to the bench. He tightened the thick,
brass-studded, leather belt round his waist, and frowned at the
restless, mumbling crowd.

"Brothers and fellow-members!" He waited until the whispering
stopped. "This meeting has been called to discuss the sharing," he

69

began. "Some fellows here seem to think they're not being treated fair. Well, now's the time to speak and get things off your chests. We don't want no one to go out from here full of bloody complaints. So let's hear what you've got to say, and clear the air."

"I've got the first complaint to make," Thomas turned his back to the brazier, "and it's a pretty general one."

"Yes?" Bull waited.

"The method we have of sharing the work," Thomas went on. "We don't consider it right, that—"

Suddenly, the cranes in the steel foundry rumbled over the girders. Bull signalled to a labourer passing by.

"Hey, Jack! Ask them fellers in there don't they know we got a meeting on, and tell 'em to stop that bloody row... Now, Thomas Hughes, you were saying?"

"The list," said Thomas, "we object to Lu choosing his own men."

"Hear, hear," came a voice from the rear. Isaiah Charles stepped forward. "Thomas is right. I'm a married man, but seems to me no one got a thought for the single chaps. They got to live, you know. Lu picks the same couple of men every week, and it's got to be stopped."

"You've got nothing to moan about," Bull countered. "You're on top of Lu's list every week."

"But I'm prepared to stand down."

"So am I," said Dick Jones, a machine moulder. "Share and share alike. We all got to live, we're all in the same union. If we let Lu have his way all the time, it's no use us belonging to any union. We've got to stand together in this."

"I'd like to say something now." Ieuan ignored Bull's aggressive scowl. "We single chaps have been prepared to let the married men have preference, and we've been satisfied with the arrangement, but this has only led to quarrelling and jealousy amongst us. What unity we had at one time is being slowly destroyed. I propose that we share the work equally and fairly, irrespective of whether a man is married or single."

70

"You are thinking of getting married?" Bull sneered, and his remark met with a few sniggers from his cronies.

"That's not bloody fair!" Thomas rushed up to the bench. He gripped Bull by the ankle. "Keep your sneers for yourself," he shouted. "This is a shop meeting where we've come to discuss trade union matters, and we don't want to get personal. But if you want it that way, let me say you're not too damned anxious to see a change. You're on Lu's list just as often as some of the others here, and you've got no family to keep."

"Hey, hey, boys! Let's carry on with the business," Dick Jones called. "This is a shop meeting, not a free-for-all. We're open for discussion, not slanders... Bull, you'd better get on with the job or let somebody else take the chair."

"P'raps you'd like to take over?"

"This is a shop meeting. Get on with it, man, not quibble like a school kid."

Bull glowered. He turned his attention to the audience. "Well, comrades," a laugh in the back-ground disconcerted him for the moment, "anyone else got some proposition?"

"I have," Ieuan spoke up. "It's this... I propose that the sharing be decided amongst the men themselves. Let everyone have an equal share, one week in, five weeks out—or two weeks in, six out, whatever is decided on."

"And what about Lu's list?"

"He has no right to choose his own men. You know as well as I do, that Lu has his favourites."

"That's a flaming lie. I suppose you're meaning me as one of 'em, like Thomas Hughes just said?"

"Yes, I do mean you. But I don't want to start a quarrel. We can settle this dispute without any bad feeling. I, for one, object to Lu having the say who's to work and who's not to. Some of the single chaps have as many responsibilities as the married men. There's Titus—he's got his mother to think of. Young Griff Owen's father is crippled with arthritis, and—"

"I've got the old woman to look after, too," Tom Pugh, a

71

young improver, protested, "and I claim my rights for a fair share."

"What about my mother?" Bull countered. "Somebody's got to look after her. She's got to live, and she depends on me and nobody else."

This started an uproar, and some of the married men, reluctant to waive their claim for preference, began to voice their objections. Then Bull called the meeting to order.

"Let's have a resolution from somebody."

Thomas raised a hand. "I propose that the Shop Committee take over the sharing list from Lu, and that the name of every moulder be put on it, then the list to be taken in rotation. The first fifteen to work one week, the other fifteen the next, and so on."

Bull accepted the resolution with obvious reluctance.

"You've heard the proposition. Any amendment?" There was no reply.

"O.K. All in favour show in the usual manner."

He counted the upraised hands. There were fifty-two.

"Resolution carried," he said. He jumped down from the bench. "You chaps who are on the Shop Committee better come with me to see Lu."

CHAPTER NINE

For the next four months the foundry continued on part-time. The men had won their victory over Lu and he was no longer allowed to control the list. Ieuan worked on the one-week-in-five basis, but his wages, combined with the twenty shillings he received from the Labour Exchange, were barely enough to meet his needs. There was no possibility of saving for his wedding, and though he accepted the situation, hoping for a sudden boom in trade, Sally became despondent.

She taxed him on the question of leaving Bevan's to take up employment in another foundry. She was anxious to marry him, and, as the weeks passed into another summer, her gaiety and confidence in the future vanished.

"It's impossible to find a job in another foundry," Ieuan tried to explain, but she appeared to look upon his explanation as an excuse, well aware of his hatred for the foundry and everything appertaining to it. "To begin with, the other foundries in Abermor already have their full quota of moulders. As for trying for a job in Swansea or Cardiff, or somewhere in the valleys, it just isn't worth it. After paying for board and lodging, bus fares, I wouldn't have enough over to pay Mam anything, and as for saving..."

"Your mother—she knows we're getting married, Ieuan. Can't she make some sacrifice? She could let you keep your money—what's over, I mean."

"I couldn't expect her to do that, Sally girl. After all, she has the home to run and Dad's wages are not much, you know."

"But you won't always be with her, Ieuan."

"No, but so long as I'm home it's only right that I should contribute something. From my first year in the foundry I've hardly earned enough to keep myself in food and clothes."

73

"Then your mother is more important than me?"

"Sally, you shouldn't say that, *cariad*. We'll be married some day. But without money, what can we do?"

"You could have worked more than you have if you hadn't let those married men take your share."

"But we're all having an equal share of what work there is, Sally."

"Yes, now. I'm referring to last year. It was only for a few weeks, but you could have saved a little bit... it all helps, Ieuan."

"You wouldn't want me to refuse giving a married man precedence, Sally? A man with a family to keep surely has more right to work than I have?"

"That's what you say now, Ieuan. You didn't say it when you had that shop meeting."

"It was different then, dear. Some of the married men had become selfish. They wanted to keep the work for themselves alone, and I certainly objected to that. I was prepared, and so were the other single chaps, to let them have the bigger share—but we were not going to allow them to keep us on the dole entirely. Oh, please don't let's quarrel over this, Sally. I'm not blaming the married men for wanting to grab every hour of work, although it was wrong and selfish. Maybe, if I were in their position, I would be just as grasping. That's what this living from hand to mouth existence does to men."

"I'm sorry, Ieuan. I'm to blame, and it's your forgiveness I should be asking. I promise you, dear, I'll never lose patience with you again. But this being out of work all the time, it's worrying. Every night I dream about it, and see no hope for our future together. If only we could have some good luck for a change. We're not asking much, Ieuan, just a chance to live happily together, with a little comfort. Someday we'll have a house of our own, with a nice garden. And we'll have children, Ieuan. That's all I ask from life. Why—why does everything seem to go against us?"

In July the last fifty-ton casting was delivered. The men waited

74

desperately, clinging to the hope that the management would have succeeded in getting further contracts. It was a hope in vain, and they knew it. The steel furnace was damped down, the ladle taken out into the yard. Tools were cleaned and oiled. The cranes were driven to the pine end of the foundry and their gears dismantled.

Lu, solemn-faced, instructed Bull to tell the men to sign for the dole. How long a spell this time, he couldn't say. Maybe a month or two, maybe more. But as soon as he would hear good news from the management he'd let the men know. He was sorry.

Lu was sorry. What a bloody good joke that was! Let him speak the truth, and say what was on his mind. A month, two months, six months, a year—for Lu it was a damn good holiday. A nice long holiday on full pay. Salmon fishing in the Towy, a spot of shooting on his brother's farm in Carmarthen. Then, there was his garden to enjoy himself in.

A good year for tomatoes, Lu. Plenty of sun about, and plenty of time to sit and watch them tomatoes ripen. No standing in the queue at Box 5, no waiting for the Union's secretary to dole out the benefit on Friday nights. The world was a grand place for Lu.

And Lu was a grand chap, one of the best, a lovely man—when all went well and there was a pay packet waiting on Fridays in the little tin box with a number on it; a tin box with a few hours overtime at time-and-a-half. Those were the days. The happy days of long, long ago, when there was so much work to be done in the foundry that one got stupid, got drunk on Fridays, and grumbled on Mondays because Saturday was such a hell of a long way off.

"Roll on, Saturday," was the headachy, tired Monday cry. But now there were no Saturdays to look forward to. Every day was Saturday, and Saturday was every day. Oh yes, Lu was a champion, fair play—when all went well. The management, too—splendid men they were. Good firm to work for, was Bevan's. A gold watch for every workman who stood the noise, the dust, the smoke, the tearing grind, the sweat and tears of fifty years.

A gold watch worth ten pounds for his pocket, enough to pay for a coffin for his grave. But that was in the good old days of prosperity, when old man Bevan was a pioneer in the industrial wilderness.

Yes, the management: Mr. Phineas Brown, Mr. Adam Pugh Price, Mr. E. M. Beynon, and the old man Bevan were decent gentlemen, every one of them—when all went well. But now it was unemployment again. What did the bastards care? They had their salaries and their big houses on the roads that led away from the smoke and dust. They had their cars, their wives had servants, and never knew the taste of neck-end-of-lamb stew. Their children went to private schools to learn how to become little ladies and gentlemen, so that in time they could exploit those who were not so fortunate as they.

Once again the shabby streets around the foundry were filled with the leaning men that lived there, a stone's throw away from the main gate through which they had trudged in sun and rain. Again the queues formed at the Employment Exchange on Mondays and Wednesdays, and the men strolled in scattered groups through the town where everyone but they were busy.

The old-age pensioners who fished in the sun from the quayside on the dock, found new company. Other legs now dangled over the quay, and younger eyes stared down at the bobbing floats in the green water.

Ieuan became one of the idle brigade. They fished with home-made, bamboo rods, broom handles, curtain poles, and sought the wily mullet and the voracious salmon bass; fishing, because there was nothing else to do, relaxing in the sunshine, because that was all that was left to do. Time was measured by no hooter. There was no morning, no afternoon. Ambition was dead, and hope was dying.

Friday evenings would find them at "New Haven" on the winding road that led to the beach. "New Haven", a double-fronted villa to which Aaron, the Union secretary, came at seven o'clock, black bag in hand, book of names under his arm; hang-dog through the busy streets, the black bag clinking with silver and coppers from the C.W.S. Bank.

Through the alphabet: "Abrahams, Adler, Barnes, Bowen, Charles, Cummings, Davies, Dyson…" One behind the other, lining up for a hand-out.

So much for the missus and kids, so much for personal expenditure. Count it up quickly, before it melts. Put a quid in this pocket, a couple of bob in the other, but for Pete's sake don't let the missus get hold of the wrong pocket or there'll be some awkward questions to be answered. Hey you, there! don't forget to pay the Union dues, your one-and-a-click. Jesus! do they think a man's a bloody millionaire? How the hell can a feller pay Union dues when he's got just over a quid coming to him?

To hell with the Union! What's it done for me, anyway? I'm on the road, tattered and torn, with no job to call me own. Let the Union go do something about finding us work. One-and-a-click a week. Where the hell's the money going to? To pay the General Secretary, the Branch Secretary, and expenses for conciliation board delegates. Trips to Swansea, and tea at R. E. Jones's. Let the Union wait for its one-and-a-click. Stick it on the arrears sheet.

Some day that wire from Littlewoods will come along. Then, to hell with all Unions great and small, and General Secretaries with their cool thousand a year. Yes, Aaron, put it down on the arrears sheet. I'll settle with you some other time. Don't worry about the disqualification. I'm bloody disqualified from a job already.

Get Guy Fawkes into Bevan's one day. He's the best chap that ever got into Parliament. Maybe he'd do the place good. What's that? What would a chap gain if Bevan's was blown sky-high? Let me ask you, Aaron—what would he lose?

Ieuan grew as bitter as his companions, and was now almost without hope. The other industries in the town were working full-time. What was wrong with Bevan's? One had served an apprenticeship—for what purpose? Of what use was a trade if one could not earn a living by it?

77

Unemployment benefit. Twenty shillings, less one-and sixpence Union fees. Keep two bob and make your plans for the week. Cut down smoking to a minimum. No more Players. Woodbines and colts-foot leaves will do.

What about your weekly treat to the cinema?

Luxury on the dole, eh?

But must go somewhere to forget. Easy life, if one had plenty of money.

Must go to the fourpennies. Never been to the fourpennies in your life? What will the girl in the pay-box think? She knows you; knows you've always been a regular patron of the ninepennies.

Fancy walking down the aisle while the lights are on. Someone might recognise you.

"Imagine *him* going to the fourpennies! Must be hard hit."

The disgrace of penury in Abermor of the Sunday School morality.

Well, you are hard hit, brother. Admit it with a song and a dance. Kill that little vestige of pride.

All right, brother, do as you will. You look the other way, hurry down the aisle, slink into your seat, conscious of your poverty—for poverty it is, brother, call it what you like.

Yes, slink into your seat, watchful for the broken spring that jabs into your posterior. Pray for the lights to dim. Ah, that's better!

The music resounds along the darkened hall. Hero and heroine are pursued. Canyon, valley, mountain, hill. Bang! Bang! Galloping hooves. Clouds of dust. Death faced ten times; ten eternities in one afternoon's performance. Thrill upon thrill. Escape from reality.

Interlude. Chatter, chatter. Rustling of paper bags, munching of sweets. Monkeys in the zoo. Two-fingered whistle, "Dai-oh! Come and sit by here, *mun*. What you doing back there?"

"Lovely picture, isn't it, Maud?"

"Smashing!

Birth of a new language: "Whassamatterwidyou?"

Overture to star attraction. The lion roars.

Super screen vamp, silken, seductive, glamorous, voluptuous, desirous, in the stupendous, gigantic, colossal production.

No longer the tiger-skin rug of the piano-and-Theda-Bara days. Gone, but not forgotten, the Nazimova theme song:

> *I'd like to sleep with Nazimova,*
> *I'd smack her—and turn her over...*

Canned music has come with progress. But the only new thing about the theme of the film is the song. Otherwise it is sex for ever and ever amen. Sex with a capital S, and spelt B-O-X O-F-F-I-C-E. Opium in the guise of a half-naked, starry-eyed siren.

Moisten your lips as she minces, poses, sways, slinks over the polished floors. See the intrigues of love and lust, the sleek, handsome men of old school tie and big business, not wretches like you with fourpence to spend.

Sit entranced. Let spirit leave you, to wander side by side with SEX on the screen before you. Take your brief moments with the shadows. You paid your fourpence, so take what you want. It's all yours for the afternoon. But dream not too deep and too long.

Flicker of lights. Stand up! stand up!

GOD SAVE THE KING.

CHAPTER TEN

The unaccustomed happiness and laughter which a temporary prosperity had brought to the Morgan household was over, and life again became the anxious and colourless routine it had been for so long to Mrs. Morgan.

The excitement of Gweneira's wedding, the introduction to Sam's parents, and a visit to Brecon where she had helped the young couple to redecorate their home, had kept her mind away from the fact that another wage-packet had been lost to her. But now that Bevan's had closed down again, she began to complain.

"Struggle, struggle, all the time. It's no pleasure to be alive, Dick. That Bevan's foundry! Indeed, it's sorry I am that I ever put Ieuan in there when he was a boy. If I'd had a bit more sense I would have sent him into the tinworks. That's the only place that seems to be working full, and good money he'd be earning there. Mrs. Thomas-next-door-but-one, over fifteen pounds comes into her house every week, and never known a day's unemployment has her Jacko."

Dick had replied quietly: "Well, Millie, you were too anxious to get the boy started. You put him into Bevan's when you should have let him stay in school for another couple of years. He would certainly be better off today, in a good job—and when I say a good job I don't mean in the tinworks either. An office job he should have had, solicitor's clerk or something. Or in the Town Hall. Something regular, Millie, with a chance of promotion. Anyway, it's a bit late to think of that now, isn't it?"

"So you're blaming me for him being out of work, eh? What about the time when nobody in this house was working? Was I to blame for that, too? Why, the pair of you haven't given me a full week's wages for more than a couple of months on end. Nineteen-twenty-four Ieuan started in Bevan's, and now it's the end of nineteen-thirty-one. Seven years, and how much money have I had in all that time? Some people have been doing well all these years. Mrs. Thomas-next-door-but-one... All right, don't look at me like that, Dick... She's bought her house, and her children are dressed as if they lived in Howard's Avenue. Yes, bought a house, and a grand piano that must have cost over a hundred pounds, even though there's not one of them can play a tonk on the instrument. And here's me, slaving all my life, and what can I buy, I ask you? Not even a rabbit hutch."

Dick tried to humour her. "You get some rabbits, Millie, and I'll build you a hutch in two ticks."

"Humph! that's right. Make jokes over everything. But I'm not the one to laugh. I don't know what it is to laugh, not since the days when we were... Oh, never mind."

"Sorry, Millie girl. I know what you've been through. It's been a bad time for all of us here in Abermor, though why it should be so, I don't know. Boom in world trade there was after Baldwin got in, then as soon as Macdonald took over, what happened? A slump."

"There's been no boom in Abermor, only in the tin works. Macdonald, indeed! Him and his Labour Government. What did I read in the papers? —something about a Royal Commission on unemployment. That's what him and his sort have done for us. Vote Labour, my foot! Daft I was when I let Ieuan talk his nonsense to me. Now that we've put the Tories back, maybe we'll get a bit more luck. P'raps what this country wants is a Five Year Plan like that Stalin man has got in Russia. Ieuan was telling me only the other day that—"

Dick laughed. "So you do listen to his nonsense sometimes, Millie? He's got a good head on him, has Ieuan, and there's plenty of people in this town know it, too. We should be proud of the boy, Millie. It's we gave him the brains, you and me."

"Proud, indeed! Ashamed I was to see his name in the paper getting to be as regular as that nonsense by Anne Mayfair who

81

was writing those bits about fashions for women. Thank goodness he's got over that craze and stopped writing again. I suppose if Sally Marvin hadn't come home he'd still be at it, so in a way I'm glad he's keeping company with her. Into trouble he'll get one of these days with that daft itch he's got to be always dabbing things down on paper. When he marries that girl he'll have to toe the line, or find himself out of a job good and proper. Bosses are not going to stand for that sort of thing. A man's duty is to stick to whatever job he's got, and not interfere with what parliament is trying to do. Let the M.P.'s run the country. They should know their work, they're getting a good wage for doing it, anyway."

The New Year came, and still there was no prospect of Bevan's restarting. Each week the Shop Committee would call at Lu's house, to be met with a shrug, a shake of the head, and a few words of sympathy. Then the long walk back to town to report to the moulders when they met at "New Haven" for their dole.

"To hell with Lu. I don't believe the bastard cares a toss when we start. We ought to go over his head, and see Bevan. Things are rotten in the state of Denmark, and a damn sight worse in Abermor. Why the hell's the foundry always closing down on us when everybody else seems to be working? It's got me beat, fair and square."

"The management, they're to blame. There's Beynon and Pugh Price—they couldn't run a bloody fish and chip shop. We chaps ought to take over from them, like those communists done in Russia. Bet we'd make the place pay, too."

"Don't talk balls, Dai, you couldn't even count up your pay on a Friday."

"I counted it all right—when I had a pay to count. But that was a hell of a long time ago."

January, February... the weekly sojourn to the suburbs continued, and Lu would meet them with doleful face.

"No, boys. Nothing doing. This is the worst spell we've ever had. Don't remember it being so bad."

"But the weather's not so dusty, Lu. How you enjoying the holiday?"

"There's no need to be sarcastic, Brin. I'm as fed up with this lolling about as you are. Only last night I was telling the wife, 'Them poor chaps I got under me in the steel shop must be feeling the pinch by this time.'"

"Squeezed to the bone, Lu. Wearing out shoe leather standing on street corners. Now, if we was getting paid for it, I wouldn't say it was such a bad life."

"Hints for me again, eh? D'you chaps think I enjoy meeting you like this every week, with nothing but bad news to tell you? I've seen the old man and done everything I could to help you boys. Even asked him if he'd let some of you come in and tidy up the place ready for the time when we start again. There's the furnace being rebuilt, the old man could have used some of you chaps to help with the labouring, but the masons' union stepped in and said it'd be breaking the constitution. Believe me, boys, I done everything possible."

"O.K. Lu. Send us a wire when you get something good to tell us. When the foundry does start up again maybe you'll be short-handed, because some of us'll be too bloody weak to hold a rammer. As for the youngsters, most of 'em'll have forgotten what they've learnt about the trade."

Another month passed. Ieuan's dream of marriage angered him with vain expectation, and his hopes of the future sneered at his present plight.

How long was this so-called temporary depression to last? The questions he had heard others ask, now troubled him. Of what use was a trade? What purpose was there in serving five years of apprenticeship when it led only to nothing? He had hands, he had a brain. They had been valued in the market-place of industry and their hire had been paid for.

But now, they were useless hands; idle and unwanted. Muscle and brawn were now for sale in Abermor, but the market was closed. Hands and brains for hire at the trade union rate, one shilling and fivepence per hour. Brains and hands that had been trained to do a specialised job. But there were no jobs; no money; only time.

Plenty of time, loads of it, bags of it, in which to walk the streets, stand on the corners, sit in the Park, fish in the dock. Time to sleep, to eat, to think, to dream; time to reap, but there was no harvest, only the wind to reap.

A March wind, cold and bitter, sighing along the streets and lanes, through the iron gateway of the deserted foundry, into the silent, casting bays. Wind whipping against the tall, corroded columns of empty moulding boxes stacked under the dusty cranes in the yard. And rain lashing on the huddled men in doorways. The men who waited for news of work. Beggars of bread.

Yes, there was plenty of time, bucketsful, sacksful. It was free, and for nothing, but it did not pay the rent or the bills for butcher, baker, milkman, coalman, and the insurance man was asked to call another week.

Ieuan's only consolation was Sally. They saw one another often. There were long walks to the woods in the evenings, Sunday afternoons in the Park, and occasionally on Friday nights they would seek the company of other young courting couples in the back kitchen of Lewis's, the Fish and Chips, where they suppered on "two two's and a middle cut."

"Aren't there any hopes at all of Bevan's making a start, Ieuan?"

Sally had asked the question so often that it annoyed him. His mother, father, and even Mrs. Marvin had asked the same thing. What could he say, other than what was told him each time the deputation returned from Lu's house?

"You don't think I like this sort of life, Sally?" he had said one evening. His abrupt manner disconcerted her.

"Did I say that you did?" she challenged. "Surely I can ask if you've heard any news without you flaring up at me?"

"But I'm tired of answering, Sally, tired and fed up with the whole business. This is the ninth month we've been on the dole, and there doesn't seem to be a single order on the firm's books.

If I could get a job elsewhere, I'd jump at it—digging ditches, anything…"

"Perhaps you—you could do some writing, Ieuan? I mean… you could earn a bit of money that way. You've always talked so much about wanting to write."

"That's a joke, Sally. I couldn't write if I tried."

"But—"

"Yes, yes, I know what you're going to say, dear. I was full of ambition once, and not so very long ago. Childish ambitions, that's what they were, Sally. Pipe dreams. What urge can one feel to write or do anything creative when we're having such a— such a damned existence?"

"That's a very selfish attitude, Ieuan, I must say. After all, there are other men in the same position as you, and worse off many of them, too, with families to keep. I asked you about your writing. You could do some… you have plenty of time, anyway."

"Plenty of time—yes, true enough. I'll write about the dole and the effect unemployment has on one's character. That should make a splendid essay."

"Oh, Ieuan, you are being cantankerous tonight. If this is how you're going to behave after we're married, then I should be sorry."

"No, don't say that, *cariad*. I'm sorry, and I apologise. I've got the old man on my shoulder proper tonight. When we get married, Sally… You think we ever will?"

"That's a hopeful attitude, indeed! And why shouldn't we get married, like most other people? You've too much time on your hands, that's the trouble, Ieuan Morgan. Bevan's is bound to re-open before long. It can't go on like this for ever. Then, when you do start, you might work for years and years."

"And in the meantime?"

"Well, there's your writing, as I said."

"And I should write a novel? A best seller?"

"You are being sarcastic now, Ieuan. There's money to be earned writing stories, if you want to know. I was reading in the paper the other week... Ellen Elaine, she earns nearly eight hundred pounds a year, writing stories for the women's magazines."

"Ellen Elaine who writes the story of Cinderella every week—is she the one you mean?"

"Yes, and her stories are really lovely. There's no disgrace in writing Cinderella stories, is there?"

"No, no disgrace—and no glory, either. And no purpose, which is of far greater importance. You want me to write Cinderella stories, Sally, when there is so much to write about that is vital?"

"Then you do think of writing, Ieuan? Your ambition is still there? Remember what I told you on the *Cefn* that day? You'll be famous one day. Some night, my boy, I'm going to bring you a whole pile of writing-paper—and a dozen pencils. See?"

When next they met, Ieuan had to suffer Mrs. Marvin's reproaches.

What was the matter with that Bevan's place? Everybody else in town was working. Why, even the roll-turning shop, and the fitters, had been back at work in Bevan's for over three months. How was it that only the men in the steel shop were still unemployed? When her Jim was alive, he used to tell her that at one time Bevan's was the most reliable firm in South Wales. Never out of work were the men there. Got gold watches, some of them, after fifty years.

That was in the good old days, though. Wages were not so high, of course, but many a man at Bevan's was known to have bought his own house. But today, well, it was another story. Always out of work were the moulders. Not much of a future for Sally if this was how it was going to be. Wales was not such a good country to be living in in these past few years, what with all the unemployment and strikes.

Trouble between master and man—sinful it was, indeed. But there! the young men of today thought of nothing but football, the cinema, and racing the dogs. The hand of the Lord had come down on them, and they had to suffer for their idolatry.

Ieuan had curbed his anger. Mrs. Marvin's outlook was dulled by her religious fanaticism. She sought an answer to every problem in her Bible and in the teachings of the disciples at the tin-roofed Church of the Christian Brotherhood where she now attended regularly.

On the occasions when he challenged her opinions, he found Sally eager to take her mother's part against him, and he had now learned to refrain from arguing, and listened in silence, tolerating her views for Sally's sake.

Nevertheless, she had spoken the truth concerning the present position at Bevan's, and it had rankled him. The other departments were working full-time. The foundry alone remained idle. He began to feel the bite of deep discontent. These men, the fitters, roll-turners, blacksmiths, pattern-makers, had drawn their wages for the past three months and showed no interest in the predicament of their fellow workers of the foundry.

"To hell with Jack, I'm all right." It was the same tale in every industry; the unfortunate few were forgotten by the fortunate majority, neglected by their fellows as well as by the masters. Each man looked upon himself as an individual concerned only with his own immediate needs.

Thus Ieuan reasoned, blinded by prejudice, embittered by the strangulation of his hopes of marrying.

Then, at the end of April, came the test.

CHAPTER ELEVEN

Ieuan found Thomas waiting for him outside the front law of "New Haven". He appeared worried.

"Heard the latest? There's going to be some great changes in the foundry?"

Ieuan smiled. "Not going to do as old Joe Taylor suggested—blow it up?"

"This is serious, Ieuan. The piecework system—it's to be reorganised, and we'll have to work a hell of a sight faster."

"I shouldn't worry over that, Thomas. Let the place start up first, then we'll face the problem."

"We are going to start, sooner than you think."

"Well, that's news. Who told you?"

"Bull. He and the boys have just been to Lu's. The old man has a new scheme bubbling in his brain-box. Wants to speed up production, cut down costs—you know the story, Ieuan. Competition, and all that. But, first of all, Bevan and his directors got to fix on a chap who's to act as their time-study clerk."

"The Bedaux system? Surely, we're not going to stand for that?"

"You think so? After being on the peg for nine bloody months?"

"Well, I'm one who's not going to tolerate any such scheme."

"Good! I'm glad to hear you say so, Ieuan. Very glad."

Ieuan frowned. "Hey, come on—what's on your mind, Thomas? What is it? And why look at me like that?"

"Nothing, Ieuan, nothing's on my mind. I said I'm glad, damned glad you're taking that attitude, because you're the fellow Bevan's going to try out."

Ieuan laughed. "That's a good one, Thomas. Can you see me walking around the foundry with a watch in my hand?"

"O.K., laugh it off, boy. The rumour is that Ieuan Morgan's the man for the job. You'll be hearing from the old man any day. He's fixed up a contract with that firm we made the fifty-tonners for, and according to Lu he's holding on to it until he can get more orders from other firms. Then, when he says the word, we start *en bloc*—first couple o' months at the old pace, so that the jobs can be timed. Afterwards, the fun'll start. There'll be some adding up and subtracting, ready for the reorganising."

"Bevan can reorganise as much as he likes. He won't find me jumping at his offer. But tell me, Thomas, how did the rumour get about? I mean, who said I was the man picked to act as Bevan's super spy?"

"Bull says so. He had it from Lu, and I suppose Lu got the story from the old man himself. There was a directors' meeting the other week. Bevan wanted a recommendation from Lu as to who was the chap most likely to take on the job."

"And Lu said I was the mutt! Well, he's got another think coming."

"That's the way to talk, man. Don't let these people buy you out. Lu praised you up to the clouds, said you were the brainiest fellow in the steel shop, figures at your finger-tips. Told the old man how you used to work out the percentages for the other chaps. But don't take notice of all that clap-trap. We know, all of us, that you're pretty smart at figures and that you've got a good head on your shoulders. Just the same, I'm a bit scared..."

"For what reason?" Ieuan's face clouded. "You don't trust me, is that it?"

Thomas was silent for a moment. He nodded to the open doorway at the top of the drive. "Come on; let's collect our winnings."

"That can wait a while." Ieuan held him back. "I want to know what's on your mind, Thomas," he demanded. "You think I'll give way, that I won't be able to resist the bribe they'll offer me?"

"It's a pretty good bribe, Ieuan... No, don't ask me what it is;

you'll find out soon enough. But listen to me—don't be fool enough to take it. Bevan's pretty cute upstairs, there's no flies on him, believe me. He wants a moulder to time the moulders, and the idea's stuck in his head. He won't budge from it. He's going to do his best to win you over, boy."

"He's got as much hope as a snowball in hell, and that's that."

On the way home that night Ieuan pondered over what Thomas had told him. Was there any truth in it? Was it just a leg-pull instigated by Bull Jackson, who hated him as much now as during the early years of his apprenticeship?

Why should Bevan mention his name in connection with this new piecework scheme that he contemplated—if any such scheme did really exist? He remembered how a few of the men had sniggered when he entered "New Haven" tonight. He recalled the hidden wink Bull had given Reg Bowen, and how Aaron, the secretary, had handed him his dole without the customary words of greeting. If there was any truth in this time-study rumour, surely he would have been approached by Bevan himself, or received a letter asking him to call for an interview?

When he got home, there was a letter for him from Beynon, the foundry manager. Mr. Beynon would be pleased if he would call at the office between ten and eleven on Monday morning next, when he would hear something to his advantage. A directors' meeting had been held recently, and in view of certain changes that were to be introduced into the steel foundry, Mr. Bevan had made a proposal.

This proposal, the nature of which Mr. Beynon would discuss with Ieuan at the interview, was most important, and concerned the welfare of every man employed in the steel shop.

Ieuan re-read the letter. His mother watched him closely.

"Good news?" she asked presently. She cast a quick glance at Dick, who sat before the fire in slippered feet, glasses perched on his forehead, a folded newspaper in his lap.

"It's from the foundry." Ieuan gave her the letter. "They want me to take on a timing job."

She peered at the typewritten page, then looked at him vaguely. "Job? There's nothing about no job in this, Ieuan. Something to your advantage it says, true enough, but that can mean something else."

"It means they're going to offer me a job that no one else would take. They want me to stand over the men with a watch in my hand, and take down the time they spend on their jobs—and off."

"Indeed? Well, that's a nice job, Ieuan, very nice, and easy, too. How much wages are they going to give you, d'you think? I must say they have a high opinion of you in the office, to be asking you to take on a job like that, and with so many other men in the foundry."

Ieuan turned to his father. "What do you say to all this, dad?"

Dick stroked his chin. "You want my opinion, boy?"

Mrs. Morgan countered with: "Never mind what your father says, it's you'll have to do the work, Ieuan. You take it. And remember this—you'd be a fool if you turned it down, for plenty of others there'll be who'll jump at the chance. Nine months you've been on the road, with nothing to do. Regular, this job'll be. Your duty it is, to yourself and me. Remember that your father and me's kept you these last nine months... not that I am going to be a selfish old woman, but, after all, there is your duty as a son. I'm telling you now, don't you go stubborn-headed and throw this chance away."

"I've made up my mind, Mam. I'm not taking it."

"Not taking it, indeed! Come, joking you are... Dick! talk to him. This is ridiculous. Giving up the chance of a lifetime, and before he knows what the job is about. A feeling I have, that he'll be out of that old foundry sooner than he thinks... That's what you've always been wanting, isn't it, Ieuan?"

Dick was hesitant to express an opinion, now that Millie had appealed to him.

"Well, if I was Ieuan, I'd—"

"Take it, of course!" said his wife. "The boy would be nothing but a fool if he was to push aside what is given him on a plate, and don't you dare advise him otherwise, Dick Morgan. It's me that's got the worries of running this house, and remember, too, that not a week's pay have I had from him since last July."

Sorry that he had implicated his parents in the discussion, Ieuan went to bed. Throughout the night he thought over the letter, and on Sunday afternoon when he walked with Sally into the country it still worried him and kept recurring constantly in his mind. He was silent and confused, replying in monosyllables to Sally's gay and light-hearted conversation.

They came to Holly Pond, its calm surface reflecting the high green banks that enclosed it, the delicate tracery of the budding trees and bushes etched against the mirrored blue and white of sky. They sat on a crude wooden bench in the shelter of a small wood that overlooked the pond, and watched the other couples pass by.

"What's the matter, Ieuan?"

He had been staring at a baby rabbit that sat on its haunches at the edge of the wood, and her voice startled him from his reverie.

"Not a word have you spoken since we left town." Reproach was evident in her tone. She touched him lightly with her gloved hand. "You—you aren't still worrying over what I said the other night?"

He picked up a stone from the grass and weighed it in his hand. "No, Sally, of course not. I've not given it another thought... Did you say anything that would make me worry?"

She smiled. "Silly! Now I know I didn't say anything I shouldn't. And to think that I was beginning to worry, too!"

He tossed the stone into the pond.

"I've got something on my mind, Sally, and I want you to help me."

"Why, yes, Ieuan... Is—is it serious?"

"I want to talk to you about it."

"Oh, please don't frighten me, Ieuan. You look so sad and

miserable. You haven't done anything," he saw her flinch, "anything bad?"

His smile, forced though it was, reassured her. "No, love, I've killed no one, nor robbed a bank, if that's what you mean. It's this, Sally—I'm going to be asked to take on a job... No, wait a minute—don't congratulate me. I want to explain to you just what sort of a job it is. I can't tell you much until I've seen Mr. Beynon tomorrow morning."

A ripple of laughter came from her throat. She sat back on the bench and fanned her face.

"Ieuan, Ieuan, there's a one you are, making me frightened. So it's Mr. Beynon you are seeing in the morning, and a big secret in your head! Keeping it from me all this time, I'm surprised at you! And pretending to be so serious, too. What next? I shall have to punish you for playing such tricks on me."

He could not bring himself to look into her eyes that were so full of expectation.

"It's a big question, Sally, whether I should take on this job. Frankly, I don't care for it."

"But I don't understand," she said. "What is wrong with it? What sort of work does Mr. Beynon want you to do?"

"Time the men," he answered bluntly. "Stand over them like a policeman, watch every move they make."

"Is that wrong, Ieuan?"

He shrugged. "Is it right to watch a man every minute of the day, make a note of what he does, and how much time he takes to do it in? Would you like to work under those conditions?"

She toyed nervously with her gloved finger-tips. "Perhaps you are exaggerating, Ieuan? A strange job it seems to me, but you could do it easily. You wouldn't have to work so hard as when you do as a moulder."

"Whether I could do it or not is immaterial."

"Then don't think of it any more if it worries you like this. I thought you were anxious to get out of the foundry?"

"I'll still be in the foundry."

"But you won't be a moulder, and a chance to get a better job doesn't come every day. Besides, it might be regular, and you'll be able to save some money for our—our wedding."

"Then you want me to take it—this collar and tie job?"

"If you want to hear the truth, Ieuan—yes, I think you'd be wise to take it. If you don't, somebody else will. It's you and I've got our future to think about, nobody else cares what happens to us. You take it, Ieuan, and don't be a fool. I know what's the matter with you... you're worrying because the other men are objecting. But they're jealous, Ieuan, can't you see? Let one of them have half a chance to get away from moulding into a cleaner job, and you'd see what would happen... What does Thomas say?"

"He wouldn't like me to do the job."

"But if he had the chance he'd jump at it, I suppose?"

"You're wrong, Sally. Thomas wouldn't consider it. He's a fine chap. I admire him a lot, and you shouldn't speak of him in that way."

"Just the same, I still say he's no different from anyone else. Chance is a fine thing, Ieuan... Take the job, you'll be better off in the long run, and then some day you'll be glad, especially when you won't have to wear those dirty dungarees again."

"I'll think it over, Sally, and by tomorrow I'll have my answer ready." He helped her from the seat. "Let's go, dear. We're not wasting any more of this lovely afternoon."

"You take the job, please, for my sake," she implored, "and we'll say no more about it. Please, Ieuan."

He led her away from the pond and into the wood.

CHAPTER TWELVE

With a nervousness that even his parents and his young sister Phyllis did not fail to notice, Ieuan got ready for his appointment at the foundry. He decided first to go up to the town. Monday was one of the signing-on days at the Employment Exchange, and anxious to avoid meeting any of the moulders he made a short cut through the back streets, arriving at the building just before nine o'clock.

The clerk at Box 5 frowned at him as he extended his franking card.

"Your time's ten o'clock. You'll have to go outside and wait."

"I've an appointment at ten," Ieuan protested.

The clerk arranged his filing trays on the counter.

"You can tell that story another time, I'm not biting," he answered. He turned his back on him. "You fellows think you can come and go here just when you like."

"I'm to meet Mr. Beynon at the foundry. Here's his letter."

"Mr. Beynon, eh?" The clerk scanned the letter. "Why didn't you say so before," he grumbled. He drew out a pink slip of paper from one of the boxes at his elbow. "I'll let you sign early today, but be here at the proper time on Wednesday. I can't go upsetting my schedule to please you chaps. You understand the rules, so next time..." He looked up to find he was addressing the air, the pink slip signed, "I. Morgan", on the counter before him.

Except for three old men and a policeman on point duty, who watched with interest the progress of a steam-roller along a strip of roadway under repair, Station Square was deserted as Ieuan hurried towards the foundry. The morning was fresh and sunny, with a breeze sufficient to slap at the long line of washing in the yard of the Railway Inn and curl a pattern of smoke from the steam-roller funnel around the three staring old men.

The Town Hall clock struck ten into the wind and the scudding clouds.

"Mr. Beynon? Yes, of course, he's expecting you. This way, please."

A young clerk, pen balanced over his ear, led Ieuan up a wide, carpeted stairway and along a polished corridor. He knocked gently on the first door he came to, and stood poised with hand on the doorknob.

"Ieuan Morgan to see you, sir."

"Come in," the voice of authority answered, and as the door opened: "Ah, Morgan! Come in, come in, my boy."

Edward Malcolm Beynon, early thirties, neat, dapper, tailor-suited, rose from his desk in the lonely room and extended a hand. An invitation to the one easy-chair: "Do sit down, Morgan."

Silver cigarette-box negligently flicked open. "Have a smoke?"

A photograph of a pretty, dark-haired young woman in a *décolleté* evening gown smiled at Ieuan from behind the cigarette-box. His fingers fumbled, the cigarette dropped into his lap.

A small, antique china clock ticked away a minute of desultory conversation. And then:

"Well, Morgan, I'm very glad you've come to see me. Mr. Bevan and I have spoken quite a lot about you lately... No, nothing disparaging, I assure you. As a matter of fact, Mr. Bevan has a very high opinion of your capabilities. You're a highly intelligent young man, and it's a shame really that you've had to serve your time as a moulder. You should have interested yourself in some other career—something that would have offered you more scope than ordinary manual labour. But, of course, it's easy for me to criticise. Opportunities do not come to every man. However, Mr. Bevan and I are convinced that you are certainly entitled to an opportunity for advancement, right now."

Ieuan rolled the crumpled cigarette between his fingers.

"Your letter, Mr. Beynon. I came here to discuss what you've written."

96

"Yes, yes, of course—the letter." The manager leaned back in his chair and knuckled his smooth chin.

"Excuse my rattling away. Board meetings, and all that—one gets into the habit of making speeches," he joked. "We'll come to the point, shall we?" He laid his well-manicured hands on the desk. "Morgan, I suppose there's no need for me to tell you that the foundry's in a bad way. For the past six years we've struggled to keep the place going. There have been times when we should have shut up shop, and it was only Mr. Bevan's consideration for his foundry-men that prevented us doing so. We are human, my boy, and we have a duty to our employees, to men who have helped to build up this—this enterprise. But now, I'm glad to say, there are brighter prospects in store for all of us, and that is why Mr. Bevan and I sent for you."

Ieuan rested his arms on the chair. "Is it true that you're introducing the Bedaux system, Mr. Beynon, and that you want me to time the men?"

The manager was embarrassed. He smiled indulgently. "That's a rather crude way of putting it, Morgan. Let me assure you that, first, we have no intention of applying the Bedaux system, and secondly, your remark about timing the men. What we want to offer you is the post of time-study clerk which, you must admit, is somewhat less drastic than what you supposed. We are anxious to have a progress chart, a reference to the number of hours spent on different moulds, and—"

"But the foundry has been working on a piece-work basis for some years," Ieuan interrupted. "Practically all the heavier work has been priced, and you know the number of hours each job has taken."

"True enough, Morgan. However, the position is now changed. We have to revise those prices. And it is in this way you can help us. We want you to make a note of the various jobs, the hours spent on them, and this means, of course, that if a man is absent from his particular job for some minutes, then that time has to be accounted for. We intend to revise completely and thoroughly.

Our prices must be lowered, otherwise we have no hope of surviving. Competition is keener today than ever, and now that we have a large stock of orders in hand, it is up to us to hold on to them. Well, Morgan—are you prepared to take on this post?"

Ieuan prepared to rise from his chair. "I'm sorry, Mr. Beynon. No—I'm afraid I can't accept."

"Sit down, Morgan, my boy. Now, listen to me. I'm a little older than you and have had quite a lot of experience in business. Believe me, I appreciate your feelings, but just let me give you some friendly advice... Here, take another cigarette."

Beynon relaxed in his chair. "Yes, I appreciate your position," he went on. "The very thought of my having sent for you has made you suspicious. There can be no co-operation between master and man— that's the foolish attitude some of the workers take. But this is the twentieth century, Ieuan. We're not back in the days of feudalism. Look at it this way. We have, as I said, a large number of orders on our books—sufficient to carry us through the next year. If we can have a detailed list of the hours taken on these jobs and come to some satisfactory arrangement— I mean, if we can cut down on our production costs, then Bevan's would be a formidable rival to any firm in the market today. It stands to reason that at present our tenders are too high, that's why you and your fellow workers in the steel shop have been thrown on the dole. Don't be a fool, Ieuan. Take this chance while it's given you. We have to choose a moulder for this particular work because—well, a moulder knows the run of the foundry, he knows the various snags that crop up from time to time on a job. And we decided on you because you are the one who's most capable."

Beynon drummed his fingers on the desk. "It's a comparatively easy job, Ieuan. Of course, we realise that you'll have to put in a few hours' work at home each evening. I mean—your job won't finish at five o'clock. There'll be some accounting to do, but to compensate you we've instructed our head cashier not to deduct anything from your pay should you arrive late some morning. I can't see how the men could hold any objection at all. If they wish to object," he shrugged, "and remain satisfied with the dole, then there's nothing I can say—except this. The work we now have in hand will have to be sub-contracted, and we'll close the foundry for good."

The manager struck a match and held it to Ieuan's cigarette. "If you accept this job, Ieuan, and cooperate with us, we'll not let you down," he went on. "Sink your personal feelings for the time being. Think of the other men, some with wives and children to keep. They've been on the dole for the past ten months. This is their opportunity as well as ours. Bevan's can get back to the position it once held in South Wales, and again become the leading engineering firm here. There would be a brighter future for every one of us. You're a young man, Ieuan, and this is your chance to climb out of a rut and better yourself, as well as make things easier for your fellowworkers in the steel shop."

Ieuan sat up.

"Very well, Mr. Beynon. I'll take the job."

"Well done, Ieuan. That's splendid!" The manager beamed. "I knew I could depend on you to see things clearly and without prejudice. Our confidence in you has certainly been justified. Remember, Mr. Bevan and I will always be ready to advise you on any difficulty which might arise—not that we anticipate any difficulties, mind you," he added hastily, "but you know how it is when one introduces something new and untried. Little snags have a habit of popping up now and then."

"What about the foundry, Mr. Beynon? When do you think the men will restart?"

"Hm!... Let me think. Four to five weeks, I should say. In the meantime, of course, you will be paid your full wages, so you'd better inform the Employment Exchange people."

Beynon escorted him to the door. "We are very grateful to you, Ieuan, and I assure you that you won't regret assisting us with this new experiment." He shook hands, and as Ieuan turned to go: "By the way, the foundry will probably re-open in the second week in June. I'd like to see you a few days before, so that we can discuss the best method of drawing up the time-study charts. Good morning, Ieuan. It's been a pleasure to talk to you."

Outside, in the sunlight of the yard, Ieuan pondered over the manager's words. While the manager had been talking, a plan had formulated in his mind. It had come suddenly, an inspiration, and he had pounced upon it.

He would arrange a system of time-study whereby the moulders benefited. He would reject whatever method Beynon eventually decided upon, and then, at the opportune moment, introduce his own scheme. It was obvious that the management were concerned only with their own salvation; the men's future counted for little.

Bevan was not a philanthropist. The time-study scheme was meant for the office files. The piece-work prices would be ruthlessly cut, production speeded up to the maximum. True, the workers would earn a bigger wage, but compared with the profits the employer would gather, the extra shillings of the moulders and labourers were infinitesimal.

He would take the time spent on the jobs, but in his own way. There would be no noting of time spent by the men while they were at the latrines, or while they took a rest period after a heavy cast. A great deal of time was wasted in searching for tackle for the various jobs, but this was entirely the fault of the management. It was their lack of organisation that had brought about this waste of production hours. He would make a special note of it and remind Beynon that unless the men were provided with the necessary equipment, the wastage would still continue to be the major problem.

The moulding-boxes were faulty; there was a shortage of tools, hand-rammers, steel wedges, cramps; the pneumatic rammers needed overhauling; there were too few labourers employed, which meant that the moulders were forced to do the labouring work as well as their own.

Boxes piled haphazardly in the foundry created congestion and took up floor space which could be utilised for other moulds. It was too obvious that the foundry needed drastic reorganising, but the lowering of piecework prices would not solve the management's problems. Production could be speeded up by the elimination of the factors responsible for delaying it. The management, and not the men, were to blame for the foundry's present plight. He would tell Beynon so when they next met, and have proof to put before him.

Later that evening, when he told Sally the result of his talk with Beynon, she was delighted.

"There! what did I tell you? Oh, you were wise to take it, Ieuan, and I'm so glad you didn't let your old stubbornness stop you. After all, what harm can you do to anyone? I still say it's only the jealousy of the other men that made you hesitate. Mr. Beynon and Mr. Bevan, they must think you're a wonderfully clever young man. And their opinion goes far, Ieuan. They're men of high position in Abermor."

He explained his scheme to her, and her enthusiasm gradually diminished.

"You will be careful, Ieuan," she urged. "This is your big chance, and I wouldn't do anything that might spoil it. A fool you'd be, to sacrifice yourself for the men, and if I were you I wouldn't be too anxious to let them benefit from your plan. You say Mr. Beynon is only using you for his own ends... I wouldn't be too sure about that. Some of the men working with you would just as soon cut your throat as look at you... What did your father say when you told him?"

"Dad had nothing to say, not tonight. Mam, of course, is as pleased as Punch, and he didn't have a chance to offer his opinion."

"Never mind, Ieuan dear. Our luck has changed at last, and perhaps now we'll be able to look forward to something... But it was so good of Mr. Beynon to offer you five weeks' wages for nothing, wasn't it? That proves how valuable a man you are to them."

He smiled wryly. "I should be," he answered, but his meaning was lost on her.

The following Wednesday morning when he met Thomas returning home from the Exchange, he suggested a walk to Dinas Wood. He wanted to discuss his scheme with him, but on the road out of town he hesitated to mention the subject, waiting for Thomas to broach the matter first.

He felt ill at ease, tortured by the thought that he was betraying his fellow workers. His motive—was it as altruistic as he had supposed? Or was it but a compromise meant really to justify his acceptance of the job? Beynon had tried to buy him with his bribe of full pay until the foundry restarted. To those who would not try to reason sympathetically, the bribe had been taken, and self-esteem and integrity sacrificed.

Would Thomas think so? Thomas, the only friend he had in the foundry; who had always stood by him since that first tortuous year of apprenticeship.

"By damn, you're quiet today, Ieuan. What the hell's up?"

They climbed the steep hill that curved into the wood; then paused a while to rest on the iron fence bordering the path.

A farm labourer, coat slung over his shoulder, wished them good day as he trudged by. His heavy footsteps faded into the depths of the wood. Then, there was a silence, disturbed occasionally by the rustling of the leaves, and the mournful bleat of a sheep.

Thomas lit a cigarette. He drew himself to the top rail of the fence and sat, knees apart, his heels levered against the lower rail. The country road they had walked was deserted. Through the laced screen of leaves, and far below them in the distance, stood the beach and the muddy estuary. There was no sun. The grey day spread over the ebbing tide and the dark pools it had left on the beach. The Gower headland disappeared into the mist, formless, the green fields and hedgerows vague and indistinct. Rain was not far away.

"Thomas, I went down to see Beynon on Monday."

Thomas nipped the cigarette end and placed the butt in his waistcoat pocket. He balanced himself on the fence rail.

"I was waiting for you to say that. You've got something on your chest. Come on, get rid of it, boy. What happened?"

His eagerness made Ieuan uneasy.

"You told him where to get off, I bet," Thomas grinned, "so don't let it worry you. Trouble with you, Ieuan, is that you're too bloody sensitive. If you gave Beynon what was coming to him, what the hell odds? I'd have told him to keep his bloody job."

"But I've taken the job."

"Taken it!" Thomas laughed. "That's a good one!" He thrust out his leg. "Here, boy, pull this."

"It's true."

Thomas's laughter froze. He swung down from the fence. "You're not serious, Ieuan?"

"Yes. I discussed it with Beynon, and I've decided to try it out."

"You've decided! I like that. What about the men? Why the hell didn't you discuss it with the Union?"

"I felt there was no need for it. But I'll see that our chaps benefit from this time-study."

"That's a laugh. Did you ever hear of a boss timing men for their own benefit? Don't you, can't you bloody well see what it's all for? We spoke about it on Friday night. You were pretty sure then, that you weren't going to take the damn job."

"But I've got a scheme worked out, Thomas, and Beynon knows nothing about it. It's my own plan to counteract—"

Thomas tossed his head.

"Plan!" he sneered. "Don't give me that kind of talk, Ieuan. You've bloody well sold yourself and sold us. How much did he offer you? What was the price you were waiting for before you clinched the bargain?"

Ieuan's fists clenched. "All right, Thomas, that's enough! I'm trying to explain. Give me a chance to say my piece."

"O.K." Thomas snapped impatiently. "But let me ask you one question. Did you tell Sally about Beynon wanting to see you?"

"Why, yes, but what has Sally to do with it?"

103

"She wants to marry you, doesn't she?"

Ieuan reddened. "You'll keep her name out of this, Thomas—I'm warning you."

"She's twisted you round her little finger, boy. D'you hear that? The sooner you get a job the sooner you'll get married. Any job, so long as the money comes in. And you've sold your principles just because she—"

Ieuan's clenched fist caught him full on the mouth. Thomas staggered back against the fence. He brushed a hand across his lips, and glanced at the splotch of blood. Dazed, he looked at his friend and shook his head slowly.

"Ieuan, boy... you shouldn't have done that. You shouldn't. We've been pals..."

But Ieuan did not wait to hear him. His anger and his tears blinded him, as he turned and hurried down the hill.

CHAPTER THIRTEEN

In the next five weeks Ieuan suffered the torment of frustration and anxiety. Thomas, from whom he had expected sympathy, had made an accusation which had forced him to raise his hand and strike him. Their friendship was over, finished. Now, there was no one in whom he could confide, no one save Sally. But he had not told her of the quarrel. He felt alone, isolated from his fellow workmen, defeated in his purpose and unsure of himself.

The moulders had been told of the interview with Beynon, and the result had not pleased them. Their resentment and anger towards him was evident in their every look and gesture when he was near. The muttered comments, "dirty bastard", "turncoat", "bloody master's man", were meant for his ears.

He had defended himself in an outburst of anger which had only served to aggravate them more, and his attempts to explain his scheme had been met with sarcasm and derision. Even the younger moulders, Titus, Reg Bowen, and Charlie, were antagonistic, while Abraham, the coreshop charge-hand, who had always respected his opinions and had agreed to listen to his explanation, was reluctant to believe him.

Dummy's contempt for him was obvious. The deaf mute, whom he hailed one night on his way to town, deliberately turned his back on him and crossed to the other side of the street.

To Bull Jackson, however, had come the opportunity he had long waited for. Within a week of Ieuan's interview he had summoned a shop meeting to discuss the Union's attitude towards the time-study plan. There had been talk of Ieuan's expulsion from the Union. He was now a member of the staff and no longer a moulder, Bull maintained. "And this is a moulders' Union, isn't it?"

His attempt to expel Ieuan failed, for, although he gained the support of a section of the moulders present at the meeting, his proposal was defeated by a majority of two.

Ieuan Morgan had been offered a staff job. To expel him for accepting it was unconstitutional, old Isaiah Charles declared. The management were determined to place a time-clerk in the steel shop, and the Union would have to accept that decision. If Ieuan Morgan had refused, another man, not necessarily a moulder, would have been engaged.

"And God help us then, it would be. A stranger to the foundry wouldn't have no sympathy for us. We must have patience, men. Ieuan says he will give to the shop steward every week a list of the times taken on the different jobs, the same list that he will give the management. A good help he can be to us in that way, and we should be giving him every bit of encouragement."

Ieuan had not attended the meeting. The enmity shown towards him had added to his feeling of frustration and dismay, and his confidence in the rightness of his decision wavered. The moulders had sneered at the suggestion that ultimately they would benefit from the reorganisation of the steel foundry. The fact that Mrs. Marvin, Sally, his mother, and Phyllis were enthusiastic and his father silent, further contributed to the weight of his uncertainty. But he had already given his word to Beynon. Let the men think the worst of him. He would show them! Yes, by hell he would!

On the Saturday morning before the foundry was due to restart he was sent a reminder from the office. Mr. Bevan and his co-directors had outlined a time-study scheme which they assumed was quite satisfactory, but there were certain adjustments to be made before it was put into actual practice. The steel shop foreman had already notified the men that they were to resume work on Monday. In view of this, and the rather short notice, would Ieuan please call at the office to discuss his new appointment?

During this second meeting with Beynon, Ieuan noticed that the latter's affability had disappeared. He was now the business man, the employer.

"Morgan, everything has been arranged. I have here a few notes taken at the recent meeting of the board of directors." He drew out a sheet of foolscap from his drawer. "First of all, I must stress upon you the importance of accounting for every minute wasted on the various jobs, and there is, as you are aware, quite an appreciable amount of time lost in the foundry."

"Yes, I understand, Mr. Beynon," Ieuan replied. "But the time you consider lost is not to be blamed on the men."

The manager looked at him enquiringly. "That's a rather challenging statement, isn't it?"

"It's true. I've worked as a moulder and I know the snags we have to put up with. The foundry is outdated, Mr. Beynon. There's no tackle, or at least what tackle there is has to be searched for—and this means that the moulders are off their jobs for practically a whole day every week. I can give you an instance of—"

"Look here, Morgan, let's face the facts. The foundry has all the equipment it needs. In the old days we had to depend on the ordinary hand-rammer. Now, we've introduced the pneumatic type, which has sped up production by ten times. There are moulding machines, a new sand-mixer, the cupola and converter have been replaced by the most modern steel furnace. There are two electric cranes, where before we had to rely on the hand jib-crane. No, I'm afraid you're trying to evade the issue, Morgan. Let me emphasise once again, the future of Bevan's foundry depends a great deal on the manner in which you will carry on with this time-study experiment. You've got to throw aside any feelings of doubt as to the men's reaction. They're not going to like this, that's obvious. But you must be quite impersonal, Morgan. We have to lower our contract estimates, or sink. Competition has become damned keen, I can tell you, and if we are to survive we must be prepared to make sacrifices... and that applies to every man Jack of us."

Ieuan offered no reply. He had tried to explain some of the production difficulties to be encountered in the foundry, but

Beynon was not prepared to listen. The same delays would still continue. The only solution was to report on them in his weekly progress chart, and force the management to take notice of them. This he would do. Talking to Beynon was evidently a waste of time and breath.

"Another point I would like to draw your attention to, Morgan," the manager ran a finger down the foolscap, "is this deliberate wastage of time in the latrines. Men go down there far too often, and for a purpose the latrines were not intended for. Heaven knows the buildings were not put up for comfort, and how the men can make use of them as a—a community centre for gossip, I can't imagine. The point is, they do. I don't think I've ever walked up the yard without seeing at least two men shuffling out from the place with their braces dangling, and returning to their departments as if they had all the time in the world on their hands. I hesitate to think what might happen if a lady visitor was escorted around the yard some day. The men could at least adjust their dress before leaving... But that's besides the point, Morgan. What I'm getting at is this—these latrine excursions must be noted, and a limit placed on the time allowed for a man's visit there, consistent, of course, with his particular urgency at that moment."

"I understand," said Ieuan, with not the slightest intention of fulfilling the manager's suggestion.

"One more item, Morgan." Beynon replaced the foolscap into his drawer. "I've noticed that the men have a habit of leaving their jobs and going out for spells. They've got hiding-places all over the foundry, and fortunately I have come to find out these *cwtches* of theirs. They congregate on the furnace landing, in the watchman's shanty, the power station, the pattern stores, and in the summer-time I've even caught some of them dozing on the foundry roof. This has to be stopped, and the only way in which it can be done is by making a note of the matter and reporting it to the office. Smoking, again, should be prohibited. I entirely disagree with allowing men to smoke at their jobs, and I told Mr. Bevan so at our last meeting. It was barred here before the war, and I see no reason why it should have been re-introduced. It's a privilege which the men have abused. How can a man work, with a cigarette dangling from his lips and smoke blowing into his eyes?"

Beynon reached for his cigarette-case.

Presently he sent for a clerk and instructed him to provide Ieuan with the necessary note-books, pencils, and a ream of foolscap.

"Monday is the day then, eh, Morgan? Good luck to you. I shall be seeing a lot of you in the future, and I trust our association will be a pleasant one."

Mrs. Morgan was highly excited at the prospect of Ieuan's opportunities for what she looked upon as further promotion, and when Monday came she had placed on his bed a clean white shirt and collar in place of the dungarees and dark blue flannel shirt he had been used to. The hobnailed boots were stored away in the cupboard under the stairs, the cloth cap replaced by his grey trilby.

"On the staff you are now, my boy. No need to go in your old working clothes. Indeed, it's proud of you I am. As I was telling your father last night, 'Not many young chaps got the brains of our Ieuan. It's out of the foundry he'll be, and into a still better job one of these fine days.'"

The previous night Sally had wished him good luck in his new job, and her wishes and his mother's words reiterated in his mind as he walked in through the foundry gates.

The men from the other departments, to whom he had always spoken on his way in, ignored him, and Pritchard, the timekeeper, was the only one who acknowledged him with a friendly, "Good morning." He stepped into the foundry, self-conscious and strained. The moulders grouped around a drying stove took no notice of him as he drew near. He was about to speak, but sensing their hostility, passed on down the shop.

Presently Lu appeared, and the men dispersed to their jobs. The foreman approached him. "First day on your new job," he said with a grin. He threw a quick glance behind him. "They've got it in for you, eh? Well, you're one of us, now—the clean-collar men, so what d'you expect? Take a tip from me, don't give a damn for what they think of you. You're in Beynon's good books, so use your head and look after your number one."

During the first break at half-past eight, Lu again approached him. "You'd better come along and have a bite in my office," he suggested.

"No thanks, Lu. I'll go over to the canteen."

"Canteen! You can't eat your food there—not now. You're one of the staff, and there's a bit of prestige about us chaps. And a dignity, too, you know."

"Thanks all the same, Lu."

The canteen door was ajar as Ieuan crossed the yard, his food tin in hand.

"Here comes the bloody collar and tie, boys."

The remark made him flinch. One of the improvers made an obscene gesture. "Tell the bastard to time this, if he can."

Ieuan hesitated in the doorway. No one spoke, but as he walked away he heard someone call his name. Titus came running after him.

"Dammit! why the hell did you take on this bloody job, Ieuan? Give it up, *mun,* and come back to us. I had a chat with Thomas just now, and he said that if—"

"To hell with Thomas, to hell with all of you," Ieuan blurted savagely. He left Titus standing with mouth agape and strode in the direction of the foreman's office.

"Changed your mind, Ieuan?" Lu drew up a chair. "I thought you would. Beynon wouldn't like it if it got to his ears that you were too friendly with the men. Suspicious he'd be, and you couldn't blame him, either."

Ieuan made no comment, but later, at nine o'clock, as they returned into the foundry, he asked for a list of the day's moulds, and classified them in his notebook, a procedure which was greeted with a prolonged hand-clapping and a loud burst of sarcastic cheering from the improvers.

Pretending to be unmoved by the demonstration he took his place on the planks covering the deep castings' pit, where he had an unobstructed view of the shop.

A labourer slouched by, an empty bucket under his arm. "Want a pair of spying-glasses?" he joked, but, finding no response, shrugged, and disappeared into the archway beneath the furnace.

Ieuan wrote the names of the men on the various moulds in his list. He would enter the daily eight and a half hours opposite each man's name, and, as each iob was completed, hand a duplicate list of the totals to Bull.

Men were being constantly shifted from one mould to another. There were heavy patterns to be carried from the pattern shop, for which a dozen or more men were detailed, and in the afternoons the moulds in the casting bay had to be prepared. It was impossible to specify every minute of a man's time, as Beynon had suggested.

Faced with the intricacies which the new job presented, Ieuan's efforts to keep a fair record of the time were obstructed by the younger moulders who refused to co-operate with him. He had promised Bull a weekly list of the total hours for each mould so that the Shop Committee, prepared with this knowledge, could counteract the management's proposal for a drastic revision of prices. The shop steward had met his offer with a certain distrust but finally he was prevailed upon by the Committee to accept it. To be forewarned was to be forearmed. Without the information Ieuan was prepared to give them, how could they hope to defeat Bevan's wage-cut policy?

The improvers, without exception, were openly hostile to Ieuan, resenting his promotion to what they regarded as a "cushy job and money for jam", envying his escape from the heavy routine work he had been accustomed to as a moulder.

When Lu directed some of them to the work in the casting bay, or sent them from one mould to another, they deliberately neglected to inform Ieuan, until finally he was forced to examine their daily time-sheets in order to check up on their hours and remedy any discrepancy in his own records.

Towards the end of the year some of the younger moulders, who had appreciated the help he was giving the Shop Committee, became sympathetic and proved eager to co-operate with him, but the majority were still suspicious, and treated him as an intruder, a spy sent in amongst them.

He failed to break down this barrier of suspicion and antagonism. Bevan and the directors had offered him the post and he had accepted it, fully aware of the dangers it held. He had been out of work. The offer had meant money—a wage. He had considered its possibilities from the employers' viewpoint as well as his own, and now he felt that he had acted rightly, since the men would certainly benefit from his position as time-study clerk. The management could say that he was favouring the workers. But even if he did, he would still have less to trouble his conscience than Bevan had when the foundry was at a standstill and the men had to exist on the dole.

He had tried to explain this to Thomas, but even he had not stopped to listen or to reason with him. They had quarrelled, and in all the months that had passed they had not spoken to each other.

This, and the continued animosity which Bull and the others showed towards him intensified the mental conflict he had experienced from that day when he had first met Beynon at the office. His health became affected and he began to feel a gnawing pain at the pit of his stomach, which grew more severe as the day proceeded. The long hours of standing in the same place caused his feet to swell, and he became alarmed at these strange symptoms.

On Sally's advice, he went to the doctor who, after careful examination, prescribed a rest.

"Nervous strain, young man. You'd better go slow, unless you want to break up."

Rest! How could he afford to rest? This was the only opportunity he had ever had to save money. He explained his position to the doctor.

"Well, you'll have to go slow, that's my advice. Your trouble is mainly psychological. However, I'll give you something that might help a little."

The medicine and tablets which the doctor prescribed for him gave some relief. The stomach pains gradually eased, and he was able to continue with his work at the foundry.

The months passed, and each week he deposited what he could afford from his wage in a savings account at the Post Office. In July of the following year his balance amounted to eighty pounds.

Eighty pounds! Sally was amazed at his wealth. Now, they could get married.

Yes, they would get married, Ieuan agreed. For what other purpose had he been putting away each week like a miser? They had waited long, but now at last their dream was to be realised.

"In August, Ieuan... next month."

"Yes, Sally *fach*. Next month—an August wedding for my lovely girl."

He held her tight and kissed her smile.

"My lovely girl."

CHAPTER FOURTEEN

Mrs. Morgan did not take with good grace the news of Ieuan's forthcoming marriage. She had expected him to marry Sally some day, but his promotion to the staff had given him the security he had never held before, and she had anticipated that he would be a good support to her for many months to come.

"You will help me to get a few things together, Mam?" he suggested one evening. She looked at him with a frown.

"Speak plainly, Ieuan. What do you mean? Get a few things together? Surely, it's the girl that gets things together. That's how it was in my time, anyway."

He smiled. "Sorry, Mam—but put it this way. I've got about eighty pounds saved. I've given notice of the wedding, and there's only a couple of weeks to go." He hesitated. "You know the custom in Abermor, Mam... when a chap is going to be married, his mother—well, she usually lets him keep his wages for a month or so before the date."

"Indeed?" she returned. "It's the first time I've ever heard of it. Now, don't you think it's a big enough loss for me as it is? Losing your pay every week I'll be from the day you and Sally are married. Yes, losing every penny, just when regular work has come your way at last."

"But, Mam—"

"I don't see how you can expect me to do what you ask, Ieuan. A lot of expense it will mean to me—your getting married. A new suit your father will be needing, a frock for Phyllis, and, of course, there's myself will be wanting a new pair of shoes. Not a swanky wedding it will be, I know, but all the same we want to be tidy. I am surprised at you asking me to let you keep your wages... not that I won't help you, mind. Oh no, I'm not the

114

selfish person you think I am. Your father and me have been talking about your future, Ieuan, and I have decided to give you a good wedding present. You know we can't afford much, but there's your bed. I always said it should be yours to keep one day. Well, there it is. Take it with you to your new home... It's not many mothers would be so thoughtful, and I—"

She burst into a spasm of weeping, and as Ieuan glanced at his father the latter held out his hands expressively and shrugged.

That night he wrote to Gweneira. Sally and he would like to spend their three days' honeymoon in Brecon, and he wondered whether Sam would care to act as his best man. Unfortunately, there was a misunderstanding between Thomas and himself, and it was rather awkward.

Gweneira's reply came by return post. Of course, Sam would be only too pleased to be best man, and as for the honeymoon, nothing would give her and Sam greater pleasure than to have them stay at Brecon.

On the wedding day the young couple and the small party of near relatives crowded into the registrar's office. The only touch of sadness Ieuan felt was at the absence of Thomas, but even this was forgotten in the greater happiness he experienced when he placed the ring on Sally's finger.

"Oh, Ieuan, there's happy I am."

* * *

Peaceful hamlets sheltering beneath the lofty blue summits of the Beacons flitted past as the train gathered speed on the last stage of its journey. The railway curved through a densely wooded valley, then suddenly, from around the bend, Brecon came into sight.

From the distance it looked like a coloured picture postcard. The River Usk flowed serenely along the green meadows and red fallow land that encompassed the town. Then, high on a bluff overlooking the river stood Brecon itself, the tall towers of the cathedral and St. Mary's Church rising above the trees and the sagging rooftops of the ancient houses.

Gweneira and Sam, who had made the return journey on his motor-bike, were at the station to meet Ieuan and his bride. They gave them a warm Welsh welcome, and Sally was greeted as a sister by Gweneira, who kissed her and laughed and cried alternately.

Ieuan was fascinated with his first view of the honeymoon town. An ancient stone bridge led past a derelict water-mill overgrown with brambles into a crooked lane of quaint, white-washed and pink-washed cottages with twinkling windows. The trees he had seen from the train seemed to grow everywhere. They reared high above stone walls mossy with age, the shadows of the leaves flickering across narrow, cobbled streets that had known the tramp of Caesar's legions and had echoed the clatter of Cromwell's cavalry.

Terraced paths and lanes, sheltered by the thick foliage, were cool and shady. Wild flowers bordered the hedges, and the scent of lime blossom filled the air.

"Lovely little place, isn't it, Ieuan?" Gweneira said with a touch of pride. "But just wait till you see our home. It's the finest sight of all, and it'll take your breath away."

But it was Sally who first expressed her delight and wonderment when they came to the street where her sister-in-law lived. The Rowlands's cottage had been built as an extension to a big, rambling house which lay back from the roadway, and from the foot of the hill which led to it, it appeared to be a blank, stone wall. The roof sagged in the middle as if it had been weighted with a heavy load and had grown tired of offering further resistance. A tall chimney-pot, painted a bright yellow, toppled drunkenly above it, and a tiny window blinked at the ivy-covered villas on the other side of the road.

Sweet-smelling jasmine festooned the yellow wall above the front door, while on the window-sill rested a wooden box of flowering mignonette.

"Make the most of your stay here," Sam smiled as they sat down to a meal of fresh trout which Gweneira had ordered from

116

a local poacher early in the morning. "You've chosen the best month of the year, anyway."

Sally and Ieuan took his advice and made the most of their three days. The peace and tranquillity of the little town and its surroundings gave them a happiness which neither of them had known or shared together in the past. They found a beauty here that was alien to Abermor and the industrial south which they had both known so well in their childhood and youth, and the three days were crowded with memories.

Memories of bird songs from the trees and hedgerows. The constant murmur of the river sounding even above the chatter of early morning women, who, leaning on their brooms, gossiped in the sunny door-ways.

Farmers in breeches and leggings, bow-legged, red-faced. Long-maned horses nodding along the quiet streets. An archway of trees glistening after a shower and casting across the lane a greenish-black cloak.

Picnic on the river bank beside a brown pool. Islands of pink stone, sun-warmed, where tall, reedy grass grew.

A freckled boy fishing for trout, his cheeks and lips purple-stained. At his feet a basket of whinberries gathered from the mountain slopes.

Laburnum overhanging crumbled walls touched with pink and green. Stone buttresses worn smooth by time and weather. Gargoyles grinning down on the narrow streets.

A walk through a field of buttercups. Shoes dusty with the yellow-green of pollen.

Along the promenade, through the shady avenue of chestnut trees. Organ music from the hidden cathedral mingling with bird songs and the rumbling of heavy lorries on the road to England.

And at night, the river again, thundering over the weir, racing over the pebbles.

The bleating of a sheep, plaintive in the silence that shrouded the Roman road to the hills.

A town of kindness, where no man was a stranger.

"You loved Brecon, didn't you, Sally?"

He asked the question as the train drew out, leaving Sam and Gweneira waving to them in the sun.

She wept a little and he teased her.

"It was like a dream, Ieuan."

The majestic Beacons floated past, purple in the summer morning. The silver ribbon of river disappeared into a wood, and the rooftops and the towers of the ancient town were gone like the honeymoon days.

"It's strange, Ieuan—I should be happy going home. But somehow, I'm not looking forward to Abermor after the wonderful holiday we've had. It was so beautiful, Ieuan... so lovely."

There was a sadness at leaving, and he, too, suffered the same *"gwendyd ysbryd"*, that "sickness of the spirit" of the Welsh. The first rapturous bliss was over. The dream had ended. Now, the reality of the foundry and the struggle to live, faced them.

How long would the new job last? What were the prospects for their future? Was unemployment to come again? Their home life with Mrs. Marvin—would they be happy there?

He took her in his arms. "Never mind, *cariad,* we've got each other."

"Yes, Ieuan... Oh, hold me tight, Ieuan *bach.* Never, never let me go." The tears came. "You will love me always?... You'll be good to me?"

* * *

Mrs. Marvin kissed them as they stepped off the train.

"God bless you, my children. It's lovely to have you back home again. I prayed the Lord to be mindful of you and to make your marriage a true and happy one."

Ieuan glanced swiftly at Sally, but said nothing.

"I've got your room ready," Mrs. Marvin continued. "I mean—

the bedroom. Just waiting now for the suite Ieuan ordered. Universal's man said it will be delivered by Saturday. Come now, children, a nice pot of tea I'll be making for you. You must be tired out after your journey."

Late that night Ieuan sat on the edge of the bed. He watched Sally as she shyly undressed. From the suitcase she took out the honeymoon nightdress of pale green satin, and tied a bow of matching green ribbon in her black hair.

Their first night at home. How lovely she looked. The green satin crackled and threw out little sparks of light as she drew it over her head. She drew close to him. His hands caressed her hair, her breasts.

"You are happy, Ieuan, love?"

Her voice intoxicated him. Her young body burned beneath the thin, glistening folds. He drew her back on to the bed.

The springs creaked. She sat up, nervous.

"Mother!" she whispered.

Ieuan became taut. Mrs. Marvin—she was in the next room, a thin wall between them. She would always be there, every night, in the next room. Her presence was an intrusion into their privacy. Her image crept into his mind, as he tenderly drew Sally into his arms.

Outside in the darkness a cat screeched, and the discordant blast of a hooter broke into the tempest of their love-making.

CHAPTER FIFTEEN

The first week passed. There had been a moment which had filled him with pleasurable anticipation. Thomas had entered the shop. Their eyes had met. Ieuan hesitated, then he smiled.

"Congratulations, Ieuan."

"Thanks... Thanks, Thomas." But no more was said. Ieuan had dropped his extended hand. The hooter had blown and the men returned to their work. The old friendship was not yet to be resumed, and the link to unite them remained to be forged.

As the months went by, Ieuan's confidence slowly returned. The preliminary negotiations for the new contract prices were made, and when the Shop Committee reported back to the moulders, their satisfaction was evident.

Beynon, on behalf of the firm, had offered his estimate for the jobs. The Committee, with Ieuan's tabulations memorised, bargained with him and succeeded in gaining far more favourable terms than they had expected.

In the meantime, the time-study work continued to affect Ieuan's health. The stomach pains returned. The physical inactivity, the tediousness of the job and the work entailed in compiling his lists at home in the evenings, made him morose and irritable.

His relationship with Mrs. Marvin threatened to develop into a bitter feud. She would insist on discussing her religious convictions at every opportunity, and her influence on Sally became more apparent each day.

He addressed her as "Mother", and at first he had assumed that they would be very happy together. But by the end of the year she had asserted herself as the dominant member of the household. The only privacy he and Sally shared was in their bedroom, and even then there was the disturbing thought that she was only the width of the room away, the feeling that she was listening to their every movement.

When he made love to Sally, he felt strained and nervous. Once, Mrs. Marvin had knocked at their door. Frustrated and angry, he had upbraided her, and it had resulted in a quarrel with Sally.

At the food table, he felt like a guest. Sally would have little say in the manner in which his food was to be cooked. His likes and dislikes were of no consequence to her mother.

"After all, Ieuan, she is my mother, and you shouldn't speak like that about her, dear."

"But damn it all, Sally ..."

"Hush, dear. Please don't use that language. If she should hear you... "

He had begun to write again in the evenings, jotting down his impressions of the foundry, the fragments of dialogue he had heard there, which he filed in a drawer in his bedroom.

Later, he found his mother-in-law reading his notes, an angry frown on her face. She had turned on him, making no apology for her intrusion.

"Ieuan, I don't care to see things like this in my house. These writings, disgusting some of them are. If men do talk like this in the foundry, then please keep it to yourself. There is enough sin and corruption in the world, and this is a Christian home. I'll have none of the Devil's words here."

"Nonsense!" he blurted resentfully. He snatched the papers from her hand. "You have no right to go prying into my drawers. Sin and corruption—yes, the world is full of it, I agree. But that does not excuse your behaviour."

"What do you mean?"

He shrugged. "Never mind, I'm in no mood to argue."

Sally heard the quarrel.

"Mam, please go downstairs," she led her mother out of the room. "I'll talk to Ieuan."

121

"It's no use, Sally," he protested, when they were alone. "The sooner we find a home for ourselves, the better. tomorrow, I'll call at the Town Hall and see if there's any hope of our getting a council house. There's a chance that things have improved by now, though, frankly, I doubt it very much... very much."

His doubts were justified. A house, indeed! Was he not aware that the waiting list was growing each day? There were three thousand applicants in 1930, so how many could he expect to find on the list now, four years later, with not a single house having been built in the meantime?

Again, there was the priority question to consider. He was a married man, yes. There were other married men, too, with families. Living in apartments? Tut-tut! There were only he and his wife. Not a child, even. He should count himself lucky, very lucky, that he was living with his mother-in-law.

Ieuan's visits to his mother's house on Sunday mornings found Mrs. Morgan with no sympathy to offer him.

"There! you went and got yourself married in too much of a hurry, Ieuan. Far better if you'd waited till things got easier in this town. Not looking too well you are these days, either. Are you getting the proper food? Young girls of today, they don't seem to know the way to do food. Can't boil an egg, most of 'em."

He smiled away her alarms. "Food is my least worry, Mam. Sally knows my tastes pretty well."

"Perhaps she does, but I say you are telling lies, Ieuan." A cunning glance. "And that Mrs. Marvin—does she throw up her religion at you on a plate every day? Met her at the wedding, I did, and my goodness! talk about a crank-pot, if ever there was one, it's her. God on her tongue every whip-stitch. I can see you joining them Christian Brotherhoods one of these days, let me tell you. But that's that—tell me, how is your job going at the foundry? Abraham's wife was telling me that Abraham was saying you were looking none too grand, and I can see you are not. Said something about your feet swelling, and gripes in your stomach."

"The job's all right. Mam. It's regular."

"Moulders are working regular these days, too. The foundry's never been going so well. I'll never forget them years you were with me. Never working you were. Always I've had to scrape to make ends meet in this house. A life of sacrifice it was for me. And now, there's you and Gweneira gone... Funny, isn't it, that Bevan's is a bit prosperous now, after losing you to this house? But there if I was Mrs. Marvin, I'd be lifting my hands to the ceiling and saying it's the Lord's will."

She drew a chair to the table. "Sit down, Ieuan. Your father will be here in a minute." She called up the stairway. "Phyllis! your brother is here. Leave them beds till this afternoon, and come down and give me a hand."

The tablecloth was spread. Ieuan got up.

"I can't stay, Mam."

"Indeed! That's what you say. A Sunday dinner you are having, whether you like it or not. Like a—a starving Armenian you look. What food can you get in that house, with her and her fads about not cooking a joint on the Sabbath, and your wife not able to—"

"Please, Mam..."

"Yes, I will say it... Not able to boil an egg. *Ach y fi!* Them Bible-thumpers! Better if they had a plateful of meat and gravy, or a basinful of broth in their bellies, an' let their souls look after themselves. Phyllis! Phyllis! Drat it, where is that girl?"

CHAPTER SIXTEEN

He stood at the foot of the bed. Her face, peeping at him from the pillows, was sad, and her eyes showed that she had been crying.

"What is it, *cariad*?" He was sorry that he had spoken so roughly to her when he came home from the foundry. She had been unwell, and he had washed and shaved hurriedly with the intention of going to the doctor's. Then her mother had interfered.

"There's no need at all to see Doctor Evans. A trifle it is, just a sick headache."

"It may be something more serious than that," he replied, "so I think it would be advisable if I went."

"You are not to go," she said.

He tried to be tolerant. "Now, Mother... surely you're not telling me what to do?"

"I am. I have no faith in doctors."

"That's a rather strange thing to say! They saved Sally's life."

"The Lord cured Sally, and brought her back to me—and you. You should be grateful, son."

"Why, of course I'm grateful... Look here, Mother, what's happening to you these days? What have I done to you?"

She clasped her hands over her breast. "You are not the righteous man I always believed you to be. You are an unbeliever."

"But, why? How? I don't understand what you're getting at."

"The Lord brought Sally back to me, I want you to understand that."

"All right, if that's what you say, I'm willing to accept it. But please, now, I have to hurry."

"You said that medical science saved her."

Her persistence angered him.

"It was the Lord who saved her," he snapped impatiently.

"Now, you mock His name. Did not the Lord bless the scientists with wisdom and knowledge?"

In the end he realised the futility of debating with her. She was obsessed with religion, and there was nothing he could do but tolerate her opinions. But this argument had continued. His visit to the surgery had been delayed. Then Sally had wept, and he had rebuked her. And now, as he watched her from the foot of the bed he saw that she had been crying again.

"What is it, Sally? Tell me."

She called him to her side. Her fingers stroked his cheeks.

"Ieuan... are you happy here with Mother?"

"Why, yes—yes, of course I am."

"You are not. You—you hate her."

"Go on with you, silly!"

"But I'm not happy, Ieuan. There's something I want to say."

"Yes?"

"Yes, dear. Bend down, and I—I will tell you."

He lay down beside her. She turned his head and whispered into his ear: "Ieuan... I—I want a little baby."

He held her close.

"Because you are not happy, Sally?"

"I want us to be happier, Ieuan. We—we are growing away from one another."

"Nonsense, sweetheart."

"But we are. If we have a baby, we can forget about Mother."

"Oh, you silly little bird."

"Mam is getting on your nerves, Ieuan, I know. But you must overlook her ways. She's my mother. She will always be with us."

He bit his lip. "Always?"

"Yes, Ieuan. I could never leave her."

"And you think I could love you more if we had a baby?"

"It—it's not that, Ieuan. I know you love me, but you hate Mam, and so long as she's with us you'll always hate her. Please,

please give me a baby." She turned back the sheets. "tonight, Ieuan... Now. I will make myself beautiful for you."

When he opened his eyes she was standing before him in the green satin nightdress. The same green ribbon she had worn on the honeymoon night was in her hair. And on the floor he saw the crumpled tissue paper that had fallen from the open drawer. She moved silently towards him. Her hands were upon his flesh. With a sigh, she lay across the bed. Her lips parted.

"Take me, take me, my love."

It was early in his second year as time-study clerk that Ieuan became aware of a change in the attitude of those improvers who previously had been unfriendly. They went out of their way to help him, notifying him of any change of job, comparing their time-sheets with his list.

At first, their consideration puzzled him, but later he realised that they now regarded him as a permanent official and were anxious to win his favour. Beynon, during his occasional inspection of the foundry, would stop to chat with him and crack a joke, and one Saturday afternoon, while he and Sally were shopping in the main street, the manager and his wife had drawn up in their car and offered them a lift home.

Probably this incident had been witnessed by one of the improvers, and the news had spread. Yes, the collar and tie and the manager's acknowledgments had established him as a person of authority in their eyes.

He saw himself as a young man whose intelligence had been recognised by the master, and now by the men.

He felt nothing but contempt for the improvers who toadied to him. They had once denounced him as a "bloody master's man". He had been prepared to help them, and they had spurned him; but now, like schoolboys who brought their shining apples to the teacher, they were seeking his favours.

He began to experience a new sensation, a satisfying feeling of power over these men. He asserted his authority over them, and felt a certain pleasure in their meek obedience. He was so fascinated by his power that he found himself using it, not only on those who had mocked him, but also on his friends.

One day Titus left his job and spent three hours in the smithy, where he had to wait for a core-iron. Quite unintentionally, he had forgotten to notify Ieuan of his absence, who, on his return to the foundry, challenged him.

"Next time you leave your job, Titus, let me know."

Titus grinned. "Come off it, Ieuan *mun*."

"I'm warning you," Ieuan replied testily. "Don't let it happen again."

"Warning me by damn!"

"Yes."

"Oh, go to hell!"

"That's enough!"

He saw Titus sneer and turn his back to him. Hell, what was he saying? What were power and authority doing to him? He was being corrupted. Who was he to order men about?

Superior intelligence, indeed! He was a snob. Soon, he would not have a single friend in the foundry.

He hurried after Titus. "Look here... I'm sorry," he began.

Titus wheeled round. "You're acting like a bloody boss, Ieuan. What the hell's come over you?"

On the way home that night Ieuan reflected on the incident. He had been a damn fool to speak to Titus in that manner. What had come over him lately? He had fallen a victim to the old saying: "Place a man into a uniform, and he ceases to become a man."

He felt guilty and ashamed, and though he tried to find excuses for himself he knew that there were none. But what was he to do?

He would speak to Sally about it.

CHAPTER SEVENTEEN

"Something's worrying you, Ieuan." She looked at him across the supper table. "Is it the trouble with the men again?"

He shook his head. "It's me, Sally... I'm forgetting myself. The job's gone to my head, and I've been behaving like a stupid fool." He told her of the incident with Titus.

"Ieuan *bach,* that's nothing to worry about," she consoled. "Titus was in the wrong to give you cheek, and I should think Mr. Beynon would say the same as me. You did quite right to tell him off."

"No, the fault lies with me, Sally... If I stick this job much longer, I'll—"

"Now, wait a minute, Ieuan." She grew alarmed. "Don't be too rash and do something you'll be sorry for." She paused. "You— you are not thinking of giving it up?"

"I don't know what to do, Sally."

"But you must stay on. It's a clean job, your money is regular, and you don't work so hard. Oh, please, Ieuan, don't do anything you'll be sorry for."

Later that same evening, still troubled with his thoughts, Ieuan went for a walk along the country road to Dinas Wood that he and Thomas had taken on the day of their quarrel.

Sally's advice had helped him little. She wanted him to keep the job. For her it meant security. She had failed to understand the conflict in his mind. But who would understand? Was there anyone in whom he could confide? Thomas, perhaps. But they had quarrelled. What a fool he had been! If only he had stopped to reason that day, and held his temper!

The shadow of dusk crept along the grass as he reached the wood, and a breeze stirred with a short, sweeping rhythm among the trees. A weasel darted across his path. He stopped to watch it as it disappeared into the tangled undergrowth.

He climbed the sharp rise which led into the middle of the wood, his head bowed, deep in reverie. The shadows lengthened, and presently the lights from the distant town flickered through the trees.

Suddenly, the silence was broken by the sound of footsteps and the crackle of leaves. He looked up sharply. A dark figure clambered down from the steep bank at the edge of the wood. He quickened involuntarily as he recognised the figure, and hurried forward, his hand extended. There was no holding back this time.

"Thomas!" He gripped his hand.

Thomas looked hard at him, nonplussed for the moment. Then his face broke into a warm smile.

"Ieuan! Hell, you gave me a fright, *mun*."

"I've been a bloody fool," Ieuan began. "That quarrel... I was a mutt."

"Hold on, boy," Thomas laughed. "It takes two to make a quarrel. We were both mutts." He grew serious. "It got me down plenty to think of it. I would have been your best man, Ieuan, and... Damn, let's forget it! Tell me, how's Sally? I've heard the news about the new arrival."

"She's fine, Thomas."

"And the job?"

Ieuan hesitated.

"Well? How's it going?"

"That's something I'd like to talk to you about, Thomas. I've been thinking of giving it up."

"What's that! You're chucking it? Now, listen to me, Ieuan— don't be an idiot. You're doing good work, as some of the chaps'll tell you. There's more jobs to be priced, and the help you're giving the Committee is something you ought to be pleased about. You stick to it, boy." Thomas clapped him affectionately on the shoulder. "I've got a pretty good idea what's been going through your mind, Ieuan. Just keep your head, and you'll do all right, you take it from me."

"No, it's no use, Thomas. today, I—"

"Look here... stick it for a couple more months. I'm telling you, you're doing a grand job."

"I'll see, Thomas. I'll think it over."

"That's the spirit."

Ieuan was too happy in his renewed friendship with Thomas to argue about the job, to bother about it even. Here were Thomas and he together again, and he laughed unrestrainedly as he listened to stories of old Abraham and Titus and the other fellows. Oddly enough, too, the job, now, no longer worried him, and he grimaced in the darkness as he remembered how he had felt about his power and authority.

One week in May, Ieuan's decision was made for him in a manner which he had not anticipated. He had not been feeling well and had arrived late at the foundry on two consecutive mornings. On the Friday of the following week he noticed that seven shillings had been deducted from his pay.

"Mr. Francis, has there been some mistake here?" He handed his pay slip to the head cashier. Francis examined the slip. "I'm afraid not, Ieuan. It's all in order."

"That's strange. I don't understand it." Ieuan glanced at the figures once more. "Were you instructed to deduct the seven shillings, Mr. Francis?"

The cashier looked at him uneasily. "Yes—yes, I was."

"Who gave you the orders?"

"Mr. Beynon."

Ieuan nodded slowly. "Oh, so that's it. Thanks, Mr. Francis."

He went into the outer office and climbed the stairs to the manager's room.

Beynon frowned as he entered. "Yes, Morgan?"

Ieuan tossed the pay slip on to the table. "I'd like to discuss this with you, Mr. Beynon."

130

"You would, eh? Well?"

"I'd like to know what it means."

"Indeed! Perhaps you'd better see Francis about it. I'm not the cashier, you know."

"I've seen Mr. Francis, and he's already explained to me. You instructed him to make the deduction."

Beynon became aggressive. "Now, look here, Morgan—what right have you to come barging in here?"

"Never mind that, Mr. Beynon... I just want to know why the deduction was made. We had an agreement, you remember?"

"Yes, yes, I know. But I don't see why you should be paid when you're not here. You were late on two occasions last week, Morgan. You pegged in at seven-thirty-five, and you know the rules as well as I do. Any workman who arrives after seven-thirty is not allowed to start work until nine."

"So that's your excuse, Mr. Beynon." Ieuan snatched the pay slip from the table and crumpled it in his hand. "Why couldn't you have been honest enough to tell me that you've made full use of me, instead of resorting to this—this underhanded way of getting me back to my old job as a moulder?"

Beynon flinched. "That's enough, Morgan! Do you realise whom you're talking to? You're a moulder by trade, and you should consider yourself lucky that I'm prepared to let you return to your job. Other employers would not be so considerate, I assure you."

"Thank you, Mr. Beynon—that's damned generous of you."

"Just a minute, Morgan... What do you mean?"

Ieuan strode from the room and slammed the door loudly behind him. Angered, yet inwardly relieved, he immediately went to Thomas. He related what had happened in the office. "So you see, Thomas, I don't have to worry any more about the job. The matter's been decided for me."

"I'm damned!" Thomas smiled wryly. "Of all the dirty tricks..." He shrugged. "Never mind, Ieuan, don't let it get you down. It's what you could have expected from Beynon. Anyway, you're back

with us again... Look here, we'll have to meet one night, and—"
The loud roar of the cranes, and the ear-splitting throb of
pneumatic rammers made further conversation impossible. A
shrill whistle sounded from the casting bay. The teemer cupped
his hands over his mouth, and the cry, "Up-ladle!" hurried
Thomas to the long row of hot moulds which were to be assembled
for the afternoon's cast.

Ieuan watched the broad-shouldered, dungareed figure skip
over the tall bank of moulding sand that ran parallel with the
casting bay. He saw Thomas glance back, a cheerful grin on his
face, his thumbs held up.

CHAPTER EIGHTEEN

"So he's back with the bloody sand rats again, is our Iron." Bull Jackson spat into his hands and gripped the heavy, pneumatic rammer. "Hope he can stick it after that holiday he's had. He had enough o' what it takes to fill that young missus of his, but from now on he'll be wanting some Life Drops to keep him going. I reckon the bastard won't be able to last the pace after that soft job he's been nursing."

"That's a bloody fine way to talk," Titus snapped. "If it wasn't for him you wouldn't be getting that fat pay packet every Friday. Fair's fair, I say."

"Oh, dry up! Tell that to the marines. What I get in my pay packet comes from my own slogging. I got no one to thank for that but my old man. He gave me my muscles."

"Pity he didn't give you no brains."

"You trying to be smart? Want to put up your fists?"

"Aw, dry up, Bull. Go fry yourself an egg."

When Ieuan went back to his former job, he was placed on daywork and had to be content with the bare trade-union rate, while the men who were employed on piecework earned a minimum of fifty per cent above the rate. He was one of five, excepting the apprentices, who were put to work on the day-rate jobs.

Of the other four men who worked with him, two of them—Joe Taylor and Bill Pugh—were too old to stand the increased pace that piecework demanded, whilst Jack Delaney, a bachelor, who lived in one of the lodging-houses in town, had no incentive to earn a bigger wage. The other, Dai Gammy, was lame, and was unable to keep pace with his fellow workers, some of whom had told him that there was no room for passengers in a piecework team, and that every man had to pull his weight.

133

Ieuan did whatever jobs Lu told him to do. He suspected that the foreman was unfriendly, and his suspicions were confirmed when the latter one day grumbled to him about the Shop Committee and his loss of authority in the foundry.

"A foreman I'm supposed to be, but damn me, ever since this piecework has come in, I got no say in the running of the shop, no say at all. It's the Shop Committee does everything. They tell me what jobs got to be done. They order me about as if I was a labourer. Proper bolshie this place has turned out to be."

"But you should be glad, Lu. It means less responsibility for you," Ieuan countered.

"I like responsibility. That's what I'm paid for, isn't it? A foreman with no dignity, that's what I'm becoming. Next thing that'll be happening is that I'll be back on the floor with the moulders—like you. It was you started all this trouble, Ieuan. If you'd stood out against Beynon and told him where to get off, there wouldn't be no piecework here today."

"And the foundry would be closed down, the men out of work again."

"They managed to live before, didn't they? Not one of them starved."

For the next few months Ieuan continued on the day-rate moulds. He had explained the position to Sally when, after a meeting with a fellow moulder's wife during her Saturday afternoon's shopping, she hinted at the meagreness of his wage compared with the earnings of the other moulders.

"Why shouldn't you have a share, Ieuan? Mam and I were discussing it the other day. With the baby coming, it's only fair that you should be allowed to earn more money. Some of the single chaps are taking home as much as seven pounds a week."

Then Mrs. Marvin had spoken. "It is your right to demand more money. A new life is to be born into this house. Sally will be needing things, and it is no time to think of your own personal feelings. No Christian would—"

"All right, all right!" he retorted, red with anger. "Sally's my wife. The child will be ours. What concerns us need not concern you. Sally hasn't wanted for anything yet, and so long as I have a pair of hands she'll not starve."

"Oh Ieuan, please don't upset Mam," Sally pleaded. "After all, she has a right to her opinion, and that's what you've always said—a person is always free to express an opinion."

"Quite right," Mrs. Marvin interjected with a sniff.

Ieuan held himself in check. He turned to Sally. "Listen, *cariad,* if earning more money will make you happier..." He saw her wince. "I'm sorry—I didn't meant it in that way... I'll ask the Shop Committee on Monday if they'll consider my case."

"I can't see why they couldn't have let you work piecework in the first place, Ieuan," she said softly. "You've done so much for the men. It's only fair that they should consider you. But please, don't let's have words about old money."

The following Monday he approached Bull. The latter bristled at his suggestion.

"Share of piecework, by Christ! You've got a hell of a nerve! Where was your principles when we were walking the roads, and you drawing over a month's pay for sitting on your arse?"

"O.K. Bull, keep your shirt on. I'm not going to beg, but remember this—you're the shop steward, and I've put my case before you. It's now up to you to report it to the Committee. The shop will have the final say whether or not I go on piecework."

Bitter though he was in his opposition to Ieuan, Bull knew that he would have to put his case before the Committee. But, before he did so, he appealed to the moulders who had objected to Dai Gammy having a share of the extra earnings. He stressed that one name less on the list meant a larger bonus for them, and reminded them of the month when Ieuan was paid a full wage.

"He didn't think of you chaps, then. He didn't offer to give you a share of his pay, so why the hell should he benefit now? Wants the cake and the biscuit, he does. Shop meeting's on Friday afternoon, so be there, all of you. And don't be bloody fools to

135

vote him on the piecework list. Remember what he done for you when you were wasting your shoe leather on the streets."

When the shop meeting was eventually called, Ieuan was told that he would not be allowed to attend.

"But I have a right to be there," he protested.

"Not this time, you haven't," Bull grunted. "And it's got nothing to do with me, so get that suspicion out of your nut. It's the Committee's decision, and it stands. I've got to report back to you after the meeting, so you'll be hearing the news, then."

When Ieuan returned to the foundry at two o'clock, he found Lu waiting in the casting bay, a deep frown on his face. A group of labourers stood near a water bosh, their shovels in hand.

Lu looked at his watch. "Another moulders' meeting?" he asked Ieuan dryly. "It's all meetings these days. Times have changed since I started here."

One of the labourers overheard the remark. He winked to his mates. "Ay, Lu," he grinned. "These modern days are to blame. Meetings everywhere, indeed to God. Looks like there's going to be a big one in Abyssinia soon. That Eytie, Musso, got something on his chest."

Presently the moulders came straggling back from the canteen where the meeting had been held, and Lu went up the shop to meet them. "Look here," he said to Bull, "I know you're the shop steward, but remember that these meetings got to be over by two o'clock in future. The furnace is waiting, and I'm behind with the cast."

"O.K., Lu." Bull sauntered towards Ieuan. "You're a lucky bastard, Iron. Shop's voted you on the list, but you wouldn't have had a smell if Tomtit hadn't opened his trap."

"What d'you mean?" Ieuan began, but Bull was in no mood to explain. Later in the afternoon he was given a full report of the meeting. The majority had been unwilling to discuss his case and were opposed to his having a share of the piecework, but Thomas had spoken vigorously on his behalf and had finally succeeded in swaying the whole shop in his favour.

The renewal of his friendship with Thomas had restored Ieuan's confidence in himself. It had helped him to overlook Mrs. Marvin's erratic behaviour and he felt far happier than he had been for some months.

Sally was quick to notice the change in him, and she was relieved to hear that the long-standing quarrel was now over.

Thomas became a frequent caller at the house, though his visits were arranged to coincide with Mrs. Marvin's weekly prayer meetings at the Brotherhood Hall, a tin-roofed shack on a waste stretch of land adjoining the chemical factory. But when he did call there was matter enough for conversation between him and Ieuan. The years of fear had begun. Fascism was spreading, and already Mosley and his Blackshirts had staged a rally in London's Olympia, a spectacle which had ended in a bloody battle which seriously discredited this new and vicious movement.

In Germany, the new President, Adolf Hitler, imprisoned the Communists; Jews were deprived of German citizenship and their marriage with Aryans forbidden. July saw the murder of Chancellor Dolfuss, Austria's pocket tyrant, the victim of Nazi putschists, while in England the National Government had introduced the Unemployment Act, the hated Means Test which aroused the hostility of the working class.

Of these things Ieuan and Thomas talked in the evenings and at their work in the foundry, and once again Ieuan felt compelled to write to the local papers.

"I don't know why you've taken to writing these letters again, Ieuan." Sally's voice was full of reproach. She held up the *Guardian*, turned to the page which contained his letter. "Your name—it's here for everyone to see. Oh, why can't you let things rest? You upset Mam, then she goes on to me about it. Honestly, Ieuan, I can't stand it—this worry all the time."

"Worry, *cariad!*" He smiled and patted her head. "Come now, there's nothing to be upset about. I wrote that letter because I felt I should. Thomas and I were talking—"

"Yes, that's just it. Ever since you've been friends again you've been talking of nothing but old politics." She placed her arms around his neck. "Please, Ieuan *bach,* don't do anything to upset Mam. If—if you want to write, why don't you do some stories? You've never written at all since that day when you and Mam had words over those silly papers in your drawer."

"Sally," he squeezed her gently, "my writing that letter—I felt I was doing some good."

"But isn't it just a… a showing off? Like… well, wanting to see your name in the papers?"

Her words hurt, and he did not answer.

"I'm sorry, Ieuan." She drew away from him. Her lips pouted. "You've got me and the baby to think of now… What if you had the sack?"

"The sack? I don't understand, Sally. Whatever made you think of that?"

"Well, Mam was saying that if Mr. Bevan should read that letter he might take offence. It says some nasty things about the employers and the Means Test. Mr. Bevan might think that you've become vindictive because you were sent back to your old job."

"Sally girl, don't be led so by your mother. What's wrong with her lately? Frankly, I think she's working herself into a state of religious mania."

"That's a nice thing to say, Ieuan. You're the last person I'd expect to make fun of Mam."

"But I'm making fun of no one, lovely."

"It wasn't a very nice thing to say, just the same." He sighed. "All right, Sally, I apologise. Your mother's the sweetest, dearest, most precious…"

"Now, now, sarky!"

* * *

Sally's confinement drew near. Throughout the summer months Ieuan had impressed upon her the importance of clinical advice, and she had regularly attended the clinic for observation. Knowing that her mother would not approve of this, the visits had been surreptitious. He had consulted the doctor and was relieved to hear that there were no complications. When he first knew she was pregnant he had been tormented by doubts.

Sally had been a patient at *Calon y Nôs* for three years. He had recognised her plea for a child. But he had not considered her physical condition. The joy of consummation had blinded him to quiet reasoning. Should he have granted her her wish? Doubt and self-reproach had driven him to consult the doctor.

"You say your wife was a patient at *Calon y Nôs*?" The doctor scribbled on his pad. "Discharged, June 1930?" He pondered for a while. "I'll get in touch with Dr. Jacobson, the medical superintendent there. Come and see me in three days' time, Mr. Morgan. I dare say there's nothing really serious to worry about. Anyway, we'll talk it over when I've had my report from Dr. Jacobson."

Ieuan had not mentioned his visit either to Sally or her mother, and the three days had seemed interminable. Then finally had come reassurance, and with it, the removal of his fears.

"I have good news for you, Mr. Morgan. Dr. Jacobson's report is most satisfactory. Indeed, most satisfactory. Sit down, my boy." The doctor motioned him to an easy chair. "There are three facts which are important," he went on, "and I would like to stress them to you. First, tuberculosis can be cured if steps are taken in time, though it may be a long job. Secondly, the condition is not hereditary; the children of tubercular parents are born free from the disease and can be brought up perfectly healthy."

The doctor glanced at a letter with an embossed heading, '*Calon y Nôs Sanatorium*', which lay on his desk.

"Thirdly, however," he continued, "the germ of the disease is conveyed from one person to another, so that a wife or child with whom a sufferer lived might become infected." To emphasise his points, the doctor picked up the letter and tapped it with his free hand. "You need have no fears at all, my boy," he smiled. "Your wife was discharged with a clean bill—completely cured. Now, go home and take care of her. Then, before the end of the year I hope to have the pleasure of bringing another young Morgan into the world."

It was on an evening in late October when Sally felt the first spasms of labour pains. She was sitting at the supper table with Ieuan and her mother. The wild look in her eyes alarmed Ieuan. He sprang to his feet.

"I'll send for the doctor, Sally... Mother, will you help me to get her to bed, first?"

Mrs. Marvin looked at him with fierce enmity, knowing only too well how he would oppose her plans for Sally's delivery.

"I'll see the girl to her bed. As for the doctor, it's not necessary."

Ieuan flashed back at her: "For God's sake, this is no time for another argument. Sally needs a doctor. This—this is not one of your sick headaches she's suffering from." Suddenly, he calmed down. Sally's eyes were closed. She rocked herself to and fro, her hands clasped over her swollen body.

"Sally, *cariad*... let me take you upstairs." He drew her arm over his shoulder and helped her to her feet. "Mother, please don't let us quarrel at a time like this," he appealed, but Mrs. Marvin made no reply.

They got Sally into bed. Ieuan pulled on his overcoat. "Mother, I'll run down to the call-box," he began. Mrs. Marvin barred his way. "You needn't waste your time going for the doctor. I've arranged everything. Mrs. Maconochie—she's coming to attend to my child's confinement."

"Maconochie! You've dared to ask that—that old harridan here?" Ieuan's fury returned. He glared at the thin, austere woman facing him. "I'll pack her out, d'you hear? I want no meddlesome women in this house. This is a matter of life and death."

He knew of Mrs. Maconochie and her unsavoury reputation. She was an elderly widow who, at one time, earned a living as a "death nurse", laying out the dead and bargaining for her fee with the undertakers. At one period, too, she had practised midwifery, until rumour had associated her with three abortion

140

cases. Since then, she had become a fervent member of the religious sect to which Mrs. Marvin belonged, hoping in this way to regain her respectability in the neighbourhood.

Mrs. Marvin bridled at Ieuan's anger.

"Mrs. Maconochie is one of the Christian Brotherhood," she retorted bitingly. "She brought my Sally into the world. She it was who prepared my Jim's body ready to meet the Lord. I have faith in her."

"To the devil with her!" Ieuan countered. He pointed to Sally, who lay pale and spent on the bed. "Don't you realise that she's your daughter? D'you think I'm going to stand by and let some disreputable, unqualified woman put her hands on my wife? You'll do as I say, Mother. ... I'm going to 'phone the doctor."

The doctor arrived at midnight. He examined Sally.

"Is—is everything all right?" Ieuan stood by, apprehensive and distraught.

The doctor completed his examination. He glanced at his watch. "I'll call again, early in the morning. There's nothing to be alarmed about, but should anything unexpected happen, then phone me, and I'll be along right away."

An hour later Ieuan sat before the kitchen fire, restless and worried. He could hear Mrs. Marvin moving around in the bedroom above. He stared at the clock, his eyes heavy with sleep.

He thought of Sally, and of the baby that was to be theirs, but especially of Sally. Was she strong enough to bear? The doctor had seemed confident, but doctors made mistakes. His fears jerked him out of the chair to the foot of the stairs, where he stood intently, and listened.

The silence wrung him dry, and he felt an emptiness in his stomach. He was trembling, and his weakness drove him back to the chair. He sank into it, and then started up again as he imagined he heard a cry upstairs. He was half-way across the kitchen floor when a low moan from the bedroom chilled him. He caught his breath and waited anxiously. Then came a muffled scream.

Unable to contain himself he rushed to the bedroom. Mrs. Marvin faced him on the landing.

"Is—is she all right?" he questioned nervously.

"Yes… Please go down, there's nothing you can do." His mother-in-law closed the door behind her. "I have sent for Mrs. Maconochie."

He felt a sudden rage sweep over him. "That woman is not to put a foot inside the house," he shouted.

He saw her face harden. Her eyes narrowed with hatred. "Mrs. Maconochie is a Christian sister," she snapped. "She will be here to see to my daughter. I have nothing more to say to you."

He was about to hurl the full weight of his anger and contempt at her, when a knock sounded at the front door. Mrs. Marvin brushed quickly past him.

From the landing he saw the elderly visitor, plump and ungainly, dressed in a rumpled, blue cotton frock and white, bibbed apron, a small leather portmanteau in her hand. The two women whispered together, and Mrs. Maconochie removed her coat.

He bounded down the stairway. Trembling, he pointed to the door. "Mrs. Maconochie, you're not wanted here. You've got to leave… Now!"

The old woman frowned. She turned to Mrs. Marvin.

"Sister Hester…" she protested.

They heard Sally moan again. The two women clattered up the stairs. Ieuan shook with emotion.

"Sally!" he cried. "Sally! Sally!"

The bedroom door opened. Mrs. Marvin appeared on the landing. "The baby…" she began. He did not wait to hear more. He rushed out into the street to summon the doctor.

When he returned to the house Mrs. Marvin was hurrying from the kitchen, a bowl of steaming water in her hands. She did not say a word, but sidled past him up the stairway.

Sally's moaning grew louder. He clenched his teeth. God! what was happening to her? He darted up to the bedroom and flung open the door.

142

The sight before him almost made him reel. Sally, her hair dishevelled, her head lolling from side to side, knelt on the bed, a tourniquet of heavy cloth knotted about her body. A stack of pillows had been placed behind her, and Mrs. Maconochie, panting from her exertions, was holding her and feverishly urging her to gather her strength.

Mrs. Marvin knelt beside the bed, mumbling a prayer: "Oh, merciful Jesus, I beg you grant us this day..."

Ieuan stumbled against the bed-rail.

"Fools! Fools!" he shouted. "What are you doing to her...? Sally! Sally, love..."

He caught her in his arms. There was no recognition in her eyes. All at once he felt her body stiffen. Her face muscles twitched spasmodically, her teeth clenched.

The two women grew alarmed. Mrs. Marvin began to weep hysterically.

"For God's sake, help me!" Ieuan appealed.

Sally's back arched. Her muscles contracted and relaxed alternately. Her eyes protruded. Saliva oozed from her lips. Then, with a convulsive shudder, she lapsed into a coma.

Mrs. Maconochie wrung her hands and stood by, quivering with fear. Ieuan laid Sally back on the bed. He untied the band around her waist and flung it to the floor. Quickly, he placed a spoon between her teeth and turned her gently over on to her side.

From outside came the hum of a car engine.

"Thank God!" he breathed.

The doctor took charge. He ordered Ieuan out of the room, and shortly afterwards the front door banged after Mrs. Maconochie.

Throughout the morning, the doctor and Mrs. Marvin remained in the bedroom with Sally, while Ieuan distractedly carried out whatever instructions they gave him, keeping a constant supply of hot water ready for their needs.

Ten o'clock... Eleven...

He could hear the doctor's peremptory commands, the clink of

143

a glass, the pouring of water. He had been horrified by the sight of the instruments which the doctor had brought into the kitchen to be sterilised.

The moments of waiting were agonising. Then the first, weak, wailing cry of the child was heard. Ieuan stood on the threshold of the bedroom. The doctor appeared, grave-faced.

"You have a daughter," he said, "but your wife is seriously ill. I had to hurry the birth, for it's clear that someone has been interfering... Your wife will have to be carefully nursed."

The doctor's words came to him across the void of his fears.

"Your wife is seriously ill..."

Trembling, he broke into the room where she lay.

CHAPTER NINETEEN

In the anxious weeks that followed Sally's confinement, Ieuan deliberately avoided his mother-in-law as much as possible. There was a silent antagonism between them from the day when they had had words about Mrs. Maconochie, though neither of them since the birth of the baby had mentioned the woman. But for Sally's sake they did not quarrel openly. The doctor had warned them that Sally had to have peace of mind. He had stressed to Mrs. Marvin the grave consequences of another visit from Mrs. Maconochie, and his warning had frightened her into submission for the time being. But her attitude towards both him and Ieuan remained hostile.

Conscious of the growing enmity between Ieuan and her mother, Sally pleaded with both and did her utmost to break down the barrier. The effort exhausted her, and her convalescence was retarded. Gradually she became absorbed in the baby, and when at last she was allowed downstairs into the front parlour, her attitude towards the two of them was tense and withdrawn.

Her illness continued into January. The baby had been christened Beth, and even in this Mrs. Marvin had influenced Sally, who, for peace, had decided to name the child after her great-grandmother.

Ieuan had determined to do nothing that might prevent her return to health.

"If your mother wants to call her Beth, then Beth she shall be. After all, dear, what's in a name? What I'm grateful for is that you're alive, and getting stronger and stronger every day. Just you wait... when the warm weather comes we'll go out walking again and have one of our lovely little picnics, you and me—and Beth."

The warm weather came. Sunny days in May, when the Park was crowded again in the evenings, and young couples sought the lonelier paths that led into the suburbs and Lovers' Lane. But with the sunshine came the gloom of unemployment. Bevan's foundry was closing down again.

Ieuan and Thomas were working on a "digging job". That afternoon a thirty-ton steel press had been cast. It was the last of a large order for a Midlands firm. Four moulders and six labourers were detailed to follow the job through from the cast to the final loosening of the mould which was necessary for contraction.

The press, encased in a massive iron moulding-box, reared up from its bed of dry sand like some huge, subdued, mechanical monster. Whiffs of steam and smoke blew from the air-holes in the mould. A shimmering haze hung over the box, and, high above, the crane-man waited for his instructions as he leaned half-way out of his cage, a handkerchief bound tightly over the lower half of his face.

"This is the last job we'll work on together for a hell of a time, Ieuan."

Thomas stripped to his vest and hung his shirt and jacket on a hook in the wall. "Lu reckons we're in for a bad spell again." He hitched up his trousers. "It's been pretty good taking home a decent pay these last months, but now we can see what piecework's really done for us. If we'd worked on the day rate, it'd have meant employment on full-time for a couple of years, and there'd been a chance of some more orders coming in. As it is, we've cut our own bloody throats."

A labourer seated on an upturned barrow spat into the slagpot. "You moulders—you're to blame," he grunted. "Working like stinko so's you can take home an extra couple o' quid every Friday. Where's it got chaps like us? Most we can expect from piecework is fifteen bob over the rate, and it ain't worth it. You were mutts to accept piecework."

"You're telling me," retorted Thomas. "Believe me, Bill, we'd

146

have been better off on daywork, but the carrot was too tempting for the old donkey."

"Ay, that's human nature all over." The labourer's mouth drooped. "Not that I'm blaming you chaps. Being on the dole takes it out of a feller worse than anything... Think we'll be out for a long stretch this time, Thomas?"

"Couple of months, Lu says. He's trying to arrange for us to work part-time—week in, week out, or, failing that, one week in three."

"Gone good Samaritan all at once, has he? Lu's looking forward to the bloody holiday. He doesn't care about us. Got his knife into you chaps, too, since you took on piecework. He's been grumbling about some of the moulders earning more'n him—and him a foreman! Oh, what the hell! Let's get this job over with."

The six labourers climbed a ladder which sloped to the top of the press, eight feet above floor level. The craneman lowered the steel chain, and the three-ton, circular, cast-iron "chill", placed across the mould to resist the pressure of the molten metal, was swung away.

Thomas, Ieuan and the two moulders each selected a six-foot, steel digging-bar, and clambered up the mould. The lengths of pig iron which reinforced a dyke of dry sand rammed around the gateway into the mould, were tossed to the floor, and the sand shoveled clear.

Clouds of gritty silica dust billowed into the air. Perspiration dripped from the men's arms and faces in the almost unbearable heat. Their movements were restricted: there was hardly room to turn in the confined area in which they worked.

Two labourers slammed heavy sledgehammers against the gatebox. The crane chain tightened over the handles, and, as the box was lifted clear, a portion of red-hot casting lay exposed.

At a signal from Thomas the men began to dig into the solid sand with their bars. They had to dig deep into the surface of the mould to allow a space for the casting to contract. The sand was hard as flint, and the digging-bars bounced and rang as though hitting against a steel surface. The sharp points grew red-hot, and bent.

Arms ached. Blisters formed on the men's hands. Eyelids, ears and hair were smothered in hot, grey dust. Moulders and labourers soaked handkerchiefs in the water bosh and bound them round their mouths, but even this measure of protection did not prevent the dust seeping through and choking their lungs.

The digging-bars became too hot to handle. Feet burned, and now and then a man would leap to the ground and wet the soles of his boots in the bosh. As the sand loosened, the labourers scooped it away with long-handled scoops and tossed it to the floor below. They worked swiftly, anxious to finish and get away from the stifling heat and dust.

From nine until midnight the digging continued. Then came the final task. The heavy steel cramps which held the joints of the huge moulding-box in position were wrenched loose, and the steel wedges collected, and returned to the moulding bay.

Ieuan felt completely exhausted. It had been some years since he had worked on a heavy digging job, and his recent spell as time-study clerk had made his muscles soft and flabby.

He was covered from head to foot with dust. It clung to his perspiring limbs; gritted between his teeth. His hair was matted with it, and in his mouth the taste of stale chocolate.

His companions were in a similar plight, and as they shuffled wearily to the canteen to wash and rest before the journey home, they cursed and grumbled to one another.

"By Jesus! To think we got to do this for a pay packet! Sand rats! The feller who said that wasn't far wrong."

"Never mind, Jack, it looks like we're in for another spell at Box 5 before long. You'll be able to sit on your backside in the Park and enjoy the fresh air."

"The way I feel right now, I don't care a pig's toss if the bloody foundry closes down for keeps. I'll try and get me a job in an ice-cream factory."

"Ice-cream! Wouldn't mind having a dollop of that."

"Give me a pint o' beer... No, a gallon's more like it. Got me a thirst like nobody's business."

On his return home from work the following day, Ieuan mentioned the forthcoming slump to Sally.

"Oh, I hope it's not true," she said earnestly. "Things have been going so well just lately. I've got over my illness, Beth is coming on lovely, and we are managing to save a little bit, Ieuan. I had planned a nice holiday in the country for the three of us when the summer comes."

"We'll have our holiday, don't you worry," he consoled. "Cheer up, love... Perhaps something may turn up at the last minute to save us from the dole."

He took her on his knee. Mrs. Marvin was attending a prayer meeting at the Brotherhood Hall, and her absence gave him a chance to court Sally. But she seemed not to want his attentions. She had become highly strung and restless since the baby's birth, and he felt that their love was being slowly submerged by the strain of living with her mother.

He knew that his outward show of unconcern for his mother-in-law's selfishness and domineering ways did not deceive Sally, and he had proved that her sympathies were for her mother, when, one day, unable to restrain himself, he had opposed Mrs. Marvin's will, and Sally had jumped to her mother's defence.

He looked forward with eagerness to the holiday they had arranged—just he, Sally, and the baby. It would give them the opportunity of regaining their love and faith in each other.

"The foundry has been working grand since we married, Ieuan. What's happened, that the men should be talking about unemployment once more? I don't understand it, frankly I don't. Mam said—"

She stopped suddenly, and he shrugged.

"What can I say, dear? There's unemployment all over South Wales. The Government—"

"Politics again, Ieuan?" There was a new edge to her voice that he had heard several times of late. It was an echo of her mother's bitter antagonism, and it shocked and frightened him. "Always, it's politics, politics, politics. Why can't people live and work in peace? Why this struggle between masters and men all the time? Sometimes, when I sit down and think, I blame the workers. They never seem satisfied. Always wanting more money, striking for this, demanding that. Mam may be taken up with her religion, but at least people seem to be happy once they have their faith, like her."

"Oh, come, *fach*. You must be reasonable," he said gently.

"I am reasonable, Ieuan," she countered. "All I want is my home, my husband and my baby, and just enough so that we can live decently, without any debts hanging over us. There's unemployment in South Wales again, yes, and trouble in the valleys. Look what happened in Merthyr at the beginning of the year when they smashed the offices of the Unemployment Board... If only the workers would be satisfied."

"Sally, Sally, you're being blind to reason, girl," he protested, disturbed by her anger. "Just think what those poor families in the Rhondda have gone through. How would you feel if I were on the Means Test, being questioned by officials and badgered and kicked around like a dog? If I'd have been with those men in Merthyr I'd have helped them to tear down those offices."

"You said as much in that other letter you wrote to the *Guardian*," she reminded him bitterly.

"Yes, Sally, I did. I felt it was only right that I should."

"But you never write anything that might bring you in a bit of money."

Her angry accusation humiliated him.

"I'll write, Sally. Yes, I'll write. I've talked about it, God knows, ever since I was a kid. I had ambitions, but never the guts nor the conviction to see them through..." He paused. "Oh, what's the use?"

His reaction touched her, and suddenly she was sobbing in his arms.

"Ieuan, Ieuan... why do we go on like this at each other lately? Why, oh why can't we be happy? I'm sorry, Ieuan *bach*... Sorry."

CHAPTER TWENTY

"Up-Ladle at Three."

"Dear Sir.
   I liked your story, but unfortunately it does not fit in with the present policy of the Daily Star."

"The Editor regrets…"

"We thank you for your story, but…"

"Owing to the pressure of space, we are unable to…"

Ieuan sat in the front parlour, pen in hand. Write! Of what should he write? Of the life he knew? Of the foundry? Of his childhood in the mean streets? Of unemployment?

"Earn while you learn. Take a course with the XYZ School of Authorship. Ten guineas for twelve lessons. Anyone can learn to write."

Earn by your pen. Write love stories—conventional love stories, in which the heroine with her deep blue eyes and smiling face is thrust into a welter of complications that *must* be unravelled before she sweetly falls into the arms of the handsome, gallant hero.

Protagonist, character, plot, situation, single effect, conflict, dialogue, thematic, didactic, atmosphere, surmounting of obstacle, climax, anti-climax…

Write if you must, but write to appeal. Write for the mill-girl, shop-girl, nursemaid, skivvy, the lovelorn spinster. Tell them of fairy worlds where improbability lives and flourishes. Take them away from reality. Write of South Sea islands, the Riviera, Park Lane, Fifth Avenue. Of poor, beautiful Cinderellas; of earls and pearls; of Ruritanian kings and wedding rings.

Fortune is thine.

"Take a course with the XYZ School of Author-ship. Earn while you learn."

At last Ieuan's perseverance was rewarded. One day he received a letter from a magazine editor.

"We have pleasure in accepting your story of Welsh childhood. Payment at our usual rates, two guineas a 1,000... Please sign accompanying receipt."

"Ieuan, there's wonderful news!" Sally flushed with pride. "I knew you'd sell your stories someday... You'll be a writer, I know you will. Then we shan't have to worry about the old foundry."

Said Mrs. Marvin: "Stories, indeed! Far wiser if he looked around for a job which'd bring him a regular wage. Working one week in four for the past year. How can a man keep a wife and child on two pounds a week?"

He ignored his mother-in-law's taunts. His first success had heartened him and he took a greater interest in the technique of writing. But first he had to have a typewriter. A letter from a kindly editor had impressed upon him that all mss. had to be typewritten. "Mss. to be typed on quarto sheets, double space, left-hand margin, name and address, title on cover page. Enclose stamped, addressed envelope."

With the few pounds that still remained in his Post Office account he purchased a second-hand typewriter. But the machine was so worn that in a month it was useless.

He took it back to the shop, and was told: "Perhaps you would like a brand new machine, Mr. Morgan? We should be prepared to allow you discount on the old machine. Next week—our representative will call to see you... Your address, please?"

A new machine! He was still working part-time. Could he afford to buy one? Sally hated being in debt. But this would be his debt.

"Yes, please ask the gentleman to call. No. 4 Crooked Row. Any morning next week will do."

The traveller called.

A sleek, polished car drew up outside No. 4. A gentleman in teddy-bear coat and fur gauntlet gloves carried a resplendent hide case into the parlour where Ieuan waited.

The traveller beamed with affability.

"Mr. Morgan, I'm awfully sorry about the rather unfortunate experience you had with the other machine. I assure you everything will be settled to your satisfaction. Now, look at this." He drew off his gloves, lifted the shining case on to the table, and clicked it open. "What do you think of it, eh?"

The streamlined model gleamed in the sunlight.

"Thirteen guineas, Mr. Morgan. Easy terms can be arranged." A be-ringed finger flashed over the machine. The sales talk continued. "'Excelsis' portable, latest streamlined model... padded key base... tabulating key... special contrivance whereby touch can be adjusted from light to heavy. Here, Mr. Morgan— See! this little lever—push it to the right. Number one, that's for a person with an extremely light touch. Number two, slightly heavier. Number three, four, five... There! That's right, Mr. Morgan. Beautiful machine, isn't it?"

Ieuan ran his fingers over the platen and the chromium-plated fittings.

"Just thirteen guineas," the traveller smiled. "Of course, we would allow you thirty shillings on the old machine, which sum will be placed to your credit."

Thirteen guineas! He couldn't possibly afford to pay so much, Ieuan thought.

"We can also arrange easy terms. Two pounds a month. Quite reasonable, don't you think?"

Ieuan shook his head. "No, I'm sorry. I'm afraid I can't do it."

"Mr. Morgan, you're not serious. Surely, ten shillings a week is not too much to ask for such a magnificent model? Ten shillings! Why, I'm positive you spend that much on cigarettes."

"I'm sorry, but we're going through a pretty lean time at the foundry where I work. I couldn't keep up the payments. It certainly is a fine machine."

"The very best on the market, you can take my word for it. Sit down, Mr. Morgan. Try it out. Incidentally, let me warn you, in confidence, of course—this opportunity won't come again... Government contracts and so on. Manufacture for private individuals will be stopped."

The traveller inserted a sheet of paper under the platen.

"Try it out, Mr. Morgan."

Ieuan sat down and typed his name.

"Now, wouldn't you like to own it?"

"Yes, I would—but I still say ten shillings a week is beyond me."

"Very well, then what about a pound a month—five shillings a week? Would that induce you to buy the machine?"

Ieuan thought over the proposition. Five shillings seemed a reasonable sum. He could afford it if he continued to work one week in four. But what if he became totally unemployed for a long spell? Or taken ill? His health was none too good, and he was never free from gastric trouble. Sickness benefit would bring in even less than the dole. Failure to continue with the payments would mean that the machine would have to be returned.

These points were explained to the patient traveller.

"Look here, Mr. Morgan, I'm determined to sell this model. I'll tell you what I'll do. Pay me five shillings weekly when you can afford it. If at any time, through illness or unemployment, you feel you can't carry on with the payments, we—that is, my firm—will take back the machine and credit you with the sum you've paid up to that time. Should your circumstances improve and

154

you felt you could continue the payments, we'd let you choose a brand new machine identical with this one, for the same price— thirteen guineas, less what you'd already paid when we took back the other."

The offer seemed too good to be true, and Ieuan became wary. The traveller smiled. "There's no catch in it, Mr. Morgan. If you agree to those terms I'll draw up a contract," he said quickly. "Believe me, we're a reliable firm, not one of these 'here today, gone tomorrow' companies that spring up all over the place."

His assurance decided the matter. The hire-purchase agreement was signed. Thirty shillings were deducted from the original price of the machine, and the traveller left, to return the next day with a promised guarantee, and the new machine.

Ieuan was delighted with his new typewriter and plunged into his work with ardour. Three stories were accepted, and now, so great was his enthusiasm, that every hour of his leisure was spent in writing others, many of which, crudely constructed and weak in characterisation, were promptly returned.

But he was not discouraged. His three acceptances had earned him fifteen pounds which helped to pay for the typewriter, and to settle other small debts that had accumulated during his partial employment.

The front parlour was taken over as a study, and he seldom went out in the evenings. He was often acutely aware of a sense of isolation. There was no one who was really interested in his writing; no one with whom he could discuss it. Sally was still preoccupied with the child, and he grew accustomed to her reproaches for the small returns he could show for his long hours of work.

"But it helps, Sally," he protested, disappointed with her changed attitude towards his writing. "The money isn't much, I know. What matters is that my work has been accepted. Can't you see, dear, what it means? In time I'll be able to pack up at Bevan's—that has always been our aim. When we were courting... that day on the *Cefn,* remember what we said?"

155

"I remember, Ieuan, and I would be the first one to want to see you get out of the foundry. But the money they pay you for the stories—it's hardly worth your time writing them—not the sort of stories you write. They're too real, Ieuan. People don't want to read about poverty, the foundry, and such depressing things..."

"But one can only write about what one knows, Sally."

"You could try writing those love stories I told you about. For instance, there's the *Woman's Weekly Mirror.*"

It was no use. He did not get the encouragement he had expected from her. Another year passed, and she began to chide him for neglecting her and the baby. Mrs. Marvin objected to his typing on a Sunday, and this led to frequent quarrels and bickering. But neither Sally's unreasonableness, nor Mrs. Marvin's displeasure could keep him from his writing, and when the foundry restarted again on full-time, he still spent in the parlour what hours remained to him after the day's work was done. He became ruthless in his desire to develop as a writer. Nothing should stop him from achieving his ambition, now... Nothing!

A political article he wrote on the International Brigade in Spain, and the growth of Fascism in Europe, for which he did not expect any payment, was published in *Left Wing,* a provincial magazine. He had taken an entire evening to draft out the article, and another evening was spent in typing the manuscript. A cheque for a guinea followed publication.

The moulders had been working overtime that week, and Sally remonstrated with him when she saw the guinea cheque.

"Two nights you worked on that article, Ieuan. You had twenty-one shillings for it. If you'd put in two nights' overtime at the foundry, you would have got three times as much."

And Mrs. Marvin supported her. "Yes, indeed. Another thing—it's not right and decent of you to let Sally be on her own all the time. You haven't once offered to take the child from her, too. This silly writing idea is becoming a nuisance. You are forgetting your duties as a husband."

"His duties as a husband," he reflected ironically. Sally no longer welcomed his love-making. She was frightened of having another child. She withdrew from his embraces, and as the months sped by even her beauty seemed to fade. The only consolations he had were in his writing, and in Beth, whose childish efforts to talk were a constant delight to him.

The hard work at the foundry began to tell on him. There were times when he was forced to stay away, but even then he would not leave his writing. Success was small. In a year he had sold only the article to *Left Wing,* and two stories to a Welsh literary periodical.

Then came a personal tragedy.

One Sunday morning, he had called at his mother's house. He found Phyllis in tears, and his father was visibly distressed.

"What's wrong?" he demanded.

"It's your mother, Ieuan... She's seriously ill."

He looked at his father incredulously. "But, Dad— what's happened? I don't understand... Why didn't you send for me sooner?"

"It came on her suddenly, Ieuan. Last night—she collapsed. I sent for the doctor, and—"

"Yes?"

"You might as well know the truth, my boy. There's—there's no hope for her."

Ieuan stood very still, afraid to speak, and unwilling to think. But the fearful import of his father's words compelled him to think. His first thought was that he must see his mother. He remembered he had been told that she was not well. But that was two years ago, just before he and Sally were married. Why had nothing been said to him since then? He had never dreamt that his mother was seriously ill. And what was really the matter with her?

He lifted his head to ask his father, but before he could do so he was led by him into the front room.

"Ieuan," his father said, and paused. "Ieuan.... your mother has cancer."

No, no, no! he heard himself cry inwardly. Then he said: "But I don't understand, Dad. She—she's been so well all these years..."

"You may think so, son. But there's a lot of things you know nothing of, Ieuan. I knew... Yes, I knew all along that there was something wrong, though she said nothing... Never complained about it, she did. Now it's too late."

"What d'you mean, too late? How can it be too late?" he exclaimed.

"I've spoken to the doctor, son. He told me—"

"Yes, yes, what did he say?"

"Your mother's going to die."

Ieuan raced up the stairs. When he saw his mother he knew there was little hope for her. The doctor called him out of the room and spoke gravely.

"It's only a matter of hours, my boy. There's nothing I can do, nothing that anybody can do—now. A few tablets to ease the pain, and that is all. It's a pity, a great pity that your mother never consulted me years ago."

Ieuan listened, and nodded vaguely.

Cancer! No hope! What a blind fool he had been. This was the cause of her anger, her frustration and unhappiness. This scourge that came without a whisper of pain, and then spread its malignant roots to destroy and kill the living flesh. From a whisper to a frenzied, tortuous and agonising pain that wracked the body and brain.

He moved near to the bed. Her face, twisted in agony, turned slowly towards him. Her lips moved, but no sound came from them. She beckoned him forward, her thin arms reaching weakly out over the coverlet.

"Ieuan!"

His head was on her breast. She breathed with effort.

"Funny it is, Ieuan... All alone I said I'd be... Now, it is me who is the first to leave."

Her fingers rested on his head. They sought to turn his face towards her, but there was no strength left. He looked at her

158

lovingly. Then she whispered again. "I haven't been a good mother... and I'm sorry."

He tried to smile. "Don't you worry, Mam." The words seemed futile and out of place.

"You forgive me, my boy?" There was a sadness that he had never heard before in her voice.

"There's nothing to forgive, Mam... Nothing."

"Yes, yes, Ieuan... there is much to forgive... I've been hard... an obstinate woman... But so much worries... illness ..."

"Please, Mam, you mustn't say anything. Rest—then you'll get better, and—"

A smile crossed her lips, and for a moment the beauty she had lost returned to her eyes. Ieuan held back his tears. The pity he felt for her overwhelmed him, and he could not bear to look at her.

"I've been a selfish mother... the struggle to make ends meet... love you all in my own selfish way... and, oh Ieuan *bach,* I—I don't want to leave you like this."

"You'll be bustling around again, Mam... Please don't say any more. You'll pull through this illness."

Words, words, words—of what use were they? She was dying. But the smile was still on her face, and her eyes had the tenderness of a mother who was leaving her children for the last journey.

"You... you will kiss me, Ieuan? Never have I kissed you since you was a little boy."

Her tears cooled his burning cheeks. He felt her tremble as he leaned lightly over the pillows.

"There's my lovely boy... Now I am going away happy... Better it is, perhaps, for not much happiness have I given any of you when I was alive... And poor Dick... poor Dick."

Her eyes filled with sudden fear. She strove to raise herself.

"Dick! Dick...! Oh, God, God, let me see him before I go... Dick, my husband ...!"

Ieuan rushed to the door. The doctor stepped into the room and hurried to the bed.

"Dad! Dad! Quickly!"

Dick Morgan came stumbling up the stairway. He gripped Ieuan's arm. At that moment the doctor came out of the bedroom. The grave look in his eyes told them that the end had come.

CHAPTER TWENTY-ONE

His mother was dead! Conscience began to trouble him as they bore her body down into the parlour, there to be laid out in the satin-lined coffin. His thoughts raced back over his boyhood. He recalled with sorrow his coldness to his mother, his quarrels with her, and tortured himself with thoughts of impatience, neglect and resentment. Understanding had come too late to console him, and he lashed himself with the bitterness of his regret.

Who was he to talk of a better world for his fellowmen when he had failed his own mother? And now, he was making Sally unhappy. He had been found wanting as a son, and he was proving no better as a husband.

He went into the parlour where his mother lay alone and at peace; and as he looked down at her his face contorted in his efforts to stem his tears.

* * *

It was the day after the funeral. Gweneira and Sam had come from Brecon, and they, Phyllis, Ieuan, and his father sadly discussed their plans for the future.

Gweneira had spoken to Ieuan soon after her arrival at the house.

"What are we to do about Dad, Ieuan? It worries me. He—he won't think of breaking up the home?"

"I don't think so. There's Phyllis—she's here to look after him."

"If I thought he'd be unhappy, I'd ask him and Phyllis to come and live with us."

He calmed her fears. "There's no need for you to worry, *fach*. Dad will be all right, so long as I'm here. In fact. I've got an idea…"

161

He had considered asking Sally to make their home with his father, but her reaction dismayed him.

"I wouldn't dream of leaving Mam," she said. "Phyllis is there to look after your father. I'm sorry, Ieuan, indeed I am—but I'm sure you understand. Just ask yourself... what if you were in my place?"

"You married me, Sally. Is your mother always to be your first consideration?"

"You are first in my thoughts, Ieuan."

"Then please, dear, think over what I've said concerning Dad and us."

"I'm sorry, Ieuan, but I'm not going to start an argument."

"Very well—we'll leave all the arguing to your mother. But listen, Sally—I'm not going to suffer any more interference from her. I've had enough."

Her tears had ended the discussion, and again he was sorry for inflicting pain upon her. If only he could make her see the futility of accepting her mother's will! Then, and then only could they find the happiness they had looked forward to together.

That night as they lay in bed, her black hair glistening in the moonlight, the child sleeping peacefully in its cot, he reflected despairingly on the past years of their marriage.

He had no right to inflict pain on another human being. Yet, if only she would bring herself closer to him and have faith in his struggle to achieve something from his writing; help him in his efforts to get away from the foundry; reject her mother's dominance! He was more alone now than in the days when, as a boy, he had entered Bevan's. There was no one who could offer him encouragement, who could understand his compelling urge to write. If only...

His desperate longing for peace of mind and the restoration of Sally's former confidence in him made him nerve-racked and depressed. Then one day the tension between him and Mrs. Marvin reached its climax. She had been to a special meeting of the Christian Brotherhood, and, on returning home, began to preach on her religious theories. Before the evening was through they were quarrelling fiercely.

"You're a hypocrite!" he blazed at her. "A hard-hearted, selfish old woman with no consideration for anyone or anything."

She was equally angry, and answered him with equal vehemence. Sally stood by, helpless, while they vented their fury against each other.

"This is the end." Mrs. Marvin was hysterical. "I'm not going to tolerate your blaspheming."

"Then do something about it." Ieuan was white with rage.

"I will, I will, you—you infidel! I'll never stay a minute longer in this house—not while you are here."

"Indeed! That's excellent news."

"I'm leaving, do you hear?" She waited, hands on hips.

"I've heard that threat often enough." He nodded to the bedroom. "Can I help you pack?"

"Why, you... you..."

Sally caught her hand. "Oh, Mam, please—"

"I'm leaving." Her mother strode out of the room. Sally appealed to Ieuan. He made no effort to follow Mrs. Marvin.

Presently she returned, a suitcase in hand. "Sally," she said coldly, "I'm going to your aunt's in Cardiff. I'll never stay a moment longer in this house. It was the biggest mistake I ever made, to let you and your husband live here with me. I'll send for my other things later."

Sally's remonstrances, her pleadings, were of no avail. Her mother was determined to leave. The crisis had come at last, and, as the front door slammed, Ieuan sank into a chair.

"Now, now we can at least live our own lives."

Sally looked at him with tears in her eyes. "Oh, Ieuan, Ieuan ..." Then she turned quickly and ran up to the bedroom.

Mrs. Marvin's angry leave-taking had been no gesture. Three days later a letter addressed to Sally arrived. Her mother was not coming back to Abermor. The home was Sally's and Ieuan's. There wouldn't be much happiness there, but that, of course, was no fault of hers. Oh, no. She had always done her best to lead a Christian life, but it was impossible to expect her to live in harmony with a man who opposed everything she said or did, a man who sympathised with communists, and whose very writings were filled with atheistic thoughts. Some day he would repent, but until that day she would remain with her sister. Sally and Beth were welcome to come and visit her, but Ieuan Morgan—well, she did not think that she could speak to him again. Let him repent of his sins and she might then feel differently. But she could make no promises. She had been hurt very much, and it was wicked of him to treat a good woman like her as he had done.

With Mrs. Marvin now gone, Ieuan's confidence in the future began to reassert itself. He plunged into his writing with renewed vigour. There was no immediate improvement in his relationship with Sally. She blamed him for her mother leaving them, and bitterly accused him of being selfish.

He did nothing to antagonise her, accepting her reprimands in silence. Each morning he would take her a cup of tea before he left for the foundry, and kiss her and the child. And on his return home from work, he would spend his first few hours of leisure with them.

Later at night he continued with his stories, writing them in longhand, and then labouriously typing the mss. during the weekends. He organised his leisure time, and gave himself one evening for reading contemporary short stories and for studying the technique of writing.

In the foundry, whenever an idea, a piece of dialogue, or a character interested him, he would scribble a note of it on a small pad he invariably carried. Cigarette packets, newspaper margins, time-sheets, scraps of paper—all were written on, and his dungaree pockets became stuffed with what Sally called "rubbishy bits".

He submitted his finished stories to various magazines and newspapers, and back they came, accompanied with the usual rejection slips. Nine months had gone before he had another sale.

164

Then one day he received a letter from a Miss Stella Courtland, editor of a leading literary magazine, *New Forum*. She had accepted a story of his and wrote:

"DEAR MR. MORGAN,

I was much impressed by your story, *The Last Hour* and I would very much like to publish it in *The New Forum*. I have had the pleasure of reading other stories of yours in the past, but this is the best one you have done. The rate of payment is £5 5s. a thousand, and a cheque for your story will be sent to you shortly. Would you be good enough to let me have a few biographical pars, and a photograph—if possible? In conclusion, may I offer a word of criticism? You have real gifts. Your stories are living and attractive because of (1) excellent characterisation, (2) recognisable situations which you make interesting, (3) invention, humour, and indignation. *But*—they are too static, and the themes are too carefully unambitious. Also, they lack implicit statement. This is not a bad thing when one is carried by the completeness or the streaming electric quality of a place or a situation. It does become dull and almost lifeless when repetition of technical facility, but nothing else, results in a photograph. Still, it is easy to criticise! Please send me more.

Sincerely,

STELLA COURTLAND."

He read the letter through several times. He showed it to Sally with pride, and she seemed pleased. Of the men in the foundry, Thomas alone knew of his determination to become a writer, but when he gave him the letter to read, Thomas made no comment except to wish him luck.

Somewhat disheartened, he returned home that evening. He re-read the letter in the privacy of the parlour, and his heart lightened. Here was one person who would understand his struggle and his aspirations.

165

He prepared the biographical notes she had asked for, and from a snapshot album in his drawer, took out a photograph of himself taken in the foundry. Then he began his letter:

"DEAR MISS COURTLAND,

Believe me, I am more than grateful for your very kind letter and helpful criticism. The fact that I am to be published in *New Forum* has been a grand tonic, for I was beginning to despair of ever attaining the very high standard which literary magazines like yours demand. I shall most certainly take your advice to heart, and once again repeat how very grateful I am for your interest. The few notes here enclosed may suit your purpose, but if there are any other details you wish to know, I shall be happy to let you have them.

Please excuse the rather blurred photograph. I'm afraid it's the only one I have at the moment. Do you think it will reproduce at all? If not, I can have another one taken. Please let me know.

Yours sincerely,

IEUAN MORGAN."

The following week he received another letter from Miss Courtland, and he noticed with pleasurable excitement that she referred to him as her "very promising protege".

"You will, of course, forgive me for taking the liberty of calling you such, but—I must stress this— I am most anxious to see other stories of yours. Do send them along, won't you? I feel I have a new discovery on my hands, and I want to help establish you as a writer. You say you have begun writing only in recent years. This has surprised me, for you already possess the accomplishments of one who has been writing for many years. I was not aware that you were a steel-foundry worker. Surely, that 'inferno' (as you so describe it) is no place for a young man of your obvious talents? You should seek release from such an environment. That you will do so, and quite soon, is apparent to me. In conclusion, please send me those stories. I am really very interested in your future.

Sincerely,

Stella Courtland.

P.S. The photograph, I regret to say, will not do. Unfortunately, it is much too dark for reproduction."

Heartened by the warmth of her letter, Ieuan looked through his files and sent her four stories which he had not previously submitted to any magazine. Of these, she decided to keep two, and her next letter to him was of a more friendly nature.

She now addressed him as "Dear Ieuan Morgan", and it gave him added pleasure and confidence. Here, at last, he had found not only an editor who appreciated his work, but a friend as well.

The two stories duly appeared in *New Forum*. Copies of the magazine were sent to him, and he wrote an appreciative note of thanks.

The warmth of her reply resulted in a regular correspondence between them, and this led to a friendship which was not to be without effect on him. She wished to know more about him, of his background, his plans for future writing. Had he contemplated writing a novel? Were there any friends in Abermor who were actively interested in his writing? Had he thought of coming to London?

Ieuan hastened to reply. He wrote her long letters in which he described his childhood dreams and ambitions and his years in the foundry. He wrote of his early friendship with Frank Jones, and of Frank's agonising death; of his association with Thomas, and his courtship and marriage to Sally.

Her letters followed quickly on his. She signed herself "Stella", and familiarised her address to him, "Dear Ieuan". She returned his confidences, and told him her story. She was the only child of Richard Courtland, the publisher. Her mother had died ten years ago. *The New Forum* was one of her father's publications, but she had edited it since its inception. Her background? Oh, the usual, dull routine one associates with the only daughter of wealthy parents—exclusive schools, university, chaperoned travels, parties. Editing *The New Forum,* however, had proved an adventure that was most exhilarating, especially when one suddenly discovered a new, rich and virile personality who wore greasy dungarees by day and the mantle of a poet by night.

Ieuan began to picture her in his mind, and was obsessed by the image he had formed. She was beautiful. That, he felt instinctively. And she was young. Her letters were spirited and lively, written in a firm hand, yet her essential femininity was revealed in the delicately perfumed note-paper she used. Later, another copy of *The New Forum* was posted to him, and in it he found a small photograph of Stella, captioned, "The Editor."

She was strikingly beautiful, dark, with classical features.

Her eyes were large, set in a slender face framed with black hair that swept to her shoulders. He assumed her to be not more than twenty-three, a few years younger than he.

He spoke enthusiastically of her to Sally, of her kindness to him, and of her position in the literary world. She had taught him much already, and if he could only improve in his writing he was sure that she would help him in every way possible. Now, at last, opportunity had come his way, and he would strive harder than ever to break away from the foundry.

Sally, however, did not share his enthusiasm.

"I'm glad you've had your stories taken by Miss Courtland, but to me it seems there's something false about her, Ieuan."

"What do you mean, Sally?" he asked, offended by her tone.

"What I say, Ieuan. She's a rich woman with nothing to do—just bored with life, as she said in one of her letters. She'll be dropping you like a hot brick one of these days. She's not genuine, Ieuan... I feel she's only amusing herself with you."

168

"That's not very kind of you, Sally, to say such things about someone who's been good enough to help me. Stella's a friend, as much a friend to you as she is to me. Just look back over the past two years, dear—how many editors have offered me a word of advice or criticism? Look at the rejection slips I've had, hundreds of them, just printed notes. I feel deeply grateful for the interest that a person in her position has taken in me."

"She certainly has taken an interest in you, Ieuan. Judging from her letters she's beginning to take a little more than that."

"Sally, you're being unfair. Don't tell me you're jealous. That would be silly."

"I'm jealous of no one, Ieuan."

"Then please, *cariad,* try to understand what Stella's interest in my work means to me. There was a time when my writing meant so much to you, too. Why have you changed so?"

"I'm the same now, as when you married me, Ieuan, and I love you. Oh, please, please don't say any more. If you want to write to Miss Courtland, you're free to do so."

"But, Sally, why talk like that?"

It was too evident to him that she was jealous of his friendship with Stella, frightened that it might develop into an "affair". Sally, with her womanly instincts guiding or misguiding her, was being hostile to his new friend. It was ridiculous! She had not even met her.

Ridiculous! Surely, as his wife, she had the right to challenge his intentions? But she must trust him, as he trusted her. Stella was prepared to help him. That was all there was to it. His future was bound with Sally's and the child's. If he could break with the foundry it would be to their benefit as well as his. Why couldn't she see this as he did?

To his dismay, even Thomas was suspicious. He had read to him some of Stella's later letters and had spoken appreciatively of her interest in his writing. But he had been annoyed to find that Thomas was not at all impressed by Stella's good opinions of his work.

"She may be an editor, Ieuan, but don't forget that first she's a woman."

Ieuan regarded him with astonishment. Was Thomas going to preach to him as Sally had? True, she was a woman. Sincere and friendly. Attractive, with a personality that won his admiration. But first, she was an editor.

Thomas referred again to the letters. "I haven't travelled much, my boy, but just enough to realise that this girl is letting you know she's more than a bit fond of you. Watch your step, Ieuan."

"Watch my step!" Ieuan rammed the letters into his pocket. "What's wrong with you and Sally? Why all this damn silly talk about Miss Courtland? The fact that she wears a skirt seems to be sufficient to make you believe that I'm going to fall violently in love with her."

Thomas held out his hands expressively. "Well, who knows?"

"Bloody nonsense!"

"Okay, boy. If that's the case, why go off the deep end about it? You told me how you got in touch with her, you got excited as a kid over her letters, and now, just because I feel that she's... Hell! let it drop, Ieuan. If you think she can help you, carry on. All the same, don't forget she's not in our class."

"Oh! No, of course not!" Ieuan flared. "You and I, and Sally— we're small-town people with a small-town outlook. Remember the plays we used to see as kids at the old Royalty—the poor, innocent village lad taken in by the smart, flashy girl from the city! I'm sorry, Thomas, but this time you've got it all wrong."

"Just as you say, Ieuan. Now, forget it, will you? I'm not in the mood to argue any more. I wish you luck, that's all."

The matter was not discussed again, and Ieuan, hurt by their attitude, sublimated his feelings by working with concentrated fury each night in the front parlour, typewriter clicking incessantly, his notes and rough drafts of stories always ready at his elbow.

He neglected Sally, purposely, and without remorse. She had hurt him. He would now hurt her. To the devil with his theories and principles! He had never wanted to harm anyone, and had

170

never done so wittingly. But she, yes, and Thomas—the only two on whom he had depended for advice and inspiration—had failed him. Stella was the only one left; the only one prepared to give him friendship and encouragement.

If only he could meet her, speak with her! A trip to London was not possible at the moment. She had asked him so many times to make the journey, but on each occasion he had to make some feeble excuse. They were still working part-time at the foundry. The little money he had earned from his stories had almost all gone. There were clothes to be bought, and food, and accumulated bills to pay.

Would he ever meet her? The answer came one day in September when the whole country lay heavy under the threat of war. There was a tension in the air; a dramatic hush of expectancy. The Prime Minister had flown to Berchtesgaden, and the nation waited anxiously for news of his meeting with the megalomaniac Adolf Hitler.

In Stella's letter there was not a hint of concern with either peace or war. Her world remained calm and cultured. Soon, she would be motoring through South Wales on a holiday tour, she wrote.

"... and, dear Ieuan, I am coming for a whole week to Abermor, your delightful little town. Yes, it's true! We are to meet at long last, and I am looking forward immensely to it. We—that is, Eddie Brownlee, my cousin, and I—have booked accommodation at the Beaufort Hotel. I shall write to you again to let you know when to expect me.

With my very fondest regards.

STELLA."

In the meantime, Bevan's foundry fell idle again. The men met at the Employment Exchange on Mondays and Wednesdays, resigned now to the periods of unemployment they had come to expect. Bevan's was a bloody washout! Why the hell didn't the management turn it into a Red Lamp? That was the only hope of making the damn place pay its way.

Ieuan secretly welcomed the rest. The griping stomach pains from which he had been free for some time had returned. Often, he was almost driven by them to see the doctor. But he was afraid of being declared unfit for work, and he could not afford that to happen. So long as Bevan's was open he struggled there each morning. Now, however, he would have to stay away, because there was nothing there for him to do.

It was not pleasant to be unemployed again. Still, if it helped him to get better it would not be without advantage to him. Morever, it would give him more time with Stella when she arrived. He waited eagerly for the day he would meet her. In the last week in September he heard from her. She was at Abermor the next Tuesday afternoon. Would he please call for her at the Beaufort at three o'clock? Oh, it was to be so delightful meeting him. They would have so much to say to each other!

CHAPTER TWENTY-TWO

Ieuan walked briskly down the High Street. On the corner opposite Brady's Emporium stood the Beaufort Hotel. As he drew near he saw a low, green sports car parked before the canopied entrance. A porter crouched over the rear of the car, then carried two suitcases into the hotel.

Presently, a young woman in a green jumper and tweed skirt appeared. Her black hair fell to her shoulders in a long bob. She was slim, and moved gracefully as she climbed into the driving seat.

Ieuan stopped a few yards distant. The woman looked up. Their eyes met, and there was an instant recognition.

He was the first to speak. "Miss Courtland?" He smiled nervously.

"Ieuan Morgan!" She stepped nimbly out of the car and came towards him, a hand outstretched. She laughed. "How wonderful to meet you at last."

They shook hands. The frank look with which she regarded him, her charm, and complete self-possession, put him immediately at ease.

"The pleasure is equally mine," he said, and for a moment the banality of his remark nonplussed him.

Just then, a tall, broad-shouldered man with greying hair came out of the foyer. He glanced at Ieuan, a shadow of a smile on his bronzed face. Stella beckoned to him.

"Oh, Eddie, this is Ieuan Morgan... Ieuan, this is my cousin, Eddie Brownlee."

Brownlee's smile widened as he shook hands, but Ieuan detected a cynicism in the other's formal, "How do you do, Mr. Morgan? Stella's told me so much about you," and he took an instant dislike to the man.

He was considerably older than Ieuan, possibly in his early fifties, well tailored, and obviously wealthy. But he seemed to lack vitality, and there was no grip in his handshake.

Stella turned to him. "Eddie, be a dear and take the car round to the garage, then come and join us in a drink... You will have a drink, Ieuan?"

Seated in the lounge, Ieuan could not take his eyes from her. She was far more beautiful than the photograph in *The New Forum* had shown. The illustration had not indicated the slender face, smooth red lips with their fascinating pout, the large, liquid brown eyes burning with excitement, and the high cheekbones slightly touched with colour. She was the most beautiful woman he had met.

When Brownlee returned they were deep in conversation. There was so much that Ieuan wished to tell her. He spoke rapidly, excitedly, captivated by her beauty as she listened, and laughed at what she termed his "native exuberance".

"Please, Ieuan..." She shook her head and fanned her face. "You've made me breathless. Tomorrow, we'll have a whole day together, and we'll be able to discuss things more rationally. My! you Welshmen," she laughed. She sipped her drink. "You'll manage to come tomorrow? We could drive out to the Gower coast. I've heard such a lot about its loveliness, that I'd like to judge for myself."

"Yes, of course. Of course I could come."

"You're sure? Your work—are you able to arrange with your employer?"

He fingered his glass. "I—I'm not working just now," he stammered. He saw Brownlee's cynical smile, and flinched.

"That's excellent," Stella smiled, "from our point of view. We'll have a lovely day out." She passed Ieuan's empty glass to Brownlee. "Eddie, unfortunately, won't be with us. He's suddenly developed a craze for fishing, and he's off to some little village away in the hills, aren't you, Eddie?"

Brownlee nodded. "Each to his own sport," he said dryly.

174

"Now, Eddie!" Stella kissed him lightly on the cheek. "You do like fishing, don't pretend it's a sufferance, you naughty boy." She took his arm. Ieuan laughed self-consciously.

"Tomorrow morning then, Ieuan. Will you call for me at ten?"

"I'll be delighted to." He shook hands with Brownlee. "I hope you'll have a good day's fishing."

"Thanks, old boy. I suppose I'll see you again, some time?"

Ieuan returned home, buoyant. Stella was really charming. Her smile, the interest with which she had listened to his excited ramblings, and her confidence in him had made the world a bright and happy place again.

He told Sally of the meeting and of his arrangements for the following day. She was silent, and the only comment she made was to remind him that he had to sign on at the Exchange.

"I'll be there at crack of dawn," he joked. "Stella's a fine girl," he enthused. "You must meet her, Sally. I'm sure you'll like each other on sight."

Later in the evening, seated in the front parlour, he recalled his meeting with Stella. She was beautiful, everything about her was beautiful—the way she spoke, the spring in her step, her poise, the vitality she possessed. He saw her again stepping towards him from the car, hand extended, and heard again her voice like music speak his name.

He awoke with a start from his day-dreaming as Sally called to him from the kitchen. But as they sat down to supper his thoughts kept returning to Stella. He could not rid himself of her.

The next morning he signed on at the Exchange. Some of his workmates who had arrived for the early queue, looked at him with surprise. He was dressed in his best suit and appeared incongruous amongst the mufflered, shabby-suited companions who lined up with him, their crumpled franking-cards in hand.

"Off to a wedding, Ieuan?"

"Won a couple o' quid on the pools, eh?"

"Not started courting again?"

He took their banter in good part and hurried through the little park behind the Town Hall, nodding genially to the old men who had come to sun themselves on the green-painted seats.

The grass and the ringed flower-beds were still gleaming with dew. The trees stood quiet. Not a leaf stirred to quicken the shadows that fell across the gravelled paths and the neatly trimmed lawns.

He crossed the Square and strode along the High Street. Stella and the green car were waiting for him outside the hotel entrance.

"Isn't it a marvellous day?" she greeted with hand outstretched. "I'm sure we're going to enjoy ourselves."

He helped her into the car after she had taken off her light grey coat and flung it over the back of the seat. She was dressed in a thin, green polo jersey and grey skirt that buttoned up the side. Flesh silk covered her slim legs, and on her feet she wore a pair of green walking shoes.

Ieuan noticed with pleasure that her figure, hands and feet were formed upon a model of exquisite symmetry with the size and lightness of her person, and his heart quickened as he felt her nearness and breathed the sweet scent of her presence.

Soon they were speeding along the main road out of town. He relaxed in his seat, watching her capable hands as she swung the car away from the traffic into the country lanes that led to the Gower. She spoke to him, and he answered, fascinated by the softness of her voice, and thrilled at each contact with her as she leaned towards him to steer the car around the bends.

At midday they lunched at a small wayside cafe on the road to Rhossili Bay, and in the afternoon they cruised round the coastline. After tea at another café beyond Langland, Stella decided to park the car and walk along the cliffs.

It was almost dark when they started on their way back. Throughout the afternoon they had talked of Ieuan's hopes, and Stella had repeatedly assured him of her confidence in his ability. They laughed and joked together, and he felt that he had found joy again, the joy and laughter that had been so long suppressed.

In the past year Sally's demeanour had worried him, and had

often left him dispirited. Now, with Stella's arrival, he had found cheerfulness again, however short-lived it might be.

Her worldly wisdom impressed him. She was much travelled, and had met many people. She spoke familiarly of strange places which had always beckoned him; of famous men, artists, writers, poets, who were her personal friends.

"Tell me honestly, Stella," he said. "Why did you come to Abermor just to help me—a man who literally hasn't two pennies to rub together?"

"You're a very gifted young man, Ieuan," she said seriously, "and I admire you. It's disgusting to think that you should spend your time in a foundry. You must break away, Ieuan. As a writer you must have wider experience."

He was heartened by her words. "I've always wanted to be free of Bevan's—from the very first day I started there as a boy," he began.

"Then why don't you? There's no future in Abermor."

He smiled faintly. "It's so easy to talk, Stella. Until I've really proved myself capable of earning enough by my writing—enough to keep my family—how can I hope to leave the foundry?"

"You should come to London," she said. "We'll see what we can do for you."

"London? I haven't the remotest chance of going there," he said bitterly.

They walked on for a while in silence. Below them they could hear the low murmur of the waves breaking against the cliff-face. The cry of a gull echoed mournfully over the bay. The clouds broke softly apart, and here and there let a star peep through their veil.

Suddenly, Stella stopped. Ieuan turned to her in the darkness. He could just see the outline of her face. Her lips were half open.

"Ieuan," she said softly, coming close to him and touching his cheeks with her finger-tips, "you're such a handsome, such a sweetly innocent boy."

He was taken aback, confused by her unexpected remark. He

177

trembled at her proximity as she slipped an arm around his neck. Her head fell back. She strove to pull him to the ground.

He made no effort to resist, but lowered her gently to the grass. His hands caressed her breasts. He touched his mouth to hers as she leaned deeper into the grass. Her mouth was warm, alive. Her breathing came and went in quick gasps. She whispered his name, passionately.

"Ieuan, Ieuan... you darling, you beautiful boy."

His fingers fumbled with the thin wool, and he felt the smooth softness of her breasts. He kissed her again and again, and murmured her name with each kiss.

Her body tossed beneath him and he felt her fingers writhing in his hair. Her hands dropped slowly to her skirt. She fumbled with the buttons, and, as he lightened his weight on her, she drew the skirt away.

He ran his hands over her naked thighs, and she quivered voluptuously. Again her arms closed round him. Their lips clung together, teeth against teeth. Her hair touched his cheeks and he shivered with ecstasy.

"Oh, Stella... Stella..."

His body flowed into hers. He heard her moan, and she gripped him fiercely. Her fingers dug into his flesh. She called his name, wildly, as she trembled beneath him. Then suddenly he felt her go limp in his arms, and she turned her face away from him and lay still.

He groped for the skirt and wrapped it around her.

A cold wind swept in from the bay. The crescent of lights on Tower Hill twinkled in the darkness, and there was silence, except for the breaking of the waves.

CHAPTER TWENTY-THREE

"Shall we go?" she said.

Ieuan felt shaken, and was trembling. Her self-composure amazed him. There was no trace of emotion in her voice. He took her arm and led her across the green to where the car was parked.

As they drove home she crouched over the wheel and silently concentrated on her driving. Once, his hand searched for hers, but she withdrew it, a strange, enigmatic half-smile on her face.

"Stella," he said.

"Please, Ieuan... the roads—I'm not familiar with them."

It was midnight when they arrived in the town.

"Well, here we are!" She was coldly composed. He stood on the pavement, at a loss to understand the sudden change in her.

The light from the lamp on the street corner shone on her face. The same half-smile curved her lips.

"Stella!"

"Yes?"

She drew up her coat collar and fastened it high around her throat.

"Shall I call for you tomorrow?"

"Oh, please, Ieuan... It's very late, and I'm tired."

Her peremptoriness further disconcerted him. What had caused this sudden and inexplicable change? The wild passion she had shown for him had gone. She was no longer the warm, seductive woman he had possessed only an hour ago.

He leaned over and caught her hands. "There's something wrong Stella. What is it?" he asked ardently.

She drew away. "Nothing, you romantic Welshman. Nothing at all." She gave a light laugh. "Very well, come and see me tomorrow after lunch." She brushed her hair back from her forehead. "Now, please let me garage the car, there's a dear."

Before he had an opportunity to say any more, she had swung the car away from the kerbside, and, with a wave of her hand, had disappeared round the side entrance of the hotel.

* * *

Sally was waiting up for him when he reached the house. She looked tired.

"You're very late, dear," she said quietly. "I've been worried." She laid his supper on the table. "Did you have an interesting day? It must have been very lovely on the Gower."

He sat down at the table and toyed with his food. Presently, he looked up. "Are you cross, Sally?" he asked.

"Why should I be?" she said sharply. Her cheeks flushed. Then, violently: "That woman—already she's the talk of the Beaufort, with her flash car and ladylike airs. And that man she's got hanging around her, he's no cousin... More like her lover!"

He jumped up from his chair. "How dare you say such a thing!" he shouted, giving way to a guilty anger. "Stella's been here only two days. The talk of the Beaufort, indeed! What a childish statement!"

"Ask the girls working there, they'll tell you," she challenged. Her lips quivered. She began to cry.

"So you even went so far as to make enquiries about her?" Her tears shamed and irritated him.

"And why shouldn't I? I'm your wife, Ieuan... I—I love you." She threw her hands around him. "Oh, Ieuan... please don't let yourself be made a fool of. She's no good, I tell you," she sobbed. "She's no good."

He patted her shoulder clumsily, his eyes deeply troubled.

"Don't cry, Sally... please. You shouldn't have waited up for me."

Suddenly he thought of the five years through which they had

180

lived together, and he said: "Stella is just a friend... She can help me."

"I don't want her to help you, Ieuan... I'm frightened. Oh, please, I beg of you, think of your little family. We can be so happy together, the three of us... I've been mean to you, I know, but I promise you everything will be different from now on... I promise you, Ieuan."

An immense pity gripped him. He took her tear-stained face into his hands.

"I do love you, Sally," he whispered.

"You—you won't see her again?"

"I can't promise that," He sighed, "Please, Sally, try to understand. I'm seeing Stella tomorrow... You must trust me."

At the moment he could not think clearly. So much had happened in the past hours that he felt dazed, elated, and conscience-stricken in turn.

The next day he called at the Beaufort. He waited in the entrance. Ten, fifteen minutes passed, but Stella did not appear. He walked round to the garage and glanced inside. The green car had gone.

Puzzled, he returned to the lounge. A porter approached, letter in hand.

"Mr. Morgan? Miss Courtland—she asked me to deliver this to you."

Ieuan tore open the envelope.

"Dear Ieuan,

I'm afraid I shan't be able to see you today as arranged. I've had a phone message from Eddie. The poor dear's completely bored, and wants me to return to London. I'm picking him up at Cowbridge this evening. So sorry I had to leave in this casual way, but I'm sure you will understand.

Stella."

The porter waited. "Any message, sir?"

Ieuan looked at him vacantly. He thrust the letter into his pocket. "No—no, thanks. There's no message."

He walked out into the street. Stella had gone! A few words scribbled in haste, and that was all! Why? What had caused this abrupt departure?

Eddie was bored? The excuse carried no conviction. She had not wished to see him again. Why? Why?

Stupefied, he found himself wandering through the Park near the Square. He sat down on an empty seat, his mind in a turmoil.

Why had she gone? She had come into his life for only a few hours, a single day, and he had thought that he had known and understood her. She had raised his hopes. Nothing had seemed impossible to him when she spoke of his ability. He had felt that his stories were worth while, and that fame was his to grasp.

Now, she had gone, shut herself away from him as completely as she had on that silent night ride from the cliffs. Had not their intimacy meant anything to her? Had it been only a new, but a casual experience for her?

He recalled their parting, the hesitancy of her answer when he had asked if he should call for her again. Her light laugh echoed in his ears. "Very well, come and see me tomorrow, after lunch," she had said.

Could it be possible that she had already been planning to leave Abermor? She had arranged to stay a week, excited by the promise of their meeting. They would have so much to talk about!

And now, she had gone!

The park-keeper passed by, thoughtfully. Two young men sat down on the seat next to Ieuan and began to argue over football. He got up and made his way home, his head swimming, his eyes staring fixedly at the ground.

Eddie Brownlee! Sally had accused him of being Stella's lover. The thought sickened him, and he strove to banish it from his mind. But it returned with a nagging insistency. Eddie Brownlee was her lover! No, there could be no truth in the accusation. And yet... Brownlee's cynicism, his cryptic remark: "Each to his own sport." What did that imply? That Stella was playing with him? That she had come to Abermor in search of a new experience?

No, it was fantastic to think of it. Sally had made the accusation in a fit of jealousy, and he was being foolish to let it worry him.

But why had Stella left so abruptly? There was no real reason for her going. She could have sent for him before she left; seen him, if only for a few minutes. Yet there had been nothing, no handshake, no goodbye—just a hurried note.

Sally was on her knees, washing the strip of pavement fronting the house when he appeared at the bottom of the street. He saw her glance at him, then quickly wipe her hands on her coarse, sack apron. She came down the street to meet him.

"You look pale, Ieuan. What's wrong?"

He did not answer.

She lifted the bucket of greasy water into the passageway and closed the door. In the kitchen, she prepared a cup of tea. Ieuan slumped into the armchair.

"It's that woman," Sally's eyes flamed. "She's said something to you."

He shook his head. "She's gone, Sally."

"Oh, my poor Ieuan..." Her face softened. She slid to her knees and took his hands. "My poor darling, I knew, I knew... All her promises to help you! I knew she didn't mean them..." Then her voice trailed into silence.

In the weeks that followed he could think of nothing but Stella. He wrote her a frantic letter, but no reply came. He became despondent, and he spent his days sitting in the park or wandering aimlessly through the town, embittered, avoiding the companionship of his fellow workmates as they signed on at the Exchange. On Friday evenings he would collect his dole at "New Haven" and leave hurriedly before Thomas or any of the others arrived.

He had placed all his hopes on his meeting with Stella. She had restored his faith in himself. There was so much that he could have accomplished with her to help and encourage him. The memory of the night on the cliffs... his complete possession of her, and her eager surrender... And now, this void, this emptiness within him.

He was consumed with thoughts of her. He knew no peace of mind; desperate in his urgency to be near her. She was the only one who had shown a true interest in his writing; the only one who seemed to know and understand the deep, compelling, creative urge within him.

The only one? What of Sally? Had she not given him the encouragement he needed? Was not her faith in him enough? His mind flew back to the early days of their courtship. She had given him her love. She had declared her faith in his struggle, and she had believed that he would win.

All this, he knew. But he could not forget Stella. She had come into his life and now he could not do without her. But what was her hold on him? Did he love her, or was he merely fascinated by her fine talk and her fine clothes? 'Fine feathers make fine birds.'

Her image filled his mind. At night, restless and fevered, he could not sleep.

He would go to London. He must see her again. He must!

And Sally, Beth? What of them? He had a duty to them. They were part of him. Where was his conscience, that he should consider leaving them?

He had another duty, too—to write! He owed it to himself. His ambition—how many times had it been thwarted by circumstances? Was he to be frustrated again?

No! He would see it through, and nothing would stop him.

Was it his writing or his consuming desire to be with Stella that made him reason in this manner? The foundry was closed. There was no hope of restarting for months to come. No longer was he prepared to wait agonisingly, suffer the degradation of the dole. His chance lay before him. Stella could give it to him. The opportunity had come, and he must take full advantage of it. Stella would help him.

He could see that Sally was gravely disturbed by the change in him. He had become moody and silent. His writing was neglected; he took no interest in the child. Then one day while they were at dinner, he startled her by saying:

"Sally, I'm going to London."

She made a clumsy effort to retrieve the knife that had slipped from her hand. He saw her bite her lip. "You—you mean that, Ieuan?"

"Yes, Sally, I've made up my mind." He thrust his plate roughly aside. "What's the use of staying here, rotting? I want to go to London. I can do so much for us there."

"It—it's not Stella?"

He looked at her, confused. Her frank gaze troubled him. There was a sadness in her eyes. He found it difficult to conceal the truth from her, and an agony of shame possessed him.

"She can help us, Sally. She said so. If I went to London perhaps she could find me a job. There's no future here... nothing."

"You've made up your mind, Ieuan?"

"It's the future I'm thinking of, Sally."

"Yes, I know," she said quietly, "but if you go—if she does help you, what of," she drew a hand tiredly over her forehead, "what of Beth and me?"

"I shall send for you... Honest, I will, Sally."

A slow smile. Then she placed a hand on his arm. "You go, Ieuan."

Her simple words almost made him weep. Then she said, "One thing I want you to remember always... I love you, Ieuan."

CHAPTER TWENTY-FOUR

The green flag waved. He felt Sally tremble, and her grip tightened around his shoulders. Her lips were cold under his kiss. The child whimpered. Almost imperceptibly, the train began to move. "Good-bye, Sally..."

She hung on to him, sobbing. There was a hardness in his throat. She called out his name distractedly as she broke away from his arms. The flutter of a white handkerchief, and the farewell had been said.

He sat back in his seat, teeth clenched and lips tightly closed. The train rattled over the points. On the hill, silhouetted against the sky, stood the school of his childhood. The playing-fields and the old stone quarry flashed by, and the pangs of nostalgia overwhelmed him. He was leaving home.

The rolling clouds chased over the autumn fields. He closed his eyes.

Sally, Stella... Good-bye, Abermor.

The shining steel rails pierced the space between his eyes.

Stella, Sally... Good-bye, Abermor.

The coach wheels rumbled. The carriage swayed, rocking his thoughts, and the tumult within him persisted.

* * *

Five hours, and the train drew in to the roofed-in-gloom of Paddington. Tensed, yet stimulated by anticipation, he stepped out on to the platform, suitcase in hand. Sally and Abermor were now behind him, and the nostalgic feeling buried in the pit of his stomach. Soon he would be with Stella again, his fears and his worries forgotten.

186

He took a bus to Fleet Street. At four o'clock he found himself in Salisbury Square. Up three flights of worn stairway.

'THE NEW FORUM.'

A knock on the door.

"Come in!"

An attractive young woman, sleek in a black, tailored costume, looked at him over the typewriter on her desk.

Ieuan cleared his throat. "Is Miss Courtland in?"

"No, I'm afraid she's just left, and she won't be here until Monday." The young woman rose from her chair. "I'm Miss Dacre, Miss Courtland's secretary. Is there any message?"

"No—no, thanks. I'd like to see her personally."

He saw Miss Dacre take a swift glance at his suitcase, and her eyes suddenly brightened.

"You are Mr. Ieuan Morgan?" She smiled. "I'm sure Miss Courtland would not want to miss you.

Have you arranged to stay over the week-end, Mr. Morgan?"

"No, Miss Dacre, I haven't. That is, I—"

"Then perhaps if I gave you Miss Courtland's home address?"

"That would be very kind of you." She wrote it down on a phone memo pad: "12, Heath Parade, Hampstead, N.W.3."

"The 24 bus from Trafalgar Square will take you there," she said, handing him the note.

"Thank you, Miss Dacre. I'm most obliged to you."

As he closed the office door Ieuan took with him a disquieting memory of her smile and the lift of her expressive brows when she had repeated softly: "I'm sure Miss Courtland would not want to miss you." The street lamps were lit when he reached Hampstead. A short walk from the bus stop brought him into a dark, deserted avenue of tall trees, their bare branches clutching at the lowering sky.

He came to the edge of the Heath and stopped to enquire his way. Through the lacy screen of willows a pond gleamed, silver-grey, its waters stilled as a sheet of ice. A flock of moorhens honked noisily out of the darkness, then skidded on to the surface, scattering the frightened ripples to the shore.

He climbed the hill bordering the west side of the Heath, to where he had been directed by a passer-by. At the top of the hill, he turned right into a wide cul-de-sac of Tudor-styled cottages which stood back from the roadway.

"Heath Parade."

From the end of the row came the sound of music. He walked along, glancing to right and left. Presently he came to a vivid red door—No. 12. His hand trembled visibly as he raised the ornamented knocker.

He felt his pulse quickening, and he quivered inwardly as he heard footsteps approach.

The door opened. The music swelled out into the roadway.

A uniformed maid stood half hidden behind the door.

"Is—is Miss Stella Courtland in, please?"

She hesitated before answering.

"Who shall I say has called?"

"I'm Ieuan Morgan, a friend," he replied. "Miss Courtland isn't really expecting me. But if you would tell her that I'm here… "

The maid asked him into the hallway and disappeared into an adjoining room from which the music came.

"Stella!"

She came towards him, and her beauty made his heart leap. She was dressed in a brilliant red taffeta evening gown, her arms and shoulders bare. The dress crackled about her, and her high-heeled slippers hissed along the polished floor.

"Why, Ieuan, this *is* a surprise!" She seemed embarrassed by his presence. He saw a momentary frown on her face. Then she smiled. "You must have dropped from the clouds. I certainly never expected to see you again… so soon. Why—"

"Stella, I want to speak to you," he broke in. "Please."

"Certainly, Ieuan." She was again the self-composed woman he had known. "But first you must come and join us. I'm giving a little party—just for a few friends. Incidentally," she paused, "how on earth did you discover my private address?"

"I called at the office, hoping to find you there."

"Oh, I see!... Well, never mind. Do come in and meet my friends."

The room was crowded with men and women in evening dress. All eyes turned on him as he entered. Stella waved a hand to a slim, fair-haired young man in the far corner. "Peter, switch off that radiogram, dear. The noise is frightful."

Ieuan stood near the open doorway, conscious of his shabby suitcase, his rumpled suit, and heavy shoes. A nervous smile flickered on his lips as Stella introduced him to the room. He nodded awkwardly, aware of the furtive smiles that greeted his appearance.

He wanted to be away from this smart, sophisticated crowd. He had come to see Stella, and her alone. Why had she brought him into this room to be exhibited before the immaculately dressed company? He strove to catch her eye, but she had left him and crossed to the far side of the room towards the fair-haired young man.

"Peter, do give Ieuan a drink, will you, pet? He's had a very long and tiring journey."

Someone laughed. Stella looked coolly around. She smiled at Ieuan. He heard her apologetic whisper as she came up to him and took the suitcase from his hand.

"Stella, please, I must talk to you."

She did not appear to have heard him.

"Stella, can I speak to you alone?"

She regarded him quizzically. "But what is there to say, my dear boy? Come, do have a drink."

The young man named Peter extended him a glass of sherry. Suddenly, Peter's hand was pushed quickly away, and another hand offered him a glass.

"Here, sonny boy, let me have the pleasure."

It was Eddie Brownlee, and he was half drunk.

"Welcome to London, young Morgan." Brownlee raised his glass and tossed back the drink. "So you've come all the way from little ol' Wales, just to have a word with Stella? Look here, old chap... you can't take our hostess away, you know." He placed an arm round Ieuan's shoulder in drunken familiarity. "Tell you what, sonny... Let's you an' me have a little talk, eh?" His voice was loud and the other guests looked at one another with faint smiles of amusement on their faces.

Stella held Brownlee's arm. She was unable to hide her annoyance. "Now, Ed, don't be boorish." She attempted to lead him away. "Please."

Brownlee shook off her hand. He swayed a little.

"Young Morgan and I... we have a lot to say to each other." He wheeled round. There was a dead silence in the room.

Ieuan noticed Stella's lips compress. The young man, Peter, approached Brownlee.

"Come on, Eddie, it's time you were leaving."

Brownlee looked at him with contempt. "If you dare lay a hand on me, Blakeston, I—I'll flatten you, you young puppy."

"Eddie!" Stella's voice cut sharply across the room. "You're being insufferable." She appealed to Ieuan. "Take him out, will you?" Her eyes blazed. "Go! Have your little chat, the pair of you."

She swept angrily to the other side of the room and switched on the radiogram. The couples began to dance.

Ieuan was dazed, tongue-tied. He made to follow Stella, but Brownlee linked an arm in his and drew him out into the hallway.

"Sonny boy, you're a fool!"

"Shut up!" Ieuan pushed him forcibly aside. He turned and walked back to the room they had left. He stood on the threshold. Stella was dancing with Peter Blakeston. They were smiling into each other's eyes.

The sight made him clench his teeth. He had come to speak to Stella and she had treated him almost as indifferently as she might a poor relation of whom she was ashamed.

Once again he felt Brownlee's hand on his arm.

"Don't be a fool, Morgan."

Ieuan swung round at him, his fists raised.

Brownlee tossed his head. He smiled wryly. "You poor, stupid Taffy—are you blind? Look!" He pointed to the dancing couple. "Do you think Stella's interested in you? Come! Let old Eddie Brownlee fix you another drink. Let's make a toast to all discarded lovers... to the pangs of unrequited love."

With a swiftness that took the unsuspecting Brownlee completely by surprise, Ieuan gripped him by the coat collar.

"What are you saying?" he demanded. "What do you mean?"

"All right, all right, son..." Brownlee jerked himself free. He straightened his lapels. He looked at Ieuan, the smile now gone, and his eyes narrowed.

"Don't play the rough stuff with me, my friend. I'm big enough to teach you a lesson."

All at once he smiled, and shrugged his broad shoulders.

"Morgan, I've told you not to be a damn fool." He led Ieuan into a small ante-room. "Sit down, boy, and listen to me." He had sobered. "First of all, tell me, what brought you here?" he asked.

Ieuan sat with his head held between his hands. He could find no words to express the revulsion he felt.

"You came to find Stella," Brownlee went on. "I know all about you and her, and I could have kicked myself for letting her persuade me to come down to Wales. That day at the Beaufort— I was her cousin." He gave a short laugh. "And you couldn't see through it. That was a hell of a joke she played on us, wasn't it?"

Ieuan listened in silence.

"I was her lover," Brownlee's tone was bitterly sarcastic. "You were—well, you were a new experience, an exciting adventure, another heart-throb. Now, it's young Blakeston's turn. Peter Blakeston, the gifted young producer... Stella has a flair for picking them out... her 'promising protégés', as she so charmingly calls them. This little party's for Blakeston, but boy! you certainly gate-crashed with a bang."

Brownlee reached for a decanter of whisky on a sideboard. He filled two glasses. "Here, sonny boy, swallow this. And take my advice—get on the next train back home to Wales. Stella's not interested in you—not any more. She's a girl who tires easily of new toys. A working man, with calloused hands and dirty overalls— it appealed to her sense of the unconventional. You were a poet, she told me. I don't doubt it, sonny boy. But you've sung your last song to her, believe me. Go home, Morgan. Get back to your wife and kid. Don't be a bloody sucker for a girl who—"

"Yes?"

Brownlee glanced quickly over his shoulder. Stella stood in the doorway, her hands clenched tightly. Suddenly she relaxed. She smiled.

"So you've sobered down, Eddie?" she said as she came into the room. "What on earth possessed you to behave in that extraordinary manner before my friends? It was most melodramatic."

Before he could counter, she turned to Ieuan. "Ieuan, my dear, I'm so sorry your welcome was not very effusive, but really I was completely stunned when you walked in. You were the last person I ever expected to see here tonight. When did you arrive?"

Ieuan shrugged. "Does it matter?"

"My! This is turning out to be a most entertaining evening." Stella waved a slim hand. "Eddie, pour me a drink, there's a lamb. I feel I've just walked into a condemned cell."

Brownlee handed her the drink. "I've been advising my young friend on the folly of placing one's faith in woman. *La donna é mobile,* you know...? A dissertation on waywardness. He should have stayed content in his little home town."

Stella's hand shook slightly, and a drop of the bright liquid ran over the edge of her glass.

"Indeed, Eddie! And what, exactly, do you mean?"

"Oh come, my dear. We'll discuss it some other time, eh? Some day when we're both tottering around, all passion spent."

She winced. "Eddie, you're a bore," she snapped. She faced Ieuan. "Please forgive me, Ieuan dear. But," she held a hand to her forehead, "everything seems to have happened tonight. I'm thrilled to see you again. That note I left you—I'm sorry our parting had to be at such short notice. You did understand?"

"Frankly—No!" Ieuan walked out of the room. He picked up his suitcase in the hallway. Stella followed and touched him on the arm.

"Ieuan, what's wrong?"

"I've been a damn fool!" he blurted. "I believed in you, Stella. I even imagined I was in love with you."

"Now, now, my temperamental little Welshman," she cajoled, "don't lose your head. Who said anything about love? I certainly gave you no cause to imagine I was in love with you. I was interested in helping you as a writer."

Brownlee's cynical glance and his expressive, "Quite!" infuriated her. She regarded the two men venomously.

"Oh, you prize idiots! You silly, childish, self-important idiots! Love!—neither of you has the remotest idea of what it means. You attracted me, yes... You, Eddie, because I felt we had so much in common. We moved in the same circles. You were as bored as I was with life. As for you, Ieuan Morgan ... I wanted to meet you. It was a new experience. I'd heard so much of you Welsh people's virility, your passionate sincerity. I led you on... Yes, I admit it, and it seems you've lost your senses. Go back to your wife. She's your kind. There's no place for you here."

Ieuan blundered out into the roadway. The suitcase bumped against his legs as he rushed down the street. His heart pounded. His brain was on fire.

Fool! Stupid, ignorant fool! To have believed he was in love with Stella! What had come over him? What had happened to his reasoning?

He had been blinded, overwhelmed by her beauty. Her praise and her promises—these were not what had drawn him to her. They might have been so at the beginning. But not after he had held her in his arms—as others had done before him. And it was for such as she that he had bidden farewell to home and had left Sally and her love for him.

What a fool he had been! Sally had been wiser than he. She had recognised Stella from the first. And he had thought it was her jealousy. What a conceited, blasted fool he had been!

Thomas had warned him, too. But Ieuan Morgan, with ambitions to be a writer, was too clever, of course, to accept advice from his wife and his friend. They were so narrow, so parochial in their outlook, and were cruelly unjust to Stella.

Were they, indeed!

Clever Ieuan Morgan!

He had believed himself to be in love with a respectable harlot… He was calling her names now. Well, he could stop doing so. That was merely a dishonest way of bolstering up his hurt pride. What would he have done if she had welcomed him, as he had hoped she would? What names would he have been calling her now? Would he have cared, then, for the amused glances of her friends as he stood in the open doorway with his cheap suitcase dangling from his hand?

And if she came to him now, and wound herself about him, threading her fingers through his hair, enticing him, would he refuse her? Was sex stronger than pride?

Now the journey was over. He had come to London to look for what he believed was love and hope, but he had found, in his brief hour, derision and disillusionment.

If Stella had welcomed him, what then? What of the future? He had entered her home, he had seen her friends. There was no place for him among them. They would look upon him as an innocent, wide-eyed country lad, awkward, rough-edged, a boor who would amuse them. And Stella herself, she would tire of him as she tired of her other lovers.

To help him establish himself as a writer! What a bloody joke! A writer?

You conceited fool! You've written a few stories. They have been published. You are a writer.

You make me laugh!

Remember that day when you strolled through the bookshop in the High Street in home, sweet home? And how the manager, with an eye to business, spotted you and bustled towards you? Then, the weekly visit to the same bookshop; the flowering of the manager's familiarity; the moment—the glorious, heart-singing moment when he mentioned your writings?

How proud you felt, vain atom.

The shop was crowded, you remember? It was the day before Christmas. The manager spoke loud enough for the whole shop to hear. "Are you writing any more stories, Mr. Morgan? If at any time you intend doing a novel, just let me know. When it's published, we'll push it through for you... Display, and all that, you know, Mr. Morgan?"

Everyone looked at you then, remember? You even blushed, didn't you? You were a writer in the customers' eyes. They could go home and tell their families and friends that they had seen a writer in the bookshop. A real, live writer.

Then, the next week you called again, and the manager, to whom you were not a writer, but just another good customer, came smile-flashing forward with his suggestion that you were privileged to open an account with him.

You were never one to open accounts... that was a thing undreamt of in your humdrum life. Accounts were for business men, and men of means, not for a tyro of a writer like yourself. Yet you swelled with pride, and fell into the net.

"An account, payable quarterly."

Why the hell didn't you pay for the books when you chose them? You had the money to pay. The foundry was actually working full-time.

Why, you had five, dirty pound notes in your wallet! Remember how you flashed them out at the slightest opportunity? If you wanted a box of matches, out would come the wallet and the small roll of notes.

Trying to be impressive, and who knew but that the seedy-looking man behind the counter could have shown you a hundred times as much in the little black book he kept in that inside pocket of his?

195

Then the following week again, when you fancied another book. Your five pounds had gone; you had no money to pay for the book... but you had an account!

When was the account payable? Yes, yes, you knew it was quarterly; but when was the quarter due?

How much did you owe for what you'd already bought?

You had paid one pound down, but since then you had chosen five other books. You'd be able to pay, you knew, but it worried you just the same, for it meant some weeks without pocket money.

Perhaps you had better sacrifice a few luxuries? Cut out the cinema? Sub a pound from the office?

The bookshop manager addressed you, "Mr. Morgan... Yes, sir," and in your pocket you had two bloody bob, and tucked in your wallet was a ten-bob note for emergency.

Ten bob!—not enough for a minute's shower, let alone a rainy day. And you felt proud to be called a writer? You, who could not afford to smoke, who went to the fourpenny seats at the pictures. You, who, at that very moment was conscious of the hole in your sock which had been turned under the heel of your foot.

You, who, apart from the suit you then wore, had but one other – to be worn on Sundays and holidays only.

You, whose very existence depended upon your being able to wake at six the next morning and every morning, and survive the daily eight and a half hours grind at the foundry when it worked!

You, a writer?

Look at those rejection slips, my boy. Don't delude yourself. For each story accepted there have been a hundred rejections.

Wake up! Wake up!

He changed the heavy suitcase from one hand to the other. He stood, a lonely figure in a deserted roadway, and glanced back. He could hear music and the distant laughter from the house he had left.

The trees on the other side of the road threw their shadows across the yellow lamp-light. Presently, a figure muffled in a fur wrap came running towards him.

196

"Oh, Ieuan... Why did you run away? Why make a scene?" Stella was breathless. "I said I'd help you... Oh, that Welsh temperament!"

Gripping the suitcase, he turned on his heels and walked away. He looked over his shoulder. She was standing on the corner, the hem of her dress shimmering in the light. He heard her call his name.

He stopped. A policeman passed by and looked at him suspiciously. Again he heard her call.

To hell! he thought. To hell with her!

He strode angrily down the hill and on to the Heath, not knowing what to do or where to go.

He came at last to the pond. Nothing disturbed the silence. The water flickered in the slanting rays of light from the houses on the far bank. He sat down on a bench, his brain throbbing, his anger still seething.

Seated there alone under the sheltered quietness of the trees, he looked up at the stars. His head began to clear, and he reflected on his rash impulsiveness.

The distant stars made him realise his own insignificance. He had acted blindly, without thought for anyone save himself. The circle he had just left in the house on the hill—he did not belong there. Stella was not of his kind. Her friends were not his "people".

For the first time in years he began to see clearly his life with Sally. He experienced her fears, her frustrations, her endless fight to maintain the home, the unhappiness she had known when her mother had lived with them. All these had contended against her, and created the barrier which had sprung up between him and her.

Sally loved him. He had accepted that love once, proudly. He had deceived her, knowing that her faith in him was deep and enduring. He had eaten of the husks. But now, like the prodigal, he would go home. Life would begin again for Sally and him, he hoped. His lesson had been learned.

197

And he would write. That much he knew. He *must* write. His place was in Wales, with Sally, his child, his own people. He must continue to study, to try to understand not only those who stood outside his personal life, but others who were bound to him by ties of love and affection. But he knew now that he would understand others only by first trying to understand himself. Then, some day, he would return to London.

Ieuan flung the suitcase on to his shoulder. He walked briskly down the long, dark avenue of trees. A taxi cruised towards the foot of the hill.

He raised his free hand and signalled to the driver.

The taxi drew up to the side of the road, and he clambered in.

"Paddington station," he said.

John Bowen (1914–2006) was born and educated in Llanelli. On leaving school he won a scholarship to Llanelli School of Art and in 1939 was appointed art master at Llanelli Boy's Grammar School, where he stayed until his retirement from teaching in 1979. He served for five years in the R.A.F. during World War II. Although his work was very much rooted in his home town, he exhibited widely across Wales and later in his career began to paint extensively during his travels in southern Europe, particularly Spain. The artist and critic Mervyn Levy referred to John Bowen as a "master of design". He was deeply serious about painting but was happy to remain out of the limelight. Many examples of his work can be viewed at Parc Howard Museum and Art Gallery in Llanelli.

Jon Gower is a writer and broadcaster who has twenty books to his name: these include *Y Storïwr*, which won the Wales Book of the Year in 2012; the coastal journey *Wales: At Water's Edge* which was shortlisted for the 2013 prize and *The Story of Wales*, which accompanies the landmark BBC television series. He has also written travel books about Chesapeake Bay and Patagonia, a psychogeography of his home town of Llanelli as well as four collections of short stories. He is currently working on a book about the artist John Selway and a noir novel in Welsh.

LIBRARY OF WALES

The Library of Wales is a Welsh Government project designed to ensure that all of the rich and extensive literature of Wales which has been written in English will now be made available to readers in and beyond Wales. Sustaining this wider literary heritage is understood by the Welsh Government to be a key component in creating and disseminating an ongoing sense of modern Welsh culture and history for the future Wales which is now emerging from contemporary society. Through these texts, until now unavailable or out-of-print or merely forgotten, the Library of Wales will bring back into play the voices and actions of the human experience that has made us, in all our complexity, a Welsh people.

The Library of Wales will include prose as well as poetry, essays as well as fiction, anthologies as well as memoirs, drama as well as journalism. It will complement the names and texts that are already in the public domain and seek to include the best of Welsh writing in English, as well as to showcase what has been unjustly neglected. No boundaries will limit the ambition of the Library of Wales to open up the borders that have denied some of our best writers a presence in a future Wales. The Library of Wales has been created with that Wales in mind: a young country not afraid to remember what it might yet become.

Dai Smith

LIBRARY OF WALES
FUNDED BY

Noddir gan
Lywodraeth Cymru
Sponsored by
Welsh Government

CYNGOR LLYFRAU CYMRU
WELSH BOOKS COUNCIL

A CARNIVAL OF VOICES
WWW. PARTHIANBOOKS.COM

WWW.THELIBRARYOFWALES.COM